Praise for Deadly Travel:

If you enjoy historical cozy mysteries (especially those set in the WWII era), you need to read Deadly Travel!
Christy's Cozy Corners

I really enjoyed the way Deadly Travel immersed me in a completely foreign world...I can't wait to read the next book in the series.   Diane Reviews Books

Filled with historical detail that is both fascinating and chilling, Deadly Travel is the best book I've read all year.
Cozy Up with Kathy

D0864940

Also from Kate Parker

The Victorian Bookshop Mysteries

The Vanishing Thief
The Counterfeit Lady
The Royal Assassin
The Conspiring Woman
The Detecting Duchess

The Milliner Mysteries

The Killing at Kaldaire House
Murder at the Marlowe Club

The Deadly Series

Deadly Scandal
Deadly Wedding
Deadly Fashion
Deadly Deception
Deadly Travel
Deadly Darkness

The Mystery at Chadwick House

Deadly Darkness

Kate Parker

JDP Press

This is a work of fiction. All names, characters, and incidents are products of the author's imagination. Any resemblance to actual occurrences or persons, living or dead, is coincidental. Historical events and personages are fictionalized.

Deadly Darkness copyright © 2021 by Kate Parker

All rights reserved. With the exception of brief quotes used in critical articles or reviews, no part of this book may be reproduced in any form or by any means without written permission of the author.

ISBN: 978-1-7332294-5-6 [print]
ISBN: 978-1-7332294-4-9 [e-book]

Published by JDPPress
Cover Design by Lyndsey Lewellen of Llewellen Designs

Dedication

For booklovers everywhere.
For the members of Triangle Sisters in Crime who have made me welcome.
For the members of Heart of Carolina Writers who have welcomed me back.
For my family.
For John, forever.

July 8, 1939

Chapter One

"Why on earth did you agree to that?" We'd been married less than twelve hours, and already I was sounding shrewish. I didn't mean to, but my dreams were being shattered before my honeymoon had truly begun.

Adam shrugged. "Livvy, remember, Sir John has been very good to us. When he asked me to drive him around to check his territory for our first mass blackout practice, I couldn't very well say no." He grinned at me, that warm, funny smile I loved. "He said it's for king and country."

My cousin, Lady Abby, and her husband, Sir John Summersby, had been kind. They had hosted our wedding, the wedding breakfast, and now our honeymoon. Even with my dreams coming true, I still wanted a wedding night that was a little more traditional.

The wedding had been magnificent. That morning, my friends in London, as well as colleagues from the *Daily Premier* newspaper and my now-husband's fellow army officers, had traveled to the local village. St. Athanasius was within a short walking distance of the train station, and those who had driven had plenty of room around the green to park.

Friends and family attended our wedding in the

medieval stone church with its stained-glass windows and eight bells in the tower to ring out when we left as husband and wife.

As my father walked me down the aisle, he said my pale blue gown was a bad choice because it made my face look ruddy and asked what idiot had fixed my hair. Nothing else. Just another day in our relationship.

I considered all the faces turned toward us and decided now was not a good moment to tell my father what I thought of his opinions. I reached the altar red-faced with anger. No one can do anything with my auburn curls, but I thought my choice of wedding gown was inspired.

Adam took one look at me seething with indignation, took my hand, and turned us both toward the vicar.

Sir John and Abby put on a magnificent wedding breakfast for our guests before we saw everyone off to return to London. My father, unfortunately, stayed on at Summersby House.

It was glorious. The sun had shone. And no one present commented on the fact this wasn't really my home parish. It was Sir John and Lady Abby Summersby's, and I was just a frequent visitor.

We'd chosen this date for our wedding since it was the first weekend available when we'd tried to book St. Athanasius. At that time, the government had not yet announced the date for the first air-raid practice drill over the southern third of England.

I wished now that we'd changed the date when we

heard. I wanted a wedding night spent with my husband, not one deferred while my husband and Sir John checked if the neighbors' blackout curtains were in place. We all knew it would soon be vitally important. But not tonight of all nights.

I straightened my shoulders and said, "If you insist on driving for Sir John down dark country lanes, I'm coming, too."

"You'll be bored. And there will be no cuddling in the back seat of Sir John's auto." He sat next to me on the bed and kissed my neck. "You'll have to wait until I return for that, Mrs. Redmond."

I smiled. "It won't be ten-thirty p.m. for an hour, Captain Redmond." It had taken him the better part of a year to convince me to agree to wed. The final nudge to marry my soldier came from Hitler's saber rattling.

Less than an hour later, I was trying to pull a brush through my tangled auburn curls while Adam was sticking his head and arms into a dark sweater. The blare of a car horn, I assumed Sir John's, urged us to hurry, which caused my hands to fumble on buttons and laces.

Five minutes later, we clattered down the grand main staircase to the front hall of Summersby House, Sir John and Lady Abby's sizable Georgian home. The front door was open, and I could see our hosts standing with my father on the front porch facing the drive.

There was a man standing by the driver's door of a sleek convertible parked in front announcing, "I'll have it annulled, that's what I'll do, Sir John."

"Too late," Adam whispered, leading me to cough and Abby to press her lips together to hide her smile.

My father glared at us.

"She's not of age, and even if she were, the family would never approve," the man continued.

I looked at the man in the light falling from the doors and windows in the front of the house. He was well into his forties, with a small mustache, and dressed in a tweed jacket and cap. Every inch the country gentleman.

"Look here, Glenfell, I haven't seen either of them," Sir John said.

"What about your boy? The oldest one."

"Matthew?" Sir John asked in a dry tone.

"Yes, him. Ask him. He should know what's going on." Glenfell waved Sir John away as if he were a servant.

Sir John turned to Abby, his eyebrows raised. She stepped inside the doorway and said to the maid, Mary, "Would you ask the boys to turn off the wireless and come here?"

The maid left, and we stood waiting. In the silence, Sir John introduced Adam and me to Philip Glenfell as his houseguests.

"Come on, Summersby," the man grumbled after a minute.

"You wanted to ask them. They'll be here." Sir John sounded unruffled. He put a match to his pipe and drew on it to get it started. I guessed he knew the boys were unlikely to know any useful information and he suspected Glenfell was to blame for his own predicament.

We heard the boys before we saw them, eight feet sounding as if forty, and four voices talking at once. The two Summersby boys and their new foster brothers screeched to a clump in front of Sir John, silent and looking innocent.

I was an only child. I found their behavior fascinating.

"Mr. Glenfell wants to know if any of you have seen Sally or know what her plans were for today," Sir John said.

"I haven't seen Sally since Thursday after cricket practice," Matthew said.

"Who was she with?" Glenfell demanded with such ferocity that the youngest, six-year-old Henry, slid behind Lady Abby.

It took sixteen-year-old Matthew a moment to find his voice. "A whole bunch of us, sir. Several girls were watching us and cheering us on. The junior village team was there, along with younger lads who wanted some batting practice."

"Sounds as if all the youngsters in the area were there." Sir John sent up a cloud of smoke from the pipe he'd finally lighted.

"Was Hal Ames there?" came next in Glenfell's belligerent tone.

"No. None of the farm workers were there," Matthew told him. "They were too busy with work. It wasn't an official practice, just some fun."

"Would you care to come inside?" Abby asked. I guessed she really wanted him to leave. That day, she'd hosted our wedding breakfast as well as directed preparations for blackout curtains in every window of the manor, and now I was certain she wanted to put her feet up. But Abby was unfailingly polite.

"No, thank you, Lady Summersby. I'm supposed to be off the road by eleven, although how I can possibly find her in complete darkness is beyond me. Be glad you've got boys, Summersby. They're easier to deal with." The man climbed back into his roadster and roared off.

At a nod from Sir John, the boys ran back inside to their radio program. My father ignored me as he returned to the drawing room and to the book he had been reading.

Adam and Sir John went off with a map, no doubt checking the route they would follow in their hunt to find houses giving off light that could be seen by German bombers. Tonight, fortunately, it would be our planes checking the landscape.

Adam and Sir John were treating this as a military exercise, addressing each other with their proper ranks of "Captain" and "Colonel."

I came in with Abby and we began shaking out the curtains to be certain no light escaped outside. "What was all that about?"

"Sally Glenfell and Hal Ames apparently fancy they're in love." Abby tugged on a curtain that wouldn't cover the window. "I blame it on Shakespeare. Romeo and Juliet. Sonnets. Apparently, the families haven't seen either one all day."

"And they won't see them until tomorrow morning with this blackout going on," I added.

"I hope you and Adam and John find Sally. Her parents are terribly worried, but this romance would have blown over before now if they hadn't carried on."

"How are his parents taking it?"

"It's just his mother. His father died in a harvesting accident when Hal was a baby. At least that's what people say. It was about the time John and I were married."

"Was there some question about the cause of death?"

"There were rumors, even after the inquest ruled the death an accident. Anyway, Mrs. Ames doesn't want Hal spending time around any of the Mannings."

"The Mannings?"

"Sally Glenfell is Sir Rupert Manning's granddaughter."

"Not Sir Rupert Manning again. I thought I'd heard the last of him." The man had insisted I wasn't a member of St. Athanasius church and shouldn't be married there because I lived and worked in London. Never mind that I came down on many weekends and attended services with Sir John and Abby. Anyone else would say "Congratulations" and consider me a member by family affiliation.

Not Sir Rupert Manning, former Arctic explorer and local celebrity.

Sir Rupert only showed up for Christmas and Easter services. I barely recognized him, and I didn't want to.

We weren't certain we'd be able to hold our wedding in St. Athanasius until after the wedding banns had been read three times, necessary for a church wedding, and everyone had become thoroughly sick of Sir Rupert and his complaints.

"Hal's father worked on Sir Rupert's farm. Hal's mother still blames Sir Rupert for her husband's death," Abby told me.

I could picture the two families feuding while the youngsters carried on behind the barn. "So, the Mannings and the Glenfells are snobs and Mrs. Ames nurses her hatred. But would the children run off? Where would they go?"

"That's what I'm going to ask Matthew. He might know something and not think anything of it." All the curtains on the ground floor checked, Abby headed upstairs.

Before I could follow her, Adam called me to join him.

I shouted up the stairs, "I'm off, Abby. I'll see you when we return. Or in the morning if you're smart and don't wait up for us." I hurried outside, not waiting for her reply.

I was eager to begin our ride around the countryside, checking that no light showed from any window, door, or lamppost. Only when Sir John was satisfied could Adam and I return and enjoy our wedding night.

Chapter Two

I climbed into the back seat of the car behind Sir John. Adam had to drive slowly since he couldn't use his headlights. It was after eleven, and there was no light visible from Sir John's home or barns. The moon was half-full, giving us a little light to show our way on the country lanes.

We drove past several farmhouses, dark silhouettes on the landscape, as Sir John mentioned who lived in each one. A few were tenants of Sir John's, while others were freehold. No lights shone from any of them. I suspected that being farmers, some of them had already gone to bed and we might learn more about whether they'd truly prepared for the blackout at some predawn hour.

Then we reached the village. All appeared to be in darkness. We were almost on top of the village constable when we saw a figure move and Sir John called out, "Stop."

Adam did, braking hard, and then he let the car roll forward to where the man stood.

"Is all well here, Constable Wiggins?" Sir John asked.

"I haven't seen any lights. No people, come to that, since the pub closed."

"Glad to hear all is as it should be. We're off to check our route. Good night, Constable."

We drove slowly on, a cool breeze coming in the front windows of the auto and blowing back on me. The withering heat of the day was gone, leaving a pleasant chill to the air.

More darkened village houses. The doctor's house was a large black shape looming on the side of the road beyond his dark gateposts. We were nearly past Jones's Garage before I realized where we were, since I was used to seeing the petrol pump globes lit up.

I felt my eyelids starting to droop. I blinked them repeatedly and looked up, leaning sideways to catch more of the breeze as we moved along. The sky was full of a million twinkling stars I never saw in London.

As we passed a field, I caught a glimpse of a bright light and thought I dreamed it. "Adam, stop." As soon as he did, I said, "Back up."

"What is it, Livvy?" Sir John asked.

"I thought I saw a light on the far side of the field."

As Adam continued to reverse, I kept a sharp lookout, hoping I hadn't imagined it. I'd only spotted it for a moment. "There it is," I said with relief in my voice.

"Well spotted," Sir John said. "That's at quite a distance, probably on the Ratherminster Road. Continue on about a half-mile and then we'll take the left," he directed Adam.

We rode on, not seeing any more lights. "Where do you think it is?" I finally asked Sir John.

"I think it might be the Manning place. If that idiot Glenfell is leaving a light burning for his daughter, he'll end up with a fine. Some people are not taking the danger of German bombers or invasion forces in our area seriously enough."

"Because this area is rural?" Adam asked.

"Exactly. But they don't seem to realize that, depending on where the invasion and the bombers are coming from, we're what stands between the Nazis and London."

When Sir John put it that way, I shivered. I didn't want him and Abby and the boys in danger any more than I wanted London destroyed. Suddenly, I found myself in one of those moments where I was overcome by dread of the imminent war. I wanted to shout and scream and cry that I wanted the threat to go away.

Adam and Sir John would think I had gone crazy. I had to take a couple of deep breaths to calm down.

"There. I think I caught a glimpse of the light up ahead on the right," Adam said.

I strained my eyes to find the bright light in the darkness. Suddenly it appeared to the right, just beyond a rise in the land.

"It's Manning Hall," Sir John said. "That fool Glenfell."

Aided by the light streaming out of the front door and one upstairs window, Adam easily found the long drive and followed it between fields, watching out for livestock or wild animals. In a moment, we were pulling up out front.

A woman in a twin sweater set and straight skirt rushed out the front door, hurrying to a stop next to Sir

John's car. "Oh," she said, putting a hand to her mouth, "I thought..."

"Mrs. Glenfell," Sir John began, "we're having the air raid practice tonight and your lights would be evident to any German bombers flying overhead."

"That's right. Oh, dear. You're here to check. We're quite frantic with worry about Sally. She's gone missing. Philip has gone out looking for her. I thought perhaps you'd found her and brought her home."

"I'm sure she's fine," Sir John said. "But I must insist you shut the door to keep the light from showing. And close the curtains upstairs."

"Oh." She looked up. "That's Father's room. We made sure those curtains were closed earlier." She paused and added, "That doesn't look right."

I rolled down the back window and stuck my head out to get a better look. It appeared that the curtain rod was hanging by one end, the fabric mostly below the level of the window. "It definitely doesn't look right."

"Is Sir Rupert all right?" Sir John said.

"I...don't know. I haven't seen him..."

"I'm going in," Sir John said.

Adam cut off the engine. "I'm coming with you."

They weren't going to leave me out here in the dark all alone. I climbed out of the car in time to follow them into the house, knowing if nothing was wrong, we'd look ridiculous.

I shut the door behind me as Sir John was asking Mrs. Glenfell if anyone else was in the house.

"Just Father and me. I think. Everyone else is looking for Sally..." Her voice drifted away.

In the light in the hallway, I could tell Mrs. Glenfell was pale under any conditions, with blonde hair and light blue eyes. Worried as she was about her daughter, she looked as though all color had been washed out of her.

Sir John shot Adam and me a look. "We'll go up and check to make sure all is well and see if we can't right the curtains so you don't get a fine." Sir John headed up the stairs, Adam next, then me, and finally Mrs. Glenfell. She hung back as if frightened of something.

Sir John knocked on the door. "Sir Rupert. Sir Rupert. Is everything all right?"

When he got no reply, he turned the doorknob and opened the door.

Sir John and Adam rushed in and knelt, allowing me to see over their heads. The blackout curtains were pulled down, with the rod yanked out of the wall on one side. Sir Rupert Manning, an older man with a neatly trimmed beard, lay on his back in front of the window. He had a strange-looking spear sticking out of his chest and one hand wrapped around the blackout curtain.

Mrs. Glenfell pushed past me, dropped into a chair by the door, and started to whine. I moved to block her view of the body while I leaned toward her, patting her shoulder and murmuring as I would to a small child.

"I knew somebody would get him one day," came a woman's cheerful voice from the room's doorway.

"Louisa, please," Mrs. Glenfell said, no longer sobbing

as she glared at the other woman.

"Oh, come on, Joan. He's certainly bumped off enough Arctic animals to annoy the wildlife at the very least." Louisa had all the color Joan Glenfell lacked. Black hair cut in a bob, dark eyes, lips painted bloodred.

The look and the voice were familiar from my distant past. "Louisa Porter from St. Agnes?" I asked the woman.

"It's Louisa Manning now." She dragged her gaze away from the body. "Olivia? Olivia Harper?" Her voice rose in surprise.

"Olivia Redmond as of yesterday."

"Congratulations. Oh!" she said as her eyes widened. "I'm *Lady* Louisa Manning now. I'm the wife of the new *Sir* Douglas Manning."

"Congratulations. Although, under the circumstances, that feels insensitive," I corrected myself.

"Don't worry about it." Louisa leaned in to take another long glance. "He has a whole hall of horrors downstairs we can get rid of now. Stuffed polar bears. Stuffed birds. Looks as if a narwhal got him in the end."

Mrs. Glenfell let out a wail.

"Oh, Joan, get hold of yourself." Louisa sounded weary.

"What is that?" I asked Louisa, ignoring Joan Glenfell's sobs. The narrow pole sticking out of the explorer was a spiral that appeared to be made of ivory.

"It's a narwhal tusk. And I'm sure the narwhal didn't give it up willingly just to prove Sir Rupert's manhood."

"I don't see how you can be so cruel, after all he's

done for you," Joan Glenfell sniffed. I noticed she was turning her sobbing on and off at will.

"Done *to* me, don't you mean?" Louisa said. "Done to all of us, including you."

Chapter Three

Louisa looked around then and realized she had a rapt audience. Reddening, she said, "If anyone wants me, I'll be in my room."

"Where were you?" Joan asked.

"Out looking for your wretched daughter. Now I'm cold, my feet are wet, and I want to lie down." She sauntered off around the corner, her stocking feet leaving wet prints on the wood floor. A moment later, I heard a nearby door shut.

"How many people were here this evening?" I asked Mrs. Glenfell.

"Not now, Livvy," Sir John said. "First, find the telephone and call the police."

"It's in the..." Joan Glenfell made small, round gestures toward the stairs and then covered her face with her handkerchief.

I found the telephone in the front hall. Just after I finished talking to a policeman at the nearest station, the front door swung open. I turned around as I hung up the receiver.

No one was there.

I looked out. The drive was empty except for our auto.

I quickly shut the door, shaking from the surprise. There was a dead man upstairs and the front door had opened on its own. I didn't want to be alone downstairs when anyone who could protect me was upstairs.

I ran up to Sir Rupert's room on trembling legs. "The police are sending out a constable as quickly as they can with this blackout."

"You won't tell them about Sally, will you?" Mrs. Glenfell whispered behind me.

"I'll let you do that."

"Oh, no. Philip wouldn't like that."

I shook my head. "Then you might want to decide how you're going to explain why the family was outside running around in the blackout while your father was murdered."

Turning back to Adam and Sir John, I ignored her wail, which now seemed more and more of an act, and said, "Was he robbed?"

"Hard to tell, but not obviously," Adam responded.

"I don't," sniff, "think so," Joan Glenfell said, sounding more in control of herself.

"Did you hear or see anyone in the house after the others went out looking for Sally?" I asked.

She shook her head.

I couldn't help asking. "Where do Louisa and her husband live?" Getting Joan Glenfell to talk about ordinary things might help calm her down.

"Here. The whole family lives here. Father wants us within reach."

"And so, they were available to search for Sally." I

gave her a smile. "How long have they been looking?"

"Part of the afternoon and then again after dinner."

"You waited here to coordinate their search?" *And wring your hands?*

"Father said I wouldn't be of any use, so I might as well see to the curtains and have someone bring him his tea."

"Who brought him his tea?"

"Our maid, Marjorie Lenard."

"And he was all right?"

She looked at me as if I'd lost my mind. "Of course he was. Otherwise, she would have said something."

Or screamed her head off.

I could see a smile in Adam's eyes when I looked at him. He must have thought it was as silly a question as Mrs. Glenfell did.

They were right.

I tried again. "How many people live in this house on a normal day?"

She sat silent for so long I thought she wouldn't answer me. "Fourteen."

"Including the servants?"

"Yes."

Before I could ask another question, footsteps could be heard pounding up the stairs. Then Mr. Glenfell, who'd been at Sir John's earlier, came in and said, "What's going on?"

Sir John stepped back so Mr. Glenfell could see the body.

His jaw worked a few times before he said, "I see." Then he turned to his wife. "Joan, you should be in your room. This is too much of a strain for you."

"Sally?"

"Not yet."

She nodded and slowly rose from the chair, walking hunched over out of the room and down the hall.

"Now," Philip Glenfell said in a decisive tone, "have you called the police?"

"Yes, they should be here soon if they don't have trouble driving out here in the blackout," Sir John said.

"Blasted blackout. Sir Rupert didn't approve, you know."

"No, I didn't know," Sir John said quietly.

"He found it pointless. He said we don't stand a chance against the Germans. They're too organized. Too well equipped. They'll walk over this area on their way to London and we can't do a thing about it," Glenfell said.

"That's defeatist talk for a man who spent weeks at a time in the Arctic. I can't believe Sir Rupert would give up so easily," Adam said.

"Oh, he was certain they'd take us over," Glenfell said. "He did most of his expeditions with Germans. He admired them."

Adam glared at the body on the floor.

"No sign of your daughter?" Sir John asked.

Philip Glenfell shook his head. "I didn't see her or that miserable Ames boy."

"The last buses ran early tonight. Perhaps they're

stuck somewhere without transportation," I suggested.

"Where?" Glenfell demanded. "Where would they have gone? And why wouldn't they have telephoned?"

"I don't know your daughter. You do. Where would she enjoy going on a summer day?" I asked.

His answer was to walk out of the room and head down the stairs. We heard the crunch of gravel on the drive and then men's voices at the front door.

The police had arrived.

Adam and I left Sir John to talk to the police while we went out into the cool night air. We leaned on the side of Sir John's car and murmured to each other, glad to be alone in the dark.

"Not my idea of how our wedding night would go," Adam said, running a hand through my curls.

"I'm sorry that someone you admired turned out to be so defeatist about the Nazis," I replied.

"I didn't admire him after he tried to ruin our wedding. But he'd been so determined, so alive. I guess when people get older, they get grumpy and want to take the safe route."

I grinned. "Such as Mr. Churchill? He doesn't seem eager to take the easy road."

A single chuckle broke through. "No, he doesn't, and good luck to him." Then he turned somber. "What do you make of that scene upstairs?"

"That must have been quite a fight, to pull the curtain rod out."

"I think he grabbed the curtains in an attempt to save

himself and his weight pulled the rod out of the wall. It might not have been put up securely. There wasn't much evidence of a struggle besides the curtain rod."

"It would be hard to surprise someone while carrying a six-foot-long spear." I couldn't imagine it.

"Unless he expected someone to bring the tusk to him," Adam said.

"We should check the 'hall of horrors,' as Louisa Porter, er, Manning called it." I gave him a smile. "The police should be busy upstairs at the moment."

Adam nodded and escorted me back inside. My heart sank when we found the police, Sir John, and Philip Glenfell in the trophy room.

In a floor-to-ceiling glass case were two narwhal tusks identical to the one upstairs. One of the policemen swung the door open and shut as he said, "And you say there should be three of them?"

"Yes. Of course, there are two. The third is sticking out of..." Glenfell came to a stop, looking as if he were trying not to choke.

Sir John patted him on the shoulder. "Yes. We saw."

The police sergeant saw us and said, "And who are you?"

Adam drew himself up with a military bearing I wasn't used to seeing from him. "Captain and Mrs. Redmond. We rode with Sir John while checking on the blackout. We stopped here when we saw light coming from the window upstairs."

He could have said "Captain and Mrs. Redmond" a

few more times. I hadn't become tired of hearing my new name yet.

"You're the couple Sir Rupert tried to prevent getting married at St. Athanasius," the constable said.

"Oh, I don't think it was anything personal," Philip Glenfell said. "He just didn't think she was a member of the congregation."

"'She' is Olivia Redmond, who has attended a great many more services at St. Athanasius than Sir Rupert ever did," I snapped at him. The dead man had caused so many headaches for the Reverend Garner that we weren't completely certain until days before the wedding that we'd be allowed to marry in the church.

"No offense meant," Mr. Glenfell said in a tone clearly meant to offend.

"I don't think you can speak for Sir Rupert," I said, finding Mr. Glenfell as obnoxious as Sir Rupert.

Adam put an arm around my shoulders with a grip that held me in place and said, "But we were married there this morning, so everything turned out fine."

I gave him a too-bright smile and said, "Yes." I didn't want to mess up our wedding night any more than it had been already. And being held on suspicion of murder would not be a tale I wanted to tell our children about our wedding in twenty or thirty years.

"Congratulations," the police sergeant said, eyeing me with some doubt in his expression. "Now, who was here earlier?"

"If you don't need us for anything else," Sir John said.

"No, you go on your way, Sir John. You have a job to do for the county tonight," the policeman said.

I turned, about to follow Adam out when I glanced down at the patterned Oriental carpet. There was something wrong with the pattern along one side by a huge stuffed polar bear. "What is that?"

"It's a shadow from the bear. Come along, Livvy," Sir John said.

"There's nothing to cause a shadow there," I told him. I walked over and bent down to touch the stain. It came off on my fingers. I held out my hand, dark red smeared on my fingers. "Is that blood?"

The police hurried over to my side. "Maybe," the detective said. "We'll get it tested tomorrow. The fight was in Sir Rupert's room. Probably no connection."

When I opened my mouth to speak, the constable said, "We'll take care of it."

"Thank you," Adam said, hustling me out of there before I could say another word, the smear still on my fingers. We were quickly followed by Sir John.

Once we were on our way, I asked, "Did anyone tell the police about the missing girl?"

"No," Sir John said. "Glenfell seems determined to keep any knowledge of the girl's wandering from the neighbors or the police. I just hope there's a simple explanation to where she's been."

"And the blood on the carpet isn't hers," I added. "It is blood. I just hope she's all right." Given her father's comments when he had first reached Summersby House,

I suspected she might have run off to London with her boyfriend and married there.

Having an unpleasant family such as the one I had just seen, I wished them well in getting very far away from the Mannings.

Otherwise, a young girl on her own in London could be in serious danger. And her father had made sure no one else was looking for her. It seemed odd he didn't want his daughter found and brought home as quickly as possible, by whatever means necessary.

Chapter Four

We drove around the rest of the district, but we didn't see any more lights. "It's past one. Time we went home and I made my report," Sir John said.

"Sounds good to me," Adam said. "Which way is home?"

Sir John was able to direct us in the general direction of the village and beyond there to Summersby House.

We'd not gone far before a man waved his arms as he stumbled onto the roadway directly into our path in front of the car. Adam slammed on the brakes.

I saw him at the same time as Adam did. I gasped and braced myself as I flew forward, but Sir John had been looking at Adam. Without time to protect himself, he only managed to put out one arm as he was thrown against the dashboard. With a hiss of pain, he grabbed his wrist.

As soon as we came to a stop, Adam said, "I'm sorry, Sir John. Are you all right?"

"No, I'm not bloody all right," Sir John snapped. I understood his anger. He was tired and in pain. "Who is that fool and what is he doing out at this hour? Good heavens, it's Douglas Manning."

Oh, great, another one of the Manning clan. The man was now leaning on the hood of our car, gasping for breath. While Adam saw to Sir John's arm, I climbed out of the car.

"Livvy, wait," Adam said.

In the light of the half-moon on the empty stretch of road, I had an impression of a pale man in his thirties with blood on his torn clothing. "Douglas Manning? What happened? What are you doing here?"

"I was looking for my niece. Foolish child." He didn't seem to take offense at my demanding tone. "I couldn't see where I was going in this blasted blackout when the moon went behind a cloud and I drove down the embankment. My car's down there." He straightened up and turned as if he was going to go down after it.

"Wait," Adam said, blocking his way. "We'll give you a ride home. You can get the car tomorrow." I helped Adam get the man into the back seat of Sir John's auto and we took off.

"Do you want me to take you home first?" Adam asked Sir John.

"No. You'll never find your way to Manning's and back again." Sir John cradled his wrist as he turned to Douglas Manning. "Any sign of your niece?"

"No. Silly girl. As silly as her father." He leaned back with his eyes closed. "This is nice of you. I don't think I could have walked the whole way home. The crash shook me up. Lucky you came by."

Sir John grunted an acknowledgment.

I said, "I'm afraid there's some bad news."

"Worse than telling my father I smashed up his car in

a ditch trying to find his foolish granddaughter? I don't think there is anything worse."

"There is."

He opened his eyes and focused on me. "What?"

I took a deep breath. "It's your father." When he said nothing as he faced me, I continued. "He's dead. Murdered."

"What?"

"Your father's be—"

"No. No. I heard what you said. I just don't understand." He shook his head as if to clear it. "Murdered him? Who? Why?"

"We don't know," I told him.

"Have the police been called?"

"We called them."

He stared at me. "You called them?"

"We saw the light shining from his window and stopped at the house. We went up with Mrs. Glenfell and found your father, and then we called the police. They were there when we left."

"Good. They'll sort things out." He shut his eyes again.

Surprised at Manning's satisfied tone, I glanced in the mirror and made out Adam's eyes watching me, his eyebrows raised. What kind of a family had we stumbled across?

When I heard that Sir Rupert had created a furor at the parish council meeting over the first mention of our wedding at St. Athanasius, I had thought he was without any family. I don't know why I'd thought that. Perhaps because he didn't attend church regularly, and his family didn't, either. Perhaps I assumed a family would tone down his unbridled nastiness, which was silly, since I'd never had any effect on my father's behavior.

With Sir John's grunted directions, Adam drove us back to Manning Hall. We pulled up in front of the house behind a police car. I watched Douglas Manning climb out of the seat with more ease than I expected, considering the blood and rips on his clothing.

A constable who we'd seen here with the first police car now hurried over to us out of the dark. "What is your business here?"

"I live here," Douglas said. "I wrecked my car on a side road toward the village looking for my niece and these nice people picked me up. I heard my father's been murdered."

"Sorry about not recognizing you in the dark. Sir Douglas." The constable added, "Looking for your niece?" He sounded surprised.

"Sally Glenfell. She's been missing since this morning. Well, it must be yesterday morning now. Didn't anyone tell you?" He gave a growl of impatience. "My stupid brother-in-law." Douglas Manning nudged the constable aside and stormed into the house.

Adam put the car in motion. "I think that's our cue to leave."

* * *

Adam and I didn't get to bed until well after two and then slept in on Sunday morning. By the time we were dressed and in the dining room for coffee, it was nearly eleven.

Six-year-old Henry strolled in and in a very polite voice asked if he could have a glass of juice. He gave Mary a big grin, now missing the teeth to the sides of his top front teeth, as she brought in more coffee.

"Of course, Henry." She gave him a wink and he sat down at the table across from us.

Once she left the room, Henry whispered, "We don't have to go to church today. Sir John's wrist hurts him something awful and you were all out so late that Lady Abby said there was no point in going to church just to sleep through the sermon."

"You were in church yesterday for our wedding. Maybe that counts," I whispered back. "Where are the other boys?"

"Matthew and Gerhard are in the barn working on an old bicycle they found in a shed. If they fix it up really well, they think they can sell it. Mark went over to Ray Long's to kick a ball around."

Ray was the son of a nearby farmer who'd been in Mark's class before Mark went away to public school. They'd stayed good friends despite the differences in their status. "Won't Ray be going to church?" I asked. Most of the local people were regular churchgoers.

"No. His father stopped going to church after living in trenches in the Great War." Henry thanked Mary for his juice and took a big swallow before a puzzled look crossed his face. "Why did he live in a trench?"

"That's where the soldiers lived during the war," Adam said.

"I wouldn't do that. I'd stay here with Lady Abby and Sir John and feed the animals." Another sip of juice and then, "I like my bed. I wouldn't want to sleep in the mud."

Adam choked on his coffee.

Suspecting Adam's reaction was because as an army officer he knew what was coming and completely agreed with Henry's point of view about living outdoors, I was mopping coffee off my husband when Abby came in. "I'd like tea, please, Mary."

"How is Sir John?" Adam asked. "It's my fault he was injured, slamming on the brakes without warning him."

"If you hadn't, you would have hit Douglas Manning. He stepped right into our path," I said.

"Didn't he see you?" Abby asked.

"He seemed pretty shaken up from driving his car into a ditch," I replied. "And we couldn't turn on the headlamps."

Abby shook her head. "I've wrapped up John's wrist and put it in a sling. While he has a large bruise, I don't think anything's broken. He has to remember not to use it for a while."

The phone rang in the hall at the same time that Mary set a cup of tea in front of Abby. The maid hurried out and returned a minute later, reporting that Mark was on the phone, calling from the Longs. "He says he needs to speak to Sir John urgently."

"I don't think that's a good—" Abby began.

"You don't need to wrap me in cotton wool," Sir John snarled from the hall. "Mark?" he said into the telephone. "Yes, it's me. What...?"

As the silence lingered in the hall, Adam and I rose and began to walk toward the hallway.

"You're certain," Sir John said. Something in his voice told me it was serious. "Yes, I'll pick you up on the way."

As he hung up the phone, Abby passed us and reached her husband. "What is it?"

"They've found Hal Ames's body not far from where they were pulling Douglas Manning's car out of the ditch. Adam, would you mind driving me again?"

"No problem, sir."

"I'm going, too," I said.

"Olivia," Sir John began.

"Two deaths, and this one a young man. I feel as if I should be doing something, anything, to help. Especially since this is the part of our honeymoon we'll always remember."

"Go on then, both of you," Abby said with a weak smile.

Sir John shrugged. "Could you give the police station a call, dear? I'm not certain anyone else has."

Abby got the details on the location and rang the police station while we went out to tell Matthew and Gerhard where we were going.

"I can certainly see more this morning," Adam said as we drove along in the sunshine.

"If that fool Manning hit Ames last night, why didn't

he say so? There might have been time to save him," Sir John grumbled.

"Any sign of Sally Glenfell?" I asked.

"Mark didn't think so, but they didn't let him get too close." Sir John shook his head. "Still, he'll probably have nightmares. He's not fourteen yet."

Following Sir John's directions, we were soon at the site. A couple of plow horses had pulled a damaged car up the slope and we could see marks where the car and the horses had flattened the weeds and bushes. Douglas Manning and his wife, who had been so proud the night before of becoming Lady Louisa, stood by the wreckage. A farmer held the reins of the horses.

At the bend in the road beyond them, we saw Mark waving to us. We waved to the Mannings as we drove past to where Mark stood with another boy his age. A police car and the doctor's car were parked along the edge of the lane, and Adam pulled in behind them.

We climbed out and joined the boys. "My dad is down the slope with the police and Dr. Wheeler. It's Hal," the other boy said.

"Are you and Ray all right?" Sir John asked Mark.

"Yes, sir. It looks as if Hal took a great whack to his head," Mark said. Both boys sounded more excited than alarmed at the discovery. I thought Sir John was wrong. His son wouldn't have any nightmares.

"Any sign of Sally Glenfell?" I asked. From what had been said by her father, I expected to find both of them together.

"No." Mark glanced down the hill. "Do you think she's down there, too?"

"I hope not." I looked at Sir John holding his arm protectively. "Adam and I will go down the embankment, Sir John. We'll let you know what we find."

When Sir John began to object, I added, "Abby will murder me if you reinjure that arm, and the slope is pretty steep."

He grimaced before he nodded.

Adam climbed down first and I followed where he had dug his heels into the bank. Dr. Wheeler was crouched next to a body sprawled at the bottom of the ditch on his side. Uniformed constables and a man in a suit who was fanning his face with his hat stood on either side of the doctor, with another man who appeared to be an older version of Mark's friend Ray standing a short distance away.

"You don't think he had anything to do with Manning running his car off the road?" the man in the suit asked Dr. Wheeler as we reached them.

"Oh, no. Injuries are all wrong. And where's the blood? A wound such as that should bleed quite freely." Wheeler stood up and dusted off his trouser knees. "No. He was killed somewhere else. With something flat. A flat shovel, perhaps? Or the bottom of a pan?"

"A shovel?" The man looked up from his small notebook similar to the one I carried for newspaper interviews.

"Or something with a flat surface," the doctor said.

"Has anyone formally identified our victim?"

"Aye, it's Hal Ames. We all know that," the man standing to the side said. "Has anyone told Eleanor? Since she lost her husband, Hal is all she has left."

"His mother?" the man in the suit asked.

The man nodded.

"You must be Mr. Long, Ray's father. I'm Olivia Redmond, and this is my husband. We drove Sir John Summersby out when Mark called him," I added for the benefit of the group as a whole. I decided I'd better explain to these strangers that we had a reason to be there. Sir John was a local magistrate and would be involved.

"Been working before the boys called me down here. That's my land, to the wall." He pointed to a low drystone wall that ran along the higher, far side of the lane. "Land on this side is Manning land." Another drystone wall ran along the top of the lower slope on the other side of the ditch.

We all turned toward the sound of a car driving fast along the road. It stopped just above us and a door slammed. Then a tall, thin woman started down the slope toward us. She had the sure-footed stride of a countrywoman.

Mr. Long hurried toward her. "You don't want to come down here, Eleanor. It's not..."

"Of course it's not pretty. And which one of the Mannings killed my boy?" she shouted. "Where's Sir Rupert? I want him arrested!"

Chapter Five

"I wanted to see for myself." Eleanor Ames pulled away from Mr. Long and paled at her first glimpse of the body. "That's my boy. That's Hal." There was so little expression on her rigid face her skin might as well have been made of granite.

"Constable?" the man in the suit said, sending the uniformed policeman over to take Mrs. Ames back up to the road. "I'm Detective Inspector Parsons. I'll be with you as soon as I can, ma'am."

"Just you be sure to put Sir Rupert in jail this time. He killed my husband and now he's killed my son." Mrs. Ames stalked toward the detective. Then she stopped and looked down at the body. From where she stood, the body was facing her. A tear ran down each of her weather-beaten cheeks. "Poor lad. You deserved better."

Inspector Parsons came forward, turning her away gently as he spoke quietly to her. I wondered what words of comfort he gave her.

"Who brought you here, Mrs. Ames?" the constable asked.

"Gary Jones. He heard at the garage and drove me here so I could see for myself." She shook her head. "And I have."

Then Mr. Long and the constable hurried Mrs. Ames up to the road and the car she'd arrived in.

"Poor woman," Dr. Wheeler said. "Husband's been dead more than fifteen years. She still blames his employer, Sir Rupert Manning. And now this."

"Any sign of who might have done this?" Inspector Parsons asked.

"None," the doctor said. "But that's for you to determine."

"Any sign of Sally Glenfell?" I asked.

"You think she did this?" the inspector asked me.

"She and Hal both went missing yesterday morning. You've found Hal. Sally may still be missing."

"You spoke to her parents last night about the death of Sir Rupert. They didn't say anything about a missing daughter," a constable said.

"Trying to avoid a scandal," Dr. Wheeler said, closing up his medical bag and starting up the hill. "I'll see if the mortuary men are here yet."

"Two suspicious deaths and a missing girl. We don't have time to worry about a scandal," the inspector murmured.

"Her uncle—now Sir Douglas Manning—mentioned that Sally Glenfell was missing last night when he came home," another constable told him as he returned from escorting Mrs. Ames into the car.

"He's the one with the car they just pulled out of the ditch?" the inspector asked.

The uniformed policeman nodded.

"And you didn't tell me?" Inspector Parsons growled.

"I didn't think it had anything to do with—"

"Your job isn't to think. It's to tell me what you know and learn. I'll talk to this Manning while you search this bank up to the road for anything that shouldn't be there." The inspector looked around. "No chance of getting footprints now."

"Seen enough?" Adam asked.

I'd deliberately kept a distance from the corpse. I could see something had smashed in the back of his head. I didn't want to see more. Glancing all around away from the body, I said, "I don't see anything that might be another body nearby. Let's hope Sally made her way home."

We climbed up the embankment as the mortuary men walked down while discussing the best way to move the body. They didn't want to drop the body, but they didn't want to fall climbing up the embankment, either.

Sir John, Mark, and Mark's friend, Ray, stood by Sir John's car waiting for us. "Well?" Sir John asked.

"Apparently, it's Hal Ames. There's no sign of Sally Glenfell," Adam said. "Do the lads want to come back to Summersby House with us?" He didn't add my thought, *That will keep them out of the way of the police.*

"Good idea," Sir John said. "Ray, ask your father if you could come over."

"Can't. My chores aren't done."

"Then Mark, you are definitely coming with us. Stop interfering with Ray doing his chores."

"I promised I'd help him." Mark sounded pleading.

"Then you two should get busy on those chores. And Mark, come home when you get underfoot." Sir John opened up the front passenger door and dropped into the seat with a muffled groan.

The two boys lingered by the side of the road until Adam crossed his arms and stared at them, his feet shoulder-width apart. The pair understood his message and climbed over the fence to head up the slope toward the barn and the chores.

Then Adam and I climbed into the car. He quickly turned it around and drove us to where Douglas and Louisa Manning stood. The detective inspector had just walked over to join them. Adam rolled down his window so Sir John could ask, "Sir Douglas, is Sally still missing?"

"As of an hour or so ago, yes," Douglas Manning called out.

"Do we need to start a search?" Sir John asked the policeman.

"It would help if we had an idea of where she was headed when she left home," Inspector Parsons said. "So far, we've not learned anything about this runaway from her parents."

"They wouldn't know," Louisa Manning said, pushing a lock of her straight black hair out of her face. "Ask Mrs. Thompson. Mrs. Lillian Thompson. She's the housekeeper. She knows everything that goes on in that house."

"Louisa," her husband said in a warning tone.

"Well, it's true. The Manning house and household

would fall apart without the wonderful Mrs. Lillian Thompson." She tapped her bloodred nails on the fender of the ruined automobile. "Who do you think will organize getting this hauled off to the garage and getting it repaired?"

"I'm sure I'm capable of seeing to—"

Louisa gave a most unladylike snort.

"—my car," her husband finished.

I was embarrassed for him. I knew Louisa's talent for scorn from our school days, but to see her treat her husband that way made me cringe.

If she was treating Mrs. Thompson similarly, I wondered how long the housekeeper would stay, now that Louisa was the lady of the house?

"Of course, dear." She turned to the policeman. "See Mrs. Thompson. She'll be able to tell you who Sally's friends are, and possibly even where she went. Unless she's retired to her room, where no one may enter."

Inspector Parsons looked at her with an expression of loathing.

"Sir John," Louisa continued, "can I get a ride with you to Manning Hall?"

"It would be my pleasure."

I had no idea if Sir John was telling a polite lie or not. When she climbed into the back seat with me, I noticed her shoes for the first time. "Those can't have been comfortable walking around in."

Louisa looked at her fashionable footwear. "Actually, they are quite comfortable if you don't get a pebble or a twig in the openings. I'm used to wearing high heels, and these sandals keep my feet cool." Her tone told me she thought I needed a lecture in how to dress.

The same tone she used in school to say aloud that I had no style. I was glad to see she was finally developing some taste, although she still leaned toward the garish.

With ankle straps and three-inch heels, her shoes were designed to draw the eye to her bare legs. Her dress was of the same blue as the shoes, but of very light material. She appeared to be ready for a day at a seaside holiday town, not pulling a car out of a ditch.

Maybe she still lacked taste.

I was resentful. This was supposed to be my honeymoon. It was hot out, but I didn't know when Adam and I would get a chance to go to the seaside.

"Mrs. Thompson isn't related to the Thompsons in Ratherminster, is she?" Sir John asked.

"She said she's from north of London, but I've heard a hint of a foreign accent. I've never heard why she came here," Louisa said.

"I suspect Sir Rupert got her from an agency. That's how people find help in London," I said to Adam and Sir John, showing off my domestic knowledge. Actually, it was the extent of my domestic knowledge, but I thought it made me sound sophisticated.

"I imagine," Louisa said in a bored voice. "Joan handled all of that until we got the irreplaceable Mrs. Thompson."

"How long have you employed her?" I asked.

"Almost a year."

"How is your husband going to get home?" Adam asked.

"I suppose he'll get a ride to the garage and then they'll take him home while they tow in the car. Douglas is quite adept at getting where he wants to go." I picked up a note of what was annoyance or anger in her voice.

I hoped I'd never come to feel that way about Adam.

Since he could see where he was going in the sunlight, Adam drove us to Manning Hall in a few minutes. Louisa hopped out and sauntered in through the unlocked front door, leaving it open for us.

By the time the three of us entered the front hall, Louisa called out, "She's back here."

Not certain if it was Sally or Mrs. Thompson she was referring to, I headed toward the back of the house, the men following me. I walked into the kitchen to find Louisa talking to a dark-haired woman of average height whose lack of color in her clothes or her face made her nearly invisible when standing next to the bright-hued Louisa.

"Sally's not returned," Louisa said.

"That's worrying," I replied. "Do you have any idea where Sally was planning to go, Mrs. Thompson? It would make searching for her easier if we had a direction in which to look."

"I'm sure she's with the Ames boy," Mrs. Thompson said, walking away from us to hang up a dishtowel by the sink.

"We knew that much last night," Louisa said.

"There was no sign of Sally when we found his body," I said.

Mrs. Thompson whipped around, her mouth open and her eyes wide. "You found his body?" Her voice went up on the last word.

What a strange way to word her reply. And what an unfeeling thing for me to say to her. I tried again. "He was killed. His body was found a short distance away from here, between this farm and the Longs's farm."

"His poor mother. Does she know?"

I nodded.

She grabbed the back of a chair at the kitchen table, her knuckles showing white against the wood. "That poor woman. First her husband, now her son. It's not right."

"No, it's not right," I agreed. "But at least Mrs. Ames has Hal's body. The Glenfells don't even have that comfort."

"You think she's dead, too?" Louisa asked. She sounded puzzled, but not upset.

"I don't know what to think. Who among Sally's friends would know her plans for yesterday?" Inspector Parsons should be here asking these questions. It might have a bearing on the murders, but he was conspicuous in his absence.

"I probably know as much as any of them," Mrs. Thompson said. "She and Hal planned to go to the seashore, it was such a nice day and he had the whole day off. His last Saturday of freedom before he had to report to camp for six months of militia training."

"He was in the first huge batch of young men called up for military service?" Adam asked.

Mrs. Thompson nodded. "The plan was to go to the parade and the pier in Brighton. They were going to meet to catch the eight-twenty bus that stopped in the village."

"That would have been useful to know last night. Too bad you didn't tell us before you took shelter in your room for the night," Louisa said, sounding as if it was a long-standing grievance.

Mrs. Thompson ignored her.

"Did anyone see her leave?" Adam asked, moving beside me.

"I saw her." I saw a moment's flash of anger as Mrs. Thompson glanced at Louisa, and then a calmer, "None of the household was up at that hour. Marjorie and I saw her leave."

"She walked to the village?" I asked.

"How else would she get there?" Mrs. Thompson asked in a tone that made it clear she found the question stupid.

"Thank you for your help." I turned to Sir John. "We need to tell the constable that Sally is still missing and help organize a new search."

We said good-bye and walked to the front door, where we met Philip Glenfell coming inside, accompanied by his wife. "Do you have any word of Sally?" he asked us. I couldn't doubt the anxiety in his voice.

"Mrs. Thompson says she saw Sally leave here yesterday morning on her way to Brighton on the bus.

There's now a starting point for the search for your daughter," Sir John told him. "Will you be calling the police station with the information now?"

All three of us stared at him while he hesitated.

I suspected he had no intention of calling the police.

Chapter Six

"Oh, Philip, call them. Sally is out there alone. She could be hurt. She could be in danger. She could—" Mrs. Glenfell's voice rose in a hysterical pitch.

"Oh, Joan, calm down." Her husband sounded annoyed.

"Call them, Philip, or I will," came out in a defiant shriek.

"All right. I'll call." He glared at Sir John as he stomped over to the telephone on a small table nearby. "We'll be the laughingstock of the county. Proud of yourself?"

We said good-bye and walked out of the house. "Yes, I am rather," Sir John quietly answered as he gingerly climbed back into the car.

Adam and I shared a smile. Sir John might appear stuffy with his military bearing, but he was a kind and sensible man.

We were near the village on our way back to Summersby House when we spotted a young girl walking along the side of the road who looked vaguely familiar from church. She had the thinness and pale coloring of Joan Glenfell. "Is that Sally?" I asked.

"I believe so," Sir John said.

Adam pulled over and I rolled down my window.

"Sally? Sally Glenfell?"

"Yes?" She sniffed, and up close I could see her face beneath her wide-brimmed hat was sunburned.

"We'll give you a ride home. Your family's been looking for you." I opened up the door to the back seat and slid over.

Sally climbed in and Adam turned the car around and headed back to Manning Hall. "Why would anyone be looking for me? Why would anyone care?"

"Your mother is grief-stricken with worry. You've been missing for over a day," I said.

"Oh, yes. Mummy. But she's the only one."

"Were you in Brighton with Hal Ames?"

"Yes." The sniffs were louder and closer together now.

"What happened?"

"We had a row. And then when I reached the bus stop, I found they weren't running the eight-forty bus because of the blackout. Hal must have taken the earlier bus without me, leaving me stuck all night at the bus shelter. How could he abandon me that way? Just because I wanted him to buy me a proper tea." She looked and sounded sulky, with her lower lip sticking out as if it were a toddler's.

"Did you try to call home?"

"Yes, and nobody answered."

That sounded odd. Her mother and grandfather were supposed to have been in the house all night until we arrived. Plus, where were the servants?

"Stupid Hal," she grumbled. "I never want to see him again."

"You won't," I told her. Then I softened my tone. "I have bad news."

"It can't be worse than what I've suffered." She sounded as if she were a tragic heroine in a movie.

"Sally, Hal's dead."

"What?" Her shout was nearly deafening.

"I'm sorry. His body was found in a ditch this morning between Manning Hall and the Longs's farm."

"Oh, no. In a ditch? Poor Hal. He was—he was my best friend, and now he's dead. What happened?" She let out one sob and then subsided into sighs worthy of the cinema. Her eyes were dry.

"The police suspect foul play," I told her. She didn't seem too upset, despite her theatrical performance. I hoped she, and her parents, had a good alibi.

"Foul play? Do you mean he was murdered?" Sally Glenfell asked.

"Possibly," I replied.

"Golly."

She didn't say another word as we reached her home. As soon as we pulled up, she jumped from the car and ran to the door, pushing it open.

Sir John looked at the police car in front of us in the drive and said, "We'd better go in."

I walked in last, and by the time I was in the front hall, Sally was already in her mother's embrace on a sofa in the front drawing room. Her father and Inspector Parsons were standing, while a constable was seated in the far corner, taking notes.

"You see? You let her go running loose and what is the result?" Philip Glenfell said in a loud voice, facing his wife. Sally's response was to bury her head further into her mother's arms and let out a loud sob.

I suspected if I could see her eyes now, there still wouldn't be tears.

"Sally is home safe and sound, so that's all to the good. Now, Sally, where did you last see Hal?" the inspector asked.

"What do you mean, 'all to the good'? Anything could have happened to her," Philip Glenfell roared.

"Since your wife has her hands full, perhaps you could request some tea for your daughter," the inspector said. He stood with a blank expression on his face, looking as immovable as a boulder.

"Why do I bother, I ask you?" Glenfell asked no one in particular as he walked out of the room.

"Now, Miss Sally, where did you last see Hal?" the inspector asked.

"Near the pier."

"In Brighton?"

She nodded.

"You had a disagreement?"

"I wanted tea. He wanted an ice cream. He said tea was too expensive."

"So, this was about tea time?"

She nodded again.

"Do you know precisely when?"

She buried her head in her mother's arms again and let out a wail just as her father came into the room.

"Will you stop bullying my daughter?" Glenfell demanded. "Get out of my house."

"I understand you want to comfort your daughter." Inspector Parsons then turned to Louisa. "Now that the family has had a chance to discuss where they looked for Miss Sally last night, has anything come out that might shed light on either of these murders?"

"I can assure you no one here wanted Hal Ames dead." Louisa walked over to the cigarette box and took one out, lighting it and taking in a long pull of smoke.

"And Sir Rupert?"

"Oh, everyone wanted him dead."

"Why would that be?" The inspector sounded as if he were humoring her.

"He was a cheapskate and a bully. None of us could stand him."

"Oh, Louisa," Philip Glenfell said. "He wasn't that bad."

"Then why were you sneaking off to London, applying for clerkships in every ministry of the government, and making certain Sir Rupert didn't know by getting the post office in the village to hold your mail?" she asked him.

"I want to do my bit for England in the times ahead."

"You'd have to keep that secret from the old man." Louisa turned to the inspector. "Sir Rupert was a Nazi. A thoroughly disgusting thug."

"He was a national hero," the inspector exclaimed, looking shocked.

"Really? Why?" she asked.

"We'll be back later. Good day," Inspector Parsons abruptly turned on his heel, and the constable quickly rose to follow him out. On his way, the inspector glanced at Adam and me and nodded toward the front of the house.

"We were surprised to find you here," I said as soon as I stepped outdoors.

"We were here to take the particulars on a missing girl who is no longer missing. Now," the inspector said with an impatient sigh as we walked onto the drive, "when and where did you find Sally Glenfell?"

"On the road from the village to here at a few minutes before twelve."

"She must have come in on the nine-forty bus," the constable said. "It's the first one on a Sunday morning."

"That would be a good place to check," the inspector replied. "Did you know it was her?" he asked me.

"Sir John did. I just thought she resembles her mother." *Acts the same way too, with overdone sobbing while I suspect her eyes are dry.*

"When did you learn Sally was missing?"

Adam explained about meeting Mr. Glenfell at Summersby House and later his wife at the time we discovered Sir Rupert was murdered, and did so in fewer words than I would have used.

Maybe that was why I could never do a proper job on my articles for the *Daily Premier*. I was too wordy.

"Anything else you can tell us that would be helpful?"

"Would you mind some speculation, Inspector?" I asked.

"Is it pertinent?"

"Yes."

"Then go ahead." He didn't sound willing. More as if he was doing his duty.

"I think this is the first time Sally has had a boyfriend, or at least one from the lower classes. He was her knight in shining armor until they disagreed over what he could afford on a laborer's wage, and she hit reality with a bump. And then she supposedly spent the night in an uncomfortable bus shelter counting her grievances. You won't see many tears, not real ones, but it doesn't make her unfeeling. Just immature."

"Thank you, Mrs. Redmond. This gives us more to follow up on Hal's movements as well as Sally's."

"You're welcome, Inspector. I was her age not too long ago."

"My wife was an anarchist," Adam said with a grin, "driving the teachers at her boarding school crazy with her rule-breaking."

"Even my father isn't aware of what a rebel I was," I told him, grinning back. Maybe I was Sally's age longer ago than I realized. I'd left my rule-breaking days behind me. More or less.

"I take it you've known Lady Louisa for a long time," the inspector said.

"We were in boarding school together."

"What did you think of her?"

"She was a tattletale in school, but truthful," I told him. "If she says Sir Rupert was horrible to his family, you can believe it."

"But Sir Rupert was a national hero. A daring explorer. I read about his exploits in the newspapers," Inspector Parsons said. "Plus, he was a baronet."

Thinking of Sir Rupert's efforts to block our wedding, I didn't share the inspector's hero worship. Adam gave me a look and I didn't say any more.

Adam and I said good-bye to the police as they walked off. I was glad to get away from them, and that I wasn't suspected of wrongdoing.

Sir John came out of the house at that moment, accompanied by a couple who appeared to be only a year or two out of university.

Sir John introduced us to Freddy and Anne Manning. Freddy had the pale coloring of the Mannings and a vacant sort of gleam in his eyes. Anne had brown hair and eyes, with untamed curls that reminded me of my own. She had an athletic stride as she walked toward us, and a no-nonsense manner as she held out her hand.

"I'm Anne Manning. Awful name, but that's what you get with marriage sometimes. All those Ns sounds similar to a machine running. You're Livvy Redmond? I hear best wishes are in order."

"Thank you. Did Louisa tell you?" It seemed likely.

"No. We were all treated to Sir Rupert cursing you and your unapproved wedding at St. Athanasius. Well done, you, for beating the old bully at his own game."

"Thank you." I lowered my voice. "I think."

"No thought required. I hope we see more of you around the Hall." She gave me a smile as she lowered her voice. "Freddy is the youngest of the three Manning children. And yes, 'children' is the best word for them. Sir Rupert saw to it they all stayed living at home under his thumb, where he could constantly remind them of how useless they were. No wonder someone murdered him."

I stared at her, amazed. I couldn't believe she was admitting all this to a stranger. She must have had a good alibi.

"It's going to be frightfully boring around here while we're in mourning for dear Papa," Freddy said, strolling over to us after ending his chat with Sir John.

"My condolences on the death of your father," Adam said.

"Oh, I won't miss Papa. I was a terrible disappointment to him. But the mourning will be too depressing. No parties. No picnics." He turned to his wife. "Ready to go?"

"Yes. Nice meeting you," Anne told us, and they walked off.

"They're cheerful," Adam whispered in my ear.

When we were finally in the car and on our way, with Adam still carrying out the driving duties, Sir John asked, "What are your plans for this week?"

"I'm committed to staying at Summersby House or at the flat so my regiment can reach me to return quickly if needed," Adam replied, his voice sounding a little strained.

"Hmmm," Sir John answered. "You are of course welcome to stay here, and we'll try to stay out of your way..."

"No, Colonel. It's your home. We need to stay out of your way and be good guests," Adam said. "It's a lot cooler and more pleasant here than in London, so if you don't mind..."

"Not at all. You and Livvy are welcome to stay as long as you want. And if we get to be too much..." Sir John sounded as if he was chuckling.

"You won't, sir. Livvy and I know this isn't a perfect time to get married, but you and Lady Abby have been more than generous. When the war's over, we'll go on a proper honeymoon."

"To the Isle of Wight?" I asked hopefully.

"To Scotland," he replied. It was an ongoing disagreement, but not one either of us considered an immediate worry. Not with two murders threatening us.

I was happy spending any time I could with my hero. I was trying to avoid the newspapers and the radio news, but I knew war was just around the corner, and with it would come separation.

We had to snatch every moment we could.

Chapter Seven

We arrived at Summersby House more than a little late for Sunday dinner. Abby was not pleased and wanted an explanation. We quickly got cleaned up and went downstairs to find all four of the boys were there, plus Ray Long. Mark and Ray were telling the others what they'd seen, earning Abby's wrath.

Mary brought in the soup. It tasted all right but didn't match the cook's, Mrs. Goodfellow's, usually excellent fish chowder. "I suppose I owe Mrs. Goodfellow an apology for making her hold up dinner," Sir John said.

"I'd wait on that until after we have the roast," Abby replied.

I saw why when Mary brought in the blackened, dried-up piece of meat for Sir John to carve. The vegetables were also crisply overcooked. My father's eyebrows shot up to his thinning hairline. The boys shot puzzled glances at each other but they ate their share speedily. Adam also ate quickly.

"We found Sally Glenfell and took her home," I announced to the table.

"Where had she been?" Abby asked, setting her fork down.

I told her the general story that I had heard, with Sir

John and Adam nodding when Abby looked at them.

"I see why you were late," she said. "I'll have to tell Mrs. Goodfellow and Mary that you were on a mission of mercy. Her mother must have been grateful."

"Mother and daughter both collapsed on the sofa, hugging each other," I said.

Either there was nothing the cook could ruin with the berries, or she and Mary were listening in, because the berries and cream were delicious, tasting of summertime and clear skies. The boys all asked to be excused as soon as they ate the last spoonful.

My father rose and announced he had packing to do because he needed to go back to town that afternoon. He thanked Sir John and Abby for a delightful weekend and said how glad he was to see Adam again. He did say he was glad I was married before he left the room.

Once the boys had escaped from the house, Mary came in with the coffee and tea. She set down the tray in front of Abby and said, "Beggin' your pardon, but cook wants to see you in the kitchen."

"Should I?" Sir John said, half rising.

"No, I should," Abby replied.

"She wants to see Mrs. Redmond, too."

"Me?" I said, completely surprised.

"Yes, ma'am."

The men both stood as we rose and walked out to the kitchen, leaving them with the coffee.

Hester Goodfellow, both plump and muscular as you'd expect in someone who does heavy work in a farm kitchen and does it well, cleared her throat as we stood across the table from her in the kitchen. "Beggin' your pardon, but I couldn't help overhearing about that Sally Glenfell's safe return."

Abby and I both nodded.

"But the question is, who's going to comfort Eleanor Ames? She's lost both her husband and son now."

"Does she have family in the district?" I asked.

"I'm her sister."

Was Mrs. Goodfellow looking for some leave to spend with the unfortunate Mrs. Ames? That was Abby's decision, not mine, so I kept my mouth firmly shut.

"I know Mrs. Redmond is on her honeymoon, but could she help find out who killed Hal? Sort of the way a private investigator would? She found the person who tried to blow up Mr. Churchill last autumn."

"Yes, she did," Abby agreed. Abby had aided my investigation into the assassination attempt on Mr. Churchill. I'd been working on orders from Sir Malcolm Freemantle, the head of British counterintelligence. Both Abby and Sir John were aware of how deeply I was involved in hunting Nazi spies on British soil without any of us directly mentioning my work.

"What do you think, Livvy? You'll be here for the next week."

"On my honeymoon." Which had been anything but what I expected. Riding around in the middle of the night looking at dark houses. Driving various members of the Manning clan home.

"So was Eleanor after the war and the influenza, and you see how much good it did her." Mrs. Goodfellow glowered at me before she added, "Beggin' your pardon."

"I doubt Mrs. Ames would want me sticking my nose in, asking questions," I told her. "I can be intrusive." From what I'd seen of her at the accident site, I didn't think she'd want me to interfere.

"Let me talk to her. Are you willing?"

Abby gave me a look that plainly said she wanted me to help.

I shrugged. "I don't know how much good I can do, but I'm willing to try. If I can involve Captain Redmond."

The cook nodded. "I'll contact her after tea. Thank you."

"Don't thank me yet. I haven't done anything." I walked back into the dining room where Sir John and Adam sat with their coffee. "Adam, we've been asked to find out who killed Hal Ames."

Abby poured tea for the two of us. "Eleanor Ames is Hester Goodfellow's sister."

"That explains dinner," Sir John said. "Well? Are you going to help the woman out?"

I didn't see where we had much choice. Between the wedding and the honeymoon, Abby and Sir John were being more than generous to us. "You don't have to, Adam, if you don't want to."

He took my hand and kissed my knuckles. "I don't mind, as long as I can spend the time with you."

"We'll see what Mrs. Ames tells Mrs. Goodfellow," I

told him and squeezed his fingers. "Why don't I finish my tea and we can go for a walk?"

We strolled down the tree-lined lane to the road, enjoying the breeze that cooled our skin when we were in the shade. When we reached the lane, Adam leaned against a fencepost and said, "We can't tell them no."

"You can. I can't."

He pulled me into his embrace. "I don't mind helping you, although I have no idea how we can be of any use," he said into my hair.

"Once we're certain Mrs. Ames welcomes our help, we can search the area around where Hal's body was found, and we can ask Sally questions away from her family."

"Do you think that's possible?" Adam asked.

"Oh, yes. She's a young lady who knows her own mind and she'll want to spend more time with her friends now that Hal is out of the picture. I don't think her parents will be able to stop her, short of sending her off to relatives."

Adam looked perplexed. "But her mother's family is all under the same roof."

I smiled at Adam. "Making it more probable she won't be sent away. Hopefully, that means we'll be able to talk to her away from the house. We'll have to find out from Matthew when the next cricket practice is. There should be plenty of young people there. Including Sally."

He shook his head. "Not if her father has anything to say about it. I'm sure he doesn't trust her an inch after she ran away to a beach resort with a young man. And Philip

Glenfell is a man who is very conscious of the family's reputation."

"Now that Sir Rupert is dead, I wonder how long all of the family will continue to live in Manning Hall? Especially since we now know Glenfell has been applying for positions in London. If the Glenfells leave the area, that could make it difficult to talk to Sally."

Talking into my curls, Adam said, "I wonder how long Sir Douglas—that's right, isn't it?—will want a brother-in-law he doesn't like living under his roof? I hope Glenfell finds that position soon."

I hoped the changes at Manning Hall wouldn't lead to more murders.

After tea, Adam and I drove my father to the train station. Adam carried his suitcase while my father walked beside me, telling me I needed to learn to cook and keep house now that I would no longer be working.

"I'm going to keep working."

He looked startled. "How does Adam feel about that?"

"Fine. He understands that's part of the agreement."

"Agreement? Agreement?" My father's voice rose almost to a shriek before he brought himself under control. "What about children?"

"I don't expect Adam to be around enough to make that an issue until the war's over."

"Don't be too certain, young lady." He glanced in front of him and said, "Good-bye, Adam. I wish you all the luck in the world."

"With your daughter, sir?"

My father looked startled. "Er, no. I was thinking of the coming conflict. But with her, too." He made me sound as if I was an afterthought. "I've done my best. She's your worry now."

I kept my mouth closed. He'd always found me to be an addendum. We saw him onto the train and I walked away, relieved that he was gone.

"He didn't mean it that way, Livvy."

"Yes, he did." I sighed, knowing I'd never be able to change him and his desire for a son. Or a perfectly pliable daughter. "Let's go back to Sir John and Abby's."

We returned to find a lively game passing for cricket on the lawn. Clear skies and long summer evenings were perfect for spending outdoors, and Abby and Sir John sat outside the French doors to the dining room, serving as both teams' loyal supporters.

Adam was chosen for Henry and Mark's team, while Gerhard and Matthew were stuck with me. "Evens things out," Mark said without a hint of sarcasm.

"Oh, Mark, really," his mother said in exasperation.

"You just better watch out, Mark," I said. "I might score a century against you."

When everyone finished laughing at my preposterous suggestion, we began a rollicking game.

Ten minutes later, while I was fielding, I saw Mrs. Goodfellow come around the side of the house toward us. I guessed she was calling someone to the telephone.

She stopped and spoke to Sir John and Abby, who

signaled Adam and me to come over. All I could think was Adam's leave had been canceled, and this beautiful summer had come to an end.

I wanted to scream at how unfair everything was.

Chapter Eight

We strolled over to where the adults waited for us, the boys fooling around playing catch as they waited. "Livvy," Abby said, "Mrs. Goodfellow has news for you."

I knew before she said a word that Mrs. Ames wanted, or had been persuaded to want, my investigation into her son's death. I breathed out a sigh. "Yes, Mrs. Goodfellow?"

"Eleanor wants you to find out who killed her son. She has no faith in Constable Wiggins or the fancy inspector they sent down from Scotland Yard or somewhere."

Knowing Sunday was Mrs. Goodfellow's half day and she had been finished with work hours ago, I said, "Then you and Adam and I need to go over to her house and speak with her. Sir John, can we borrow your car?"

He glanced at Abby and then said, "Of course."

About ten minutes later, we had dressed for making a call and reached the village. We followed Mrs. Goodfellow's directions to pull up on the verge in front of a stone cottage. The fence around the front was covered with honeysuckle. Looking up the hill, I could see the roof of St. Athanasius over the tops of other houses. "Both Mrs. Ames and Hal lived here?" I asked.

"Of course," the cook replied.

"Rented?" Adam asked.

"Yes, but not from Sir Rupert. Eleanor would never have rented from him, and he's never wanted anything to do with them since Hal's father died."

"Who owns it?" I had no idea why it seemed important, but it did.

"Mr. Long. It was his grandmother's. When she died, he inherited it and rents it out to Eleanor."

We climbed out of the car and I saw a curtain twitch in a downstairs window. Mrs. Goodfellow walked up to the doorstep and banged twice with the knocker while we waited on the flagstone path from the road.

The tall, thin woman we'd seen when we drove Sir John to see the site of Hal's body opened the door. Dressed the same as she'd been that morning, she stepped back wordlessly and we walked straight into a low-ceilinged drawing room.

"Hester says you can find out who killed Hal. That you're good at this sort of thing," Eleanor Ames said, standing on the far side of the room and not offering us a seat. There was only a sofa, two chairs, and a couple of small tables by the chairs, but they filled the small space.

"I've been more lucky than good," I told her, "but I'm willing to try."

"You can't make things any worse." Mrs. Ames kept her arms crossed over her chest.

"When did you last see Hal alive?"

"Saturday morning early. He was off work and planned to take the bus to the beach."

"Did you know he was going with Sally?"

She nodded.

"When did you expect him home?"

She shrugged. "He was old enough to find his way home when he was ready."

"Had he been out all night before this?"

"A few times. Off with his mates."

"Could you tell me who his mates were?"

She rattled off a few names. None of them were people I knew.

"Who did he work for?"

"Mr. Long, when he had any work on offer. He worked at Jones's Garage two days a week as an apprentice. Between the two, he was in pocket money. Both men put great store in Hal, but there's not much work going around here. Not for a young lad such as Hal. He was looking forward to a regular salary from the militia."

"He was in the group who'd been called up for six months' military training starting next Saturday, correct?" Adam asked.

"Yes, he and Gary Jones. Crazy kids. Best mates. They were looking forward to it." Her voice softened at the memory.

"And you, Mrs. Ames? Who do you work for?" I asked.

"The doctor. Cooking and cleaning."

"Dr. Wheeler?"

"What other doctor is there around here?" she asked, as if she thought I was foolish.

"Who do you think killed Hal?"

"The Mannings. Who else?"

"Why?"

"How would I know why that lot does anything?"

"Neither of you work for them. There's no real reason why you'd be in contact with them except around the village or in church." It made no sense to me. "There's always a reason why someone kills. Revenge or fury or theft. Something. Why would one of the Mannings be so upset with Hal that they'd kill him?"

"They didn't want Hal around Sally. They were afraid he'd corrupt her."

"The Mannings could have just told Sally to stay away from him. There was no reason to kill him." That seemed extreme.

"Tell Sally Glenfell anything? I want to see you try. Her mother is a doormat, and her father—all bluster, he is. The whole family is under the thumb of Sir Rupert, but even he couldn't keep Sally from seeing Hal. And that really made the old devil angry."

* * *

Eleanor Ames couldn't give us any more information, and she made it clear she didn't want to talk to us anymore. We left and Mrs. Goodfellow directed us to the Jones cottage, just down the road from the garage Mr. Jones owned.

Gary Jones, a young man the same age as Hal, answered the door. Mrs. Goodfellow immediately told him, "Mrs. Ames wants these people to investigate Hal's murder. This is Captain and Mrs. Redmond and they're staying at Summersby House."

"I didn't have anything to do with it," he exclaimed, stepping back from the doorway.

"Hey, what's this?" an older image of Gary said, opening the door wider to take a look at us.

"I'm not saying you had anything to do with Hal's death, but both you and your father knew Hal. You knew his character. You knew who he got along with, who he avoided, whether he owed anyone money. All information that may lead to his killer."

Mr. Jones looked out beyond us to the lane. "You best come in."

We were invited to take seats in the small drawing room. Through the doorway into the kitchen, I could see the remains of their evening meal on dirty dishes on the wooden table. "We're not interrupting your dinner, are we?"

"We've finished." Mr. Jones's voice was flat, disinterested.

"Well, I'll just go in and help Ellen," Mrs. Goodfellow said and headed toward the kitchen.

"Come in, Hester," a woman's voice said as Mrs. Goodfellow shut the door behind her.

"Gary, you first. Tell me about Hal."

"What do you want to know?"

I couldn't tell if he was unimaginative or being difficult. "Was he a good friend?"

"Yeah."

"Did he owe you money?"

"Nah. I don't have any money to lend."

"Did he owe other people money?"

"He and his mum were always owing on the cottage. That's why Mr. Long hired him so often. Hal worked for Mr. Long more to pay the rent than to put money in his pocket."

"An honest young man," I said.

"Yes, he was," Mr. Jones growled at me as if I'd been implying otherwise.

"How long had he been seeing Sally Glenfell?"

"Couple of months."

"Did you think that would last?"

Gary snorted. "Did you?"

"I didn't know either of them, Gary. I need you to tell me."

"She was always hanging on him, and she bossed him around. Hal was getting tired of her, even before they went to the beach."

"Whose idea was that?"

"Hers, of course. Everything was always her idea, once she started nagging. He was trying to avoid her."

"Did her family know the relationship was starting to fall apart?"

"Don't know how they could have. They'd only have heard Sally's side, and she was crazy about him. And she would have been, until she decided it was over."

Interesting, but I didn't see how this would lead us to Hal's killer. "How did they meet?"

"At a cricket match. Hal liked cricket, and he was a good batsman. He impressed Sally, and she set her cap for him. He liked anything in a skirt, and he was more than willing to take what was on offer. Called her his bit of posh."

"Even though his mother blamed Sally's grandfather for Hal's father's death?"

"Hal didn't set any store by that. Every year or two we lose a farmworker in an accident at harvesttime. He thought it was an accident, no matter what people thought."

More interesting. "What was the gossip at the time that made Mrs. Ames think Sir Rupert killed her husband?"

Mr. Jones broke in. "One of the old farmworkers, long dead now, said he saw Ames stay behind at the end of the day and corner Sir Rupert. They exchanged some sharp words and then walked off together toward the house. That was the last anyone saw Ames alive."

What I'd heard made no sense to me. "I thought his death was a farm accident. If work was done for the day, how was the accident explained?"

"Sir Rupert said Ames asked for more work. Said he needed money. Sir Rupert said he told him to clean out the harvesting machinery and left him to it. Ames was found next to a piece of machinery with wounds that might have, maybe, matched where blood was found on the blades." Mr. Jones's voice was gruff.

"'Might have' matched?"

"Depends on how he fell, and where he fell from. Most people either found it hard to believe, or didn't believe it at all. Eleanor never did."

"Was it likely it was an accident?" That had to have been the central issue of the coroner's inquest.

Mr. Jones shrugged. "It was the end of the day. He was tired. Probably slipped and fell."

"Who found him?"

"Mrs. Ames and Sir Rupert's farm manager, when Eleanor Ames came looking for him."

"Did the farm manager know about this extra work Sir Rupert gave him?"

"No, but it wasn't unheard of, Sir Rupert doing things and not telling his manager. It was his farm. He could do what he wanted. And he did," Mr. Jones added.

"Did anyone witness the accident?"

"No."

"And the decision of the coroner's jury was...?"

"Exactly the way Sir Rupert said." His tone was flat.

"Eleanor Ames never accepted it?"

"Most people didn't, but there was nothing to say what happened. In the end, we all just went on with our lives."

"Did you know Hal's father?"

"We were in school together. Went to war together. Came back together, and grateful to have survived."

"I didn't know that, Dad," Gary said.

"That's why I kept an eye on both you lads. Felt it was what I could do for him. I worked for Sir Rupert that day. Mighta been me."

"But you didn't ask him for extra work," I said, trying to keep my voice as level as his.

"I had the garage to keep me going. Mick Ames knew he could come get extra work from me if he wanted. He was supposed to come help me that night after tea. Wondered at the time why he didn't come by."

Chapter Nine

"He was supposed to work for you that evening? What did the police say when you told them?" I was curious about Hal's father's death, and whether it had anything to do with Hal's.

"He changed his mind." Mr. Jones shrugged.

"Dad." Gary scowled at his father.

"Wasn't nothing I could do. He was dead."

"Dad…" Gary started again, half pleading, half arguing.

Mr. Jones rose and headed for the door. "We've got chores to do. We've answered your questions. Hal was a good lad. Didn't deserve killing. I hope you find which one of the Mannings did it."

He opened the door and stood next to it, pointedly staring at us. We rose and took a few steps in that direction. "Mrs. Goodfellow? We're leaving," I called out.

She opened the door from the kitchen. "Oh, dear. Just a—"

"We'll take her back to Summersby House," Mr. Jones said. "Good-bye." We stepped over the threshold and felt the door shut against our backs.

As we walked toward the car, I said, "I wonder what Mrs. Ames knew of his plans for that night."

"She went looking for him at the Manning farm. She must have known he'd be there." Adam opened the car door for me and shut it again before he said, "We won't get any further tonight. Let's head back."

* * *

The next morning, along with a second cup of tea, came a request for me to visit Mrs. Goodfellow in the kitchen. I finished my eggs, tomatoes, and toast and gave Adam a smile. "I'll be back in a minute."

"Do you need me?"

"No. Enjoy your breakfast. We can discuss this later." I walked into the kitchen to find Mrs. Goodfellow sitting on a stool in front of the big oak table, chopping vegetables. "How can I help you?"

She didn't pause as she said, "What did Roger Jones tell you?"

"That Mick Ames was last seen with Sir Rupert asking for extra work."

"Mrs. Jones told me Mick was supposed to help Roger on a big job at the garage."

"Mr. Jones mentioned that, too. He also said he told the police, but they weren't interested."

"Of course they weren't," Mrs. Goodfellow scoffed. "Sir Rupert had just returned from an impressive Arctic exploration with some Germans and Finnish fellows. He was in all the papers. He was a hero. Whatever he said was taken as gospel from on high."

"Who ran the farm while he was gone?" I should have thought to ask Mr. Jones the night before.

"Ah…the farm manager. Can't remember his name now." The knife came down on the pole beans.

"He was the man Eleanor Ames went to when she was looking for her husband that night?"

"Yes, after she talked to Roger Jones and found out Mick wasn't there." The knife blade banged as it cut through the carrots as if Mrs. Goodfellow wanted to decapitate someone.

"Is this farm manager still around?"

"Shortly after the inquest, Sir Rupert found him a job as a farm manager in the West Country. That's where he was from. Sent him packing and found some man from Yorkshire to fill in before Sir Rupert set off for the Arctic again. Or traveling somewhere. Sir Rupert was always traveling."

"Anyone know where that farm manager is now?"

"No. Sir Rupert saw to that."

I gave the cook a puzzled scowl. "Do you think he knew more than he said at the inquest?" Then I realized what I didn't know and added, "Exactly what did he say at the inquest?"

"He said he didn't know Mick Ames was working that night. That Sir Rupert was free to hire anyone he wanted to do any job that needed doing. He didn't need to clear it with his farm manager. Then the coroner excused him." *Whack.* The blade came down again on a potato.

"He wasn't asked anything else, even though he was there on the farm?" I found that surprising.

Mrs. Goodfellow's expression told me how skeptical

she was.

"Who was the coroner?"

"Dr. Reynolds, the headmaster at Percy Vale School. And before you ask, he was a good friend of Sir Rupert and a lenient headmaster to Sir Douglas, as he is now, and to young Freddy. Especially Freddy. Sir Rupert knew he could trust Dr. Reynolds."

"Is Dr. Reynolds a medical doctor?"

"No, he was a doctor of Latin. Dr. Wheeler, the father of the present Dr. Wheeler, was our doctor then and did the autopsy. He said he didn't think it was possible for Mick Ames to fall on the thresher that way, and besides, the wounds didn't match up. He and Dr. Reynolds got into it, right there in the inquest."

"Why? What was said?" This inquest was sounding very odd.

"Dr. Reynolds said Dr. Wheeler wasn't an expert and should confine himself to the cause of death. Dr. Wheeler said any medical man could see the wounds didn't line up with the blades that had blood on them, and if the death was caused the way Dr. Reynolds seemed to think, then poor Mick Ames would have been impaled. And nobody says they removed the body.

"Then Dr. Reynolds had Dr. Wheeler's testimony taken out of the record. Dr. Wheeler called Dr. Reynolds a bloody fool right in front of God and everybody. Dr. Reynolds said he was coroner and he could decide anything he wanted.

"Dr. Wheeler said he could decide the sky was green,

but that didn't make it true. The two men never spoke again."

Wow. I knew most inquests were dry, low-keyed affairs. I would have enjoyed watching this one. "Wasn't there a coroner's jury?"

"All men whose livelihoods depended on Sir Rupert. No one from our side of the village was on the jury." *Whack* went the knife again.

"Our side of the village?"

"The Summersby Farm side. Men who depended on Sir John more than Sir Rupert for work."

No wonder Eleanor Ames thought Sir Rupert was guilty of her husband's murder. The inquest had certainly not been impartial.

I thanked her and walked back out to the dining room to find Sir John and Abby had left, leaving Adam on his own. He rose and said, "What's wrong?"

"How do you know…?"

"It's written all over your face." Adam knew me all too well.

"Let's take a walk."

We walked down to the road while I told him what Mrs. Goodfellow had said. By the time I finished, we had walked a distance along the lane past the gateposts.

"But Livvy, that was more than fifteen years ago. I admit the inquest sounds questionable, but that's not what we were asked to investigate. I don't see how we could investigate that death all these years later. And how would that help us figure out who killed the Ames lad or

Sir Rupert?"

"I don't know, but I think these murders are all tied together." A little voice inside me was saying, *They have to be. Otherwise, there haven't been any murders in this village.*

"Even if they are, at least with Hal's murder we have the suspects right here to talk to and the motives possible to find. In his father's death, witnesses have moved away, have died, have had years to forget details." Adam gave me a hug. "Who do you want to talk to next?"

His arms around me felt safe and comforting. I buried my face in his shoulder and inhaled his scents of clean laundry and shaving soap. "Mr. Long. Hal lived in a cottage owned by him and worked for him. I wonder what Mr. Long knows about him. And we need to find out from Matthew when the next cricket practice is that Sally Glenfell might attend."

"Sounds good." He didn't let me go.

We stood there, locked in an embrace, feeling the sunshine warming our skin, until we heard running feet and Henry's voice shouting, "Cousin Livvy. Cousin Adam. I get to go to cricket practice today."

We dropped our arms and stood shoulder to shoulder to face the child. "When is practice?" Adam asked.

"After lunch. It gives some of the lads a chance to finish their chores so they can join us." He smiled at us, his fair hair blowing over his eyes and ears.

"We'll try to get down there to watch the practice. Right now, we'll see about borrowing bicycles to ride over and talk to Mr. Long," I told him.

"Gerhard and Matthew have fixed them up so they fly." He jumped on his toes in excitement. "You'll get over there really fast."

"Good," Adam said. "Lead the way to the bicycles."

Henry did exactly that, skipping, running, and jumping while constantly talking. When we reached the barn where the bicycles were stored, we found we had a choice of four.

"Please tell Lady Abby we've ridden over to the Long farm. We'll be back in time for lunch."

Henry nodded and raced to the house.

Adam and I rode off, the bicycles gliding easily along the rough road. We reached the Longs's farm quicker than I expected and rode up to the house. The woman who introduced herself as Mrs. Long, with two young girls arguing behind her and holding scrub brushes as if they were weapons, told us Walter was in the barn and to check there.

We thanked her and left the bicycles by the house as we walked down to the barn. Walter Long, with Ray and a younger son, were stacking hay bales.

"Hello, Mr. Long," I said as we stood in the entrance to the barn. "We met when Hal Ames's body was found. We're Captain and Mrs. Redmond."

"Staying at Summersby House," Mr. Long said.

"Yes. Mrs. Ames has asked us to look into what happened to her son," I told him.

"Why?" The question fell as if it were iron onto the

barn floor.

"We've been known to investigate things for the government. Mrs. Ames wants us to use our experience for her."

I stared at Mr. Long, who studied us for a moment and then gave one sharp nod. Sitting on a hay bale, he said, "What do you want to know?"

"Everything you can tell us about Hal," Adam said.

"Good young man. Willing to work hard. Respectful to his elders. Not wild."

"I've heard he owed money," Adam continued.

Mr. Long snorted. "I can imagine where you heard that. Eleanor and Hal never had two farthings to rub together since Mick died. She did a great job of raising that boy."

"You rent their cottage to them."

"So?"

"So?" I echoed back to him.

"Yes, I rent them their cottage."

"Do they keep up on their rent?"

"Yes."

"How much is their rent?" Adam asked, reminding me that he interrogated people as part of his duties for the army. I wouldn't have dared ask a man that question.

Long stood up and said in a scornful tone, "None of your business. Ask Eleanor if you want to know and think she'll tell you."

"I will." Adam and Walter Long faced off, staring hard at each other.

"I imagine you give her favorable terms, since Mick was a friend of yours," I said.

"Of course I do. Wasn't right, Mick working so hard he had an accident and died. He was a good man."

"You served in the Great War together, you and Roger Jones and Mick Ames," Adam said.

"Yes, and we all made it back. Counted ourselves lucky." Walter Long sat back on a hay bale. "We all got married to our sweethearts and started to put our lives back together. I helped my dad on our farm, Roger Jones worked in the garage with his father, but Mick didn't have anywhere he belonged."

"You both helped him out with part-time work." I guessed they had, the same way they'd helped out his son.

He nodded.

"Where had he worked before the war?"

"The Manning estate. He was a gardener for the old lord, Sir Rupert's father. When the old lord died of influenza, Sir Rupert took over. Sacked most of the staff. He wanted the money for his traveling. Didn't want to pay it out in salaries. Didn't care how the place appeared. He didn't plan to be in residence much except between trips to the Arctic.

"And if it were up to him, the gardens would still be a jungle today." Long shook his head. "Sir Rupert was a horror. No wonder someone finally did him in."

Chapter Ten

"Sir Rupert hadn't gone on any expeditions in years. Had he brought in more staff?" In rural areas, the big estates were important employment centers. I was glad I lived in a city, although with the lingering effects of the depression, jobs were still scarce even in London.

"He didn't have much choice. The children demanded it, so they'd be able to use their tennis court and have gardens that weren't a wilderness. I heard Sir Rupert fought with them about hiring more staff, but the children prevailed in the end. Douglas—Sir Douglas now—sees the sense in keeping the farm profitable, and that requires hiring gardeners and stockmen. Especially since there's another war coming. Britain will have to survive on the products of its own farmland, and the young men will be leaving the fields again." Walter Long slowly shook his head. "The way we did. I wish them luck."

We thanked Mr. Long for his time and started toward the entrance to the barn, stopping when he spoke again.

"Has Sir Douglas told you about the arguments he'd been having with his father over his travels?"

We turned. "No. Whose travels? Where?" I asked, taking a few steps toward him. I could guess, but I wanted corroboration.

"I heard this from someone at the house. Sir Rupert kept traveling to visit his expedition friends even after he stopped going on expeditions, and apparently, his travel was as expensive as his trips to the Arctic had been. Sir Douglas told his father they couldn't afford it, and to stop traveling to Germany."

"Who told you about this?" I asked, but I couldn't get anything else out of Mr. Long.

He folded his arms and shook his head. "Those people need their positions. Can't have you starting trouble and getting them fired." And with that, he showed us to our bicycles.

We said good-bye to Ray, waved to his mother, and rode off along the lane. The day was dry and warm with a nice breeze, and we took the long way around to return to Summersby House, arriving just in time for lunch.

When Mary brought in the soup, I was so hungry from my morning exercise I could barely contain myself from falling on it before grace was said. I understood why Adam was always so hungry when he returned from his army duty.

"How are your investigations coming along?" Sir John asked.

"Interesting," I told him. "What do you remember about Sir Rupert's expeditions?"

"I remember they were a big deal. Everyone around here was proud of him drawing maps and hunting Arctic animals and setting endurance records and speed records across the Arctic. I have a book on the reports of the last two expeditions he went on. You're welcome to read it if you want."

His travels sounded tedious and uncomfortable to me, and probably made boring reading. "Who went with him?"

We all finished our soup and began on our chicken and vegetable stew before Sir John answered. "Friedrich von Marten was the leader of the expeditions Sir Rupert went on. Quite a famous man in international scientific circles. He raised the majority of the funding, with Sir Rupert putting in a share along with one or two others. Germans, all of them," he said with scorn. "Then they'd get native Greenlanders or Finns for bearers and to manage the dogs."

"Was Sir Rupert good friends with his fellow explorers?"

"He and Jürgen Wolfenhaus were close and remained that way, even now when they were both too old for that sort of thing. Sir Rupert had just returned from a visit to Wolfenhaus's castle when he started his nonsense about you not being a member of our congregation and so not being eligible to get married in St. Athanasius."

"Did Wolfenhaus ever come here?" I was trying to get an image in my mind of what Sir Rupert had been doing lately.

"He was here just a month or so before Sir Rupert went over there. Sir Rupert took him around to visit friends and see the sights, driving up and down the coast."

There was silence for a while. "And no one thought

that was strange, a German driving up and down the Channel coastline? A German in 1939," Adam asked after finishing his lunch.

Gerhard, who still remembered he was German even if Henry didn't, turned to look sharply at Adam.

Sir John looked at Adam for a moment, his expression growing dark before he said, "No."

"Did any of his other German friends come here?" Adam asked.

"No. We never saw any of the other explorers here or heard of them coming to England," Sir John said. "Just Wolfenhaus."

I understood what Adam was thinking. "And Sir Rupert didn't think we should put up a defense if the Germans invade. Was he a follower of Oswald Mosley?"

"No," Sir John said, scowling. "The Duke of Marshburn."

"Oh, him," I said with a sigh. The Nazi agent known as the French Assassin, a pleasant-looking woman hiding lethal talents, and I had crossed paths more than once in the preceding year. I suspected, although I couldn't prove, that the Duke of Marshburn was hiding her despite an arrest warrant for her on attempted murder and espionage charges.

"You realize I have to report this at HQ as soon as possible," Adam said.

At least he didn't say he was going to cut our honeymoon short, thank goodness, because his office could handle any investigation without him. After all, Sir

Rupert was dead and Wolfenhaus was back in Germany.

"Yes, I can see that you do," Sir John said. "I'm sorry, Adam, but I didn't think. I've known Wolfenhaus as Sir Rupert's friend and an explorer for ages. Never thought of him as a German. Not really."

I watched all four boys eat quickly and listen intently while trying to act nonchalant.

"Any idea of specifically what they toured?" Adam said a moment before I would have asked.

"None at all. All I heard was the coast," Sir John said. "You, Abby?"

"No, but Marjorie Lenard, the maid at Manning Hall, might know. She's a niece of Mrs. Goodfellow's. Or a cousin, I forget which."

"Is everyone in town related to Mrs. Goodfellow?" I asked.

"It certainly seems that way. Until the war, the local farmers and servants had intermarried for hundreds of years. That was especially true before the train reached our village. Even then, no one traveled far from home. So, everyone is related if you go back three or four generations." Abby's tone said this was how life was in their rural corner of England.

It certainly made it easier for Adam and me to ask questions, since Eleanor Ames wanted us to, and Eleanor Ames was related to all these people.

I supposed I needed to add Marjorie Lenard to the list of people I should speak to. And that meant more questions. "I need to ask Mrs. Goodfellow when Marjorie has her day off and how to get in touch with her."

"Who else would know about this tour of the coast?" Adam asked. "Sir Douglas? Someone else in the Manning household?"

"Douglas might," Sir John said. "He seems to be the only one with some sense."

"Then I need to give Sir Douglas a phone call, see if I can't set up a meeting." Adam glanced at me. "It'll give you a chance to catch up with your old school chum."

"We weren't that close," I admitted. "I was always breaking the rules. Louisa turned me in."

Out of the corner of my eye, I saw Mark nudge Matthew.

"Make the meeting for after the cricket practice. Can we go down to the practice field with you four?" I asked the boys.

They nodded before Henry said, "Are you going to talk to Sally again about running away from home?"

"I don't think she was running away from home," I said, surprised. Henry seemed to know what everyone was saying and doing, and he wasn't shy about asking questions. As the youngest, and a darling little boy, he could get away with it. "It sounded more as if it was a day's outing to the pier and then she missed the last bus."

"May we be excused to go to practice?" Matthew asked after a second shove from Mark.

Sir John took a glance at their empty plates and nodded.

The boys vanished.

"What are you going to ask Sally?" Abby asked.

"Whether she has any idea of who would have murdered Hal Ames. Who his good friends were. If she saw where he headed when they split up. Who in her family was most against her being friends with the Ames lad." Sally had to have some idea of what happened, now that she'd had time to think.

We excused ourselves, and Adam made a call while I went upstairs and got ready for our hike. With low boots and a hat to shade my face, I was ready. When I came back down, Adam was off the phone.

"Do you want to go to Manning Hall for tea this afternoon with the new lord and lady of the manor?" he asked.

"Absolutely."

"I made a second telephone call. To my office."

"It's a party line."

"We have a code to cover that. They'll start looking into Wolfenhaus, Sir Rupert, and their travels along the Channel coast immediately." Adam looked grim.

I nodded. At that moment, we didn't know how much damage those two men had done to Britain's security. Hiding my concern behind a pleasant expression, I found Abby and told her our plans for tea. Then I joined Adam and the boys and headed off along centuries-old paths to the village green.

I saw when we arrived that we were in luck. Sally was sitting on an embankment with another girl her age. As we were the only females present, I told Adam I'd see him in a bit and walked over to join the girls.

Adam quickly fell into the role of umpire as the boys divided up into two teams.

"Hi, Sally, are you doing all right?" I asked.

She looked at the other girl, a freckle-faced girl with brown hair and eyes, and said, "Um hum."

"Your parents aren't still crying and having fits?"

That made both girls smile. "No. Father's still trying to order everyone around, but Mum's fine now. First, she had to deliver a massive lecture, but it could have been much worse."

"Mrs. Ames wants me to figure out what happened to Hal, since she has no faith in the police," I said. "Could you talk to me about him?"

She shrank away and narrowed her eyes. "What do you want to know?"

"What was he like? He was your friend. You talked. What was he interested in? What were his hopes?"

"He was interested in himself, mostly. He wanted to leave here. He wanted to move to London and be rich."

I wondered if that was how he saw everyone in London. "How was he planning to become rich?"

"He didn't tell me," Sally said, a serious expression on her face making her look even younger than usual. "He said the fewer who knew, the better."

"He was barmy," the brown-haired girl said.

"No, he wasn't," Sally said. "Mum said he was a dreamer, but I appreciated that. If only he hadn't been so cheap."

"Cheap?" I suspected I knew where this was going.

"He wouldn't buy me tea. We'd only had chips for lunch and it was tea time and I was hungry. That's why we fought." Her eyes seemed to plead with me to understand.

"Hal had demands on the little money he had. Rent. Food. Bus fare and chips for a girl." I smiled at her.

"But he was living at home. He should have been able to save all his money or spend it any way he wanted." Sally sounded very definite about what living at home meant.

"Neither he nor his mother made much money. They had to pool their money to pay their rent."

"But it's just a poky little cottage. Two up and two down," the brown-haired girl said. Her tone made her scorn evident.

"What's your name?" I asked.

"Rose."

Time to explain household finance to two pampered, sheltered young ladies. "Rose, their rent wasn't much, but it was all they could afford. They don't own land. They don't have wealthy relatives. All they have is what they earn day to day. You two are very lucky to have families who can afford to buy you anything you want, including tea in a shop. That was something neither Hal nor his mother ever got to enjoy."

Both of the girls fell silent.

"I don't think I'd enjoy being poor," Rose finally said with a shudder.

"Sally," I continued, "what did you do after your fight with Hal over tea?"

"I went inside the tea shop and had tea and cakes."

I guessed she didn't ask him to join her, but I had to ask before I thought her spoiled. "Did you invite Hal to join you? Your treat?"

"I asked if he wanted to come in with me, but he said we needed to catch the bus home. It was still early, so I went inside."

"Which way did Hal go?"

"Toward the bus stop."

I needed to find out if the police learned if Hal had been on the last bus. "Did he ask you to go back on the bus with him?"

She nodded, looking down.

"What did you do after you finished your tea?"

"I walked to the bus stop, but I'd missed the last bus."

"Any sign of Hal?" I knew that was wishful thinking.

"No. He was gone. No message. Nothing."

"Did you try to telephone home for a ride?" I hoped Sally was smart enough to make a trunk call from a phone box.

"Of course. I'm not daft. I tried twice. Once when I found out the last bus had already left, and once after it grew dark and they turned off the lights on the pier and all over town."

"Did anyone answer?"

"No." She sounded miserable. "Neither time."

"So, you stayed in the bus shelter all night?"

She sniffed and nodded.

"That was brave."

She sat hunched over, staring at a blade of grass she'd picked. "All the lights were out. I didn't know where anything was in the town except the pier and the bus shelter, and I couldn't stay on the pier because they'd put a gate up to close it off. At least no one could see me in the bus shelter and I could hide in the corner so no one could grab me. At least it wasn't cold and rainy."

Sally's mother and grandfather and possibly the servants had been in the house. Why hadn't anyone answered the telephone? Especially with a young girl missing.

Chapter Eleven

Adam walked over to join us. "If we're going to go to tea, we need to head back to the house and get ready," he told me.

"Who are you?" Rose asked, staring up at him with wide eyes.

"Adam Redmond. Livvy's husband."

Such beautiful words. Made sweeter by the sinking of Rose's shoulders. I thanked Sally and said good-bye, and then Adam and I started walking, hand in hand once we were out of sight of the cricket pitch. We managed to get back to Summersby House and cleaned up in time to ride bicycles to Manning Hall.

"Won't they be surprised that we rode over here on two wheels?" Adam asked.

"No more than if someone visiting you in London took a bus or the Underground to see you. Besides, it's a lovely afternoon."

"It is. It'll be a shame when my leave runs out."

He sounded so depressed I didn't know what to say. "I'll miss you too," I stammered.

"Oh, Liv, why are we spending time on this investigation when we could be spending time together?" He sounded frustrated.

"Because we owe Sir John and Abby for their kindness

to us, and because if we hadn't started sticking our noses where they don't belong, we wouldn't have learned about a German touring the south coast just a short time ago. And that has now led to an obligation to have tea with the new baronet and his wife, who is my old school—well, not nemesis." I suppose I sounded annoyed, probably because I thought he was right.

And I hadn't completely forgiven Louisa for telling on me at every opportunity while we were at school.

He pedaled a little ahead of me. When I hurried to catch up, he said, "When this war is over, I want to find a desk job and come home to you every night by six or seven. To eat with you every evening at our dining table. To wake up with you, in a bed, every morning. A dull life."

"Golly, I hope so." I thought of Henry's words and smiled. "I'm not partial to sleeping in a trench."

When he glanced at me, he looked glum. "Neither am I, but before this war is over, I know I will be, and you might be, too."

His description, and what he left out, was so grim that we rode the rest of the way in silence.

We left the bicycles in front of Manning Hall, and after Adam slipped off his bicycle clips, we walked up to ring the bell. Mrs. Thompson, the Mannings' capable housekeeper, opened the door and announced us in that faint accent of hers. I couldn't place it. It couldn't have been important, but it nudged at the edge of my mind anyway.

Louisa Porter, now Lady Louisa Manning, came to the

doorway of the drawing room to greet us, her black hair gleaming and her lips as red as her nails. "Douglas will be here in a moment. He's just spending a few extra minutes roughhousing with the boys after their tea."

"I didn't realize you had children," I blurted out. With her fashionable bob and stylish frock, she didn't look matronly to me. "Do you want to spend more time with them? We can come back later."

"No, thank you. You can't imagine what a mess two little boys can make with sticky fingers and pulling at my skirts."

"How old are they?"

"Natty is five years old and Tommy is three."

"I bet they're a handful," I replied with a smile.

"Thank goodness for nursery maids." Louisa strolled into the drawing room, took a cigarette out of the box, and sank gracefully into a chair. "Sit down," she told us before striking her lighter.

Adam and I took seats on a sofa under the double windows. "Lovely weather we've been having," I said. "I'm glad we're not in London at the moment."

"And here I thought you weren't as conventional as the rest of the villagers," Louisa said, blowing a smoke ring. "Always discussing the weather. You've changed from school."

"Just testing out the waters," I replied. I didn't want to get thrown out of Manning Hall before I'd had a chance to ask questions.

Her eyes narrowed. "Why did you really come over?"

"I wondered if you know whether your late father-in-law was as pro-German as he was rumored to be." I scooted back slightly in my seat and crossed my legs at the knee.

"Oh, still outspoken. I appreciate that now. We're going to get along fine," Louisa said with a laugh. "He was Nazi to the core. He and that slimy Wolfenhaus with his nose in the air."

"Louisa." We all turned and looked at Sir Douglas, who'd just walked into the room. "His body's hardly cold."

"Wolfenhaus is still very much alive," Louisa reminded him.

"But he's causing trouble elsewhere, thank goodness, wherever he is." Douglas turned to us and said, "Meanwhile, we seem to have attracted the attention of the police inspector on his hunt for the killer. The inspector visited again this morning with questions for all of us. And Louisa was busy telling him how Sir Rupert deserved to die with a narwhal tusk through his chest. And Joan. Still going on with that 'He killed my son' business. Would you prefer tea or something stronger?"

"Something stronger," Adam said without hesitation.

I was speechless at how daring Louisa and Joan were. They were inviting, practically daring, the inspector to get the wrong idea about them.

If it was the wrong idea.

"Sir Rupert killed Joan's son?" I asked. My tone was more demanding than asking.

"You'll have to ask Joan about that," Sir Douglas said,

giving his wife a glare.

The men had scotch, which Adam proclaimed mellow, and I followed Louisa in having white wine. Once we had our drinks, Louisa pulled the bell rope and Mrs. Thompson came in a minute later.

"We want the tea sandwiches brought in here, Mrs. Thompson." Louisa had perfected the lady of the manor tone.

"Very good, milady," Mrs. Thompson replied with no inflection whatever and walked out.

"Where did your father and Wolfenhaus go on their travels while he was here?" Adam asked.

"You've heard," Douglas said, leaning his head against the back of the chair. "Up and down the south coast. If it's there, assume Wolfenhaus saw it and my father showed it to him." He sounded disgusted.

"But you don't know specifically?" Adam asked.

"No. The pair of them didn't take anyone into their confidence. Whatever my father showed Wolfenhaus, it remains their secret."

"I take it you don't share your father's defeatist attitude," I said.

"No. I know we've got a fight on our hands, but I've never been close mates with Germans the way my father was. I don't see any point in surrendering without putting up a good resistance."

"I followed your father's expeditions in the newspapers. He never sounded as if he was the type to just give up," Adam told the new baronet.

"He wasn't giving up. He was hoping for a position in the new British government. The Duke of Marshburn had been in contact. Very theoretical, you understand, as they gave each other a wink." Sir Douglas gave Adam a grimace.

I looked at Sir Douglas in horror. "I didn't realize anyone was planning that far ahead. For a German victory over England or a new government led by the Nazis. How awful." I shuddered.

"That's why Wolfenhaus was here," Louisa said. "To take back information about this new government Marshburn has been organizing, and to find the weak points in our defenses."

The room fell silent as Mrs. Thompson came in with a tray of tiny sandwiches and biscuits with jam. She set down the food along with small plates and napkins and walked out of the room.

Once the door shut behind her, Louisa said, "And I don't trust that woman, either."

"Why not?" I asked, keeping my voice lowered.

"She's German," Louisa whispered.

"She's been in Britain since the late twenties or early thirties, I think. Years, at any rate," her husband said. "I don't think she's a danger."

"And she was much too friendly with your father."

We all stared at Louisa. My first thought, hearing Louisa's snippy tone, was that Mrs. Thompson had been Sir Rupert's mistress.

"Oh, Louisa," Douglas said. "All they did was talk. She was the only one who would listen to his long, boring expedition stories."

"And I bet he had a host of those tales," Adam said, sounding as if he wished he'd heard a few of them.

"Didn't he just?" Louisa said, reaching for a sandwich.

Encouraged, Adam and I did, too. Adam's was cucumber. Mine was fish paste. Abby's tea was much better than this, but she was feeding four hungry boys as well as us.

"I get the feeling Sir Rupert annoyed everyone in this house at one time or another," I said, trying to sound conversational.

"Not Freddy. But that's because he doesn't pay attention to what anyone else thinks or says," Douglas said, sounding frustrated. I had to remember to think of him as Sir Douglas. "Freddy's good at flattery and pointless conversations and singing and playing show tunes on the piano, but that's it."

"He's shallow. Thick as two planks and completely self-absorbed," Louisa added.

"Is there anyone in this house you like?" her husband asked, his eyebrows raised.

Louisa ignored him, telling me, "He can't even carry on a conversation. He's never read a book in his life or had a thought past the time and location of the next party. And he spends money," here she dropped her voice, "that we don't have."

"I prefer people who can keep their own counsel. But do you care for anyone?" Douglas said in a raised voice. "Do you like me?"

Chapter Twelve

Lady Louisa looked shocked. Sir Douglas shook his head, held up one hand and said, "Sorry."

"Of course, I care for you, darling. There are some people here that I love and appreciate. You and the boys. And Marjorie and cook and Mrs. Hudgens. She's the nursery maid," Lady Louisa added for my benefit. "Anne's not too bad, except she adores Freddy, who can annoy me no end. I'd like Philip if he'd stop letting Joan and Sally wrap him around their little fingers."

"Sally told me she called the house twice, and no one answered. I know you two were out looking for her, but her mother and grandfather were both here, as were the servants."

"Mrs. Hudgens doesn't leave the nursery at night, particularly when we're out. When the rest of the servants go off duty at night, they don't come back to our side of the house for anything," Douglas said. "Especially the telephone."

"I envy them," Louisa muttered.

"What was that, darling?" Douglas asked.

"Sir Rupert didn't answer the phone. Thought it beneath him, but you would think Joan would, wouldn't you? Her daughter was missing and she was genuinely worried," Louisa said, adding, "despite the phony fainting and hysterics."

"We were here when Sir Rupert was found. Mrs. Glenfell's hysterics felt a little..." I was aware of Adam freezing in position next to me on the sofa.

"Forced? We've all noticed that. I just wish Philip would." Louisa crossed and uncrossed her legs, showing them off to advantage.

"Oh, darling..." Douglas began.

"All I'm saying is that it would make for a quieter house," Louisa said, giving him a bright smile.

"Where did everyone look? Was there some sort of plan, or did everyone just wander off and use their best guesses?" I asked.

"Philip went out before dinner and drove around without any luck. At dinner, we discussed where she might be. We ended up choosing tasks. Anne and Freddy walked over to look around the village, I hiked around the estate, Douglas drove around the district until he put the car down a ravine, and Philip went to call on a few of her friends."

"Leaving Sir Rupert and Mrs. Glenfell here."

"Yes," Douglas said. "In case Sally should return."

"Sir Rupert made it clear we were wasting our time, but for once Joan got her way. We did her bidding and looked for the brat," Louisa added. "But searching for his granddaughter was beneath Sir Rupert. Shame, really. If he had gone out to look for her, he'd be alive now."

"Why do you think that?" I asked, surprised at her

conclusion.

"It stands to reason. He was killed at home with one of his trophies while the rest of us were gone. If he'd been out with us, whoever broke into the house wouldn't have found him here."

She was right. And more logical than she had been when we were in school together. "Did you see anyone moving around outside on the estate?" I asked her.

"No. No, wait. I saw Jim Eggerton, the farm manager, out in the farm lorry along the fence line. It was too dark to repair any fences, but he must have been out checking something."

"When and where was this?" When I saw Louisa's expression change, I quickly added, "He's someone else who might have seen something."

"It was around nine. The sun had already set, but there was still light in the sky. I could make out the old lorry and Eggerton's figure in the distance. And the lorry seemed to be stopped by our fence along the road to Sykes's Mill."

I filed that information away to talk to the farm manager later while I wondered what Joan Glenfell had been doing to miss both the murder and her daughter's telephone calls. "Did Joan call her friends or do anything to find her daughter?"

"Not that I know of." Louisa seemed to put some effort into sounding bored, but to me she appeared just a little uneasy.

"What was she doing?" I asked.

Douglas said, "Would you care for another sandwich? Or perhaps another drink?"

We declined, and then Louisa said, "Would you enjoy seeing the gardens and the tennis court?"

I immediately agreed, ignoring a hissed breath from my husband. Anything we learned might be useful.

We went out the front door and around the side of the building. "This is quite a large house," I said.

"It has to be to house all three of Sir Rupert's children and their families, as well as Sir Rupert's gigantic ego," Louisa told me. We were a distance ahead of our husbands, so perhaps she thought it was safe to comment to me on Douglas's father. "When we first married, Sir Rupert was still traveling on his expeditions, so I didn't realize at first how terrible it would be to live under his roof."

"Did he have a lot of rules, or did he invade your privacy, or was he tight with money?" I asked. I didn't know how this information might help find a killer, but anything might be of use. And this would give me a clearer image of Sir Rupert.

Her dark eyes blazed. "All of that. We lived to his schedule, and his budget, and had to praise his every utterance. He scorned us all, calling us weaklings, not worthy of space at his table. Everything we said he called foolish. Any plans we made were called stupid. I am so glad Sir Rupert is dead."

A dangerous statement when the police were searching for his killer. "Where is the trophy room?" I asked, looking at the windows on this side of the house.

"It's on the other side, tucked in against the kitchen and servants' wing. Behind that wing is where the barns for the animals and the barn for the vehicles and equipment are located." She pointed toward the back of the house where we were headed.

Douglas and Adam caught up to us. "My grandfather built the kitchen wing as part of his attempts to modernize the house at the dawn of the century. He built the tennis court at the same time," Douglas added.

As we walked out to the tennis court, Louisa said, "We'll have to have you over for a game as soon as the weather cools a little and the blasted funeral is behind us."

"Keep it up, darling," Douglas said, "and the police will be looking at you as chief suspect."

Louisa gave us a smile and said nothing.

Standing beside the court, I looked back at the house. I remembered what Sally had said. "When the telephone rings in a big house such as this, you must hope someone is standing near the front hall, or someone will have to run to answer before the telephone stops ringing."

"The phone isn't far from the estate office, which is where I am if I'm in the house during the day," Douglas said.

We saw a black car pull up the drive and swing around the front of the house. "More policemen," Douglas said with a pinched look, and began to march down the side of the house toward the front.

Louisa, looking flustered for once, hurried after him.

Adam glanced at me and then strolled after our hosts.

When we reached the front of the house, we found a stranger had climbed out of a taxi, rather than a police car. "Ah, you have company. Were you friends of Sir Rupert, too?" the stranger asked, his voice carrying a heavy German accent. He was in his fifties, judging by his silver and blond hair and his lined face. He held out a lean hand to Adam, who shook it.

"No, we hadn't met Sir Rupert until a few weeks ago," Adam said, not mentioning my desire to choke him when he tried to derail our wedding.

"You missed an opportunity to get to know a truly great man. Sir Rupert was an original thinker and a giant in the brotherhood of explorers," the man said.

"This is Herr Jürgen Wolfenhaus," Sir Douglas said, gesturing to the older man while keeping his face a mask of civility. "And this is Captain and Mrs. Redmond."

Louisa was having nothing to do with social chitchat. "Herr Wolfenhaus, what are you doing here?"

"I am here for the funeral of my great friend," Wolfenhaus said.

"How did you hear he died? We only found him very early yesterday morning," Douglas said.

"And how sad that must have been for you. Such a loss."

"But how did you know?" Louisa persisted.

"Your publican, Mr. Black, and I are friends. He let me know of Sir Rupert's death."

"How much did you pay him?" Louisa asked in an

annoyed tone.

"My dear frau, he is glad to be a friend to me, since I am inheriting his building from Sir Rupert."

"What?" Louisa gasped, turning pale.

"You can't," Douglas said.

"Oh, but I can," Herr Wolfenhaus said. "It is not entailed, is it?"

"No, but—"

"If it is not entailed, then he can give it to anyone he wants in his will."

"Well, yes," Sir Douglas admitted, his face now displaying his distaste.

"He wanted to give it to me." Wolfenhaus smiled. He had a cat's smile. I could imagine feathers hanging from his mouth. "He wanted to give me all his unentailed properties. Money, jewels, land, buildings. It is written in his will."

"Sir Rupert didn't tell me anything about it, and I am his heir," Sir Douglas said, standing a little straighter.

"Have you read the will yet?" Wolfenhaus asked, his eyebrows raised.

"We won't see or hear the will until after the funeral," Sir Douglas said. "We have no idea what he left you."

There was that smile again. "Then you'll just have to take my word for it. Now, I want to see the properties Sir Rupert left me."

Chapter Thirteen

Sir Douglas went red in the face and said, "We need to have a talk about these claims of yours."

"They aren't just claims. They are Sir Rupert's final wishes," Wolfenhaus said, still smiling.

"Come into my study." Sir Douglas stomped off into the house without another word.

Wolfenhaus gave us a formal nod and followed him inside.

Louisa said, "I suppose..."

We made our good-byes and left. Cycling away, Adam said, "That was interesting."

"Poor Douglas and Louisa. Those properties make up a large part of their inheritance." I couldn't imagine Sir John doing something so odious to Matthew.

"I'll definitely have to mention Wolfenhaus's presence in our country as soon as I report back to my unit. This could create a dangerous situation."

"Did you note the name of the road where Louisa saw the farm manager with the old lorry?" I asked him.

"The road to Sykes's Mill. Where Sir Douglas ran his car off the road the same night, and where Ames's body was discovered."

"Why didn't Joan Glenfell answer the phone? What

was she doing?" That was going to bother me until I had an answer. It was probably a clue to how the murder was accomplished.

"I think you're going to have to ask her. Without me."

"Why without you?" This flat stretch of roadway made it easy to ride abreast so I could hear his answer.

"Perhaps it's something personal. Some female business. You know." He visibly shuddered. "She wouldn't want me there."

I suspected Adam would be embarrassed. I pictured Joan Glenfell and decided Adam was right. They'd both be too red-faced to talk. "I'll give it a try, but I don't hold out much hope that she'll tell me. I wish I could think of someone who would know what she does at night or where she goes that would prevent her from answering the phone or seeing a stranger walking about her house."

"Ask Lady Abby. She seems to know everything that occurs in this county."

"She's a good place to start." We were starting to pedal uphill, and I was finding it harder to talk at the same time.

"Maybe she couldn't answer the phone because she was busy killing her father," Adam suggested and then pedaled hard to speed up the hill.

As the gap between us widened, I was trying to see Joan Glenfell as a murderer. With a narwhal tusk.

I could imagine it, if she was telling the police her father murdered her son.

We rode back to Summersby House in time for dinner.

With all the exercise and a tiny tea, I was hungry and I could hear Adam's stomach growl. We hurried to get cleaned up and dressed in nicer clothes for the evening meal. Abby insisted the boys dress for dinner, too, as part of their education in how to be gentlemen. It was only our church clothes and not formal attire, but we made a festive-looking group around the table.

During the roast and vegetable course, Abby asked, "How was tea at Manning Hall?"

"Informative. I want to discuss it with you after dinner," I said.

"Everything all right with the younger Mannings?" Sir John asked, shed of his sling and using both hands again.

"Seems to be," Adam said. "Arm all right now?"

"A little sore. Much better," he told us.

"What do you know about Joan Glenfell?" I asked.

"A woman who's had a difficult time of it," Sir John said.

"Really? What happened?" I asked.

Abby shot her husband a look. "We'll discuss it over coffee."

The boys tried to hide their smiles. I wondered if they were aware of what Abby and Sir John wanted to keep them from hearing, or only that the adults would be discussing things they shouldn't hear that they had already heard from their friends.

I doubted the boys had any interest in what we would discuss, but Sir John would make certain they wouldn't linger, just in case my questions were not appropriate for young ears. On the other hand, the older boys might have a good idea what the answers to my questions about their neighbor would be.

After a berry pie with whipped cream for last, the boys asked to be excused to listen to the wireless and the adults headed into the drawing room, where Mary brought in the coffee.

"Now," I said, "I have the feeling you have quite a tale to tell me."

"Oh, no. Not at all," Abby said. "Well, it's very sad, but I wonder if Mrs. Glenfell wouldn't be a little stronger if her father and husband weren't so protective."

"Her husband seems to want to wrap her in cotton wool," Sir John said. Then he glanced at Abby and said, "Not that that's a terrible thing."

"The Glenfells had a son. He went to Scotland for some hiking with his grandfather and Wolfenhaus last summer. The boy fell off a cliff and died. He was only sixteen or seventeen." Abby shuddered as she glanced toward the ceiling in the direction of the four boys upstairs.

"No wonder Mrs. Glenfell was so upset when Sally went missing." I couldn't imagine what that poor woman had gone through and was still going through. "He was Sally's older brother?"

"Yes. Joan Glenfell hadn't wanted the boy to go with them. I don't think she liked or trusted Wolfenhaus. She hasn't spoken a word to him since, and barely spoke to her father, holding them responsible."

"Did his father want him to go?"

"No, and I don't think the boy wanted to either. Jack, the boy, asked if Matthew could come with them. They were good friends. Joan warned me against sending Matthew, hoping if Matthew couldn't go, then Jack wouldn't either."

"If the parents were both against it, why did the boy go?"

"You saw how Sir Rupert behaved if he wanted something, and you not being wed in the local church was nothing compared to his grandson hiking with him."

"Did no one in that family stand up to him?" I was incensed on behalf of Matthew and his friend.

"Sir Rupert, by having his children live in the manor house and constantly cutting away at their self-esteem and ability to earn a living and live independently, made certain they didn't disagree too strongly." Sir John had his pipe lit now, and he shook his head sadly.

"But Mrs. Glenfell, having lost her son, was having none of her father's orders. Sir Rupert's response was to call in the doctor." Sir John raised his eyebrows as if to punctuate his words.

"Dr. Wheeler?"

"No, some quack from London. What we heard through local gossip was the doctor was going to put her in a sanitorium if she didn't take the drugs he prescribed," Abby said.

"No wonder she seemed so strange when we met her at the house. I thought it was just worry over her missing daughter. Maybe she'd taken some of her pills," Adam said.

"If her pills knocked her out, then she wouldn't have heard Sally ringing on the phone or the murderer walking around her house," I suggested.

"Lucky for the murderer," Sir John said.

"Or was it luck?" This time I raised my eyebrows.

"There are probably quite a few people in the district who know about Joan Glenfell's pills, and they could guess she would take them when her daughter went missing," Abby said.

"But how many people around the village knew the rest of the family would be out after dinnertime looking for Sally and that they'd have a clear path to Sir Rupert and his trophies?" I thought these details pointed directly at one of the family as the murderer.

Abby set down her coffee cup. "It would be a good guess. Philip was asking everyone if they'd seen her. Knowing how Joan suffered after Jack died, the rest of the family would do anything they could to bring Sally home as quickly as possible."

"Even Freddy and Anne?" I asked.

"Yes, especially Anne. She has twice as much sense as her husband and ten times the brains, plus she's kind to Joan," Abby told me.

"They were supposed to be checking around the village that night for Sally." I set down my cup. "Is there anything open beside the pub at this time of night?"

"No."

"Great. Adam, care to stroll down to the pub and ask a few questions about last Saturday night?"

"Sure. It'll be light out for a while longer." He turned to our hosts. "Anyone else want to come along? My treat."

"In that case, I'm sure we want to come. Let's take the car," Sir John said.

Since it was a Monday night, the Hawk and Anvil wasn't too busy. Sir John parked just off the green and we walked over to the Tudor-era half-timbered building with the sign hanging from the roof above the entrance. Both the hawk and the anvil appeared freshly painted.

"What's that shed?" I pointed to a roofed structure next to the pub. It looked as if it was a good place to store firewood.

"The bus shelter. That's the stop for the village on the London to Brighton route," Abby told me.

"Where Sally and Hal Ames left from and presumably returned to?"

"Yes."

It was safe to assume Ames had returned to that spot. But when? And where did he go next? "Where is the Ames cottage from here?"

Sir John pointed. "Across the green, behind that Victorian monstrosity."

The four of us walked through the main bar of the Hawk and Anvil. Smoke was thick in the pub under the low, brown-stained ceiling and I immediately began to cough. Abby and Sir John greeted customers seated about as well as the middle-aged man behind the bar before we entered a side room that I was certain was the snug. The wooden tables were heavy, polished, and dented, probably from fights in Jacobean times. The few chairs had cushions, while the benches were uncomfortably sturdy but smooth wood. The ceiling here was even lower, and I was afraid Adam would hit his head on a beam.

Adam took our orders and went up to the bar. Sir John lit his pipe. I was anxious to start my investigation and asked Abby, "Who should I ask to learn when Freddy and Anne Manning were here on Saturday night?"

"Here's the lady you should speak to," Abby said, smiling at someone behind me.

I turned around in my seat and looked up at a woman of about eighteen holding a menu. "Anything you want to order, Lady Abby?" she asked.

"Some chips would be lovely, Jane. Oh, Jane, this is Olivia Redmond. Mrs. Ames has asked her to look into what happened to her son, and Olivia wants to know whether Freddy and Anne Manning were in here Saturday night."

"Oh, now, they wouldn't have harmed Hal," the barmaid began.

"No, I want to rule them out. They were in here, weren't they?" I asked.

"Right in that corner, from before eight-thirty until closing time. Honestly, a bit past. Dad was talking to Freddy after the place had pretty much cleared out about…" Her voice drifted off.

"Jane's father is the landlord," Abby said.

"About?" I asked.

She hesitated for a moment and then seemed to make a decision. "Sir Rupert wanted to raise our rent again. That's the third time this year." She made a face and snorted in disgust. "I know it's not done to talk ill of the dead, but for someone as wealthy as Sir Rupert, he certainly was making life miserable for everyone in this village."

Chapter Fourteen

"Does Sir Rupert own the village?" I looked from Jane to Abby.

"This side of it," Abby said. "Sir John owns the other half. There are parcels that have been bought by their owners over the centuries, but many of the buildings are still part of the two estates."

"Has Sir Rupert been raising everyone's rates, or just yours?" It might increase the number of people with possible motives.

"Everyone's, and been nasty about it while he's at it," Jane said.

"What do you mean?" I asked.

"Don't go sharing tales about a man who can't defend himself," the barman warned as he brought two of the glasses. Adam followed with the other two.

"This is Mr. Black, Jane's father, and the owner of the pub," Sir John said.

"But not the owner of the building?" I added, looking at Mr. Black.

Black shot a glare at his daughter. "My daughter seems to be filling you in on all the gossip."

"Olivia wanted to know when Freddy and Anne Manning were in here Saturday. She's looking into what happened to Hal for Mrs. Ames," Jane told him.

"That's police business. Nothing to do with the rest of us."

"Mrs. Ames doesn't think so," I told him.

"Well, her, yes, poor woman," he agreed in a grudging tone.

"She wants to find out what happened to her son, and I hope to make sure she knows."

"Won't bring him back," Mr. Black said.

"But it'll give her a sense of completeness she didn't get with her husband." I stared hard at the landlord.

"That old business." Mr. Black stomped back to the bar.

"Do you think Hal's death had anything to do with his father's?" Jane asked.

"Do you?" I replied. She'd have a much better idea about that than I would.

She chewed on her lower lip for a moment. "I'll get the chips." She turned and fled.

"Oh, dear." I hadn't planned that my asking questions would cause problems for Abby and Sir John. They lived here full time. These people were their neighbors.

"It's a sensitive point for Black," Sir John said. "The lease on this pub came available about three months after Ames died. There were several who wanted it, but Black had been called to testify at the inquest. He said Ames told him when they finished work the day he died that he, Ames, that is, was going to ask Sir Rupert for more work, since he wasn't getting paid enough at the garage."

"I don't see why it would upset Mr. Black."

"There were many people who wondered why it took Black so long to remember that conversation. It was almost a week, until the day before the inquest, before he mentioned it to anyone. Some people still don't believe it." Sir John took a swig of his beer. "He does pull a good pint, though."

"Are Mrs. Ames and Mr. Jones two of the people who still don't believe it?" I asked.

Sir John nodded.

"Was there anything odd about the lease coming available at that time?" Adam asked.

"Old Mr. Croft fell down the basement steps and needed to be cared for after that. Broken leg that took a long time to heal. He had to go to his daughter in Brighton, who was his closest relation. No family was in line for the lease, but there were several people who were interested. Black was the only one of Sir Rupert's employees who wanted to take it over, but even with that in his favor, there were some who were surprised when he won the lease."

"Why?" I asked.

"Because he hadn't the foggiest idea what he was doing." Sir John laughed. "The first few years, he was in danger of going bankrupt nearly every month."

"Wasn't Sir Rupert worried about not getting his rent?"

"There were those who thought he'd already been paid handsomely for the rent of this place. Mostly the people who lost out on getting the lease here." Sir John took another swig of his pint. "Some of them couldn't make sense of how they lost out to a man with no experience."

Just then, Jane came back with our order. "My father was the only local. That's why he won." She slammed the plate of chips down and stormed off.

"They wanted the gossip," Sir John said to her retreating back.

"Oh, dear," Abby said.

Oh, dear, indeed.

We could hear male voices talking in the main bar. There was nothing unusual in that, except they sounded as if they were pretending to be friendly and sociable when they actually couldn't stand each other. One of the voices had a thick German accent.

After they quieted, Jane came back in to see if we wanted refills.

"Who was that talking to your father?" I asked.

"Herr Wolfenhaus. He came in earlier looking for a room for a few nights, until after Sir Rupert's funeral. Apparently, they don't want to put him up at the Hall the way Sir Rupert always did. I don't blame them, either." Jane took our orders and walked off.

After Abby and Sir John had greeted another couple from the village, I asked Sir John, "Is it dangerous for Mr. Black to lodge a German this close to the coast?"

"Not terribly wise, but not illegal. We're not at war yet," Sir John said.

"And his money is as good as the next man's," Mr. Black said, setting down two filled pint glasses. "Good English money."

"I hope he wouldn't try to pay you in German money," I said.

"Can't spend that around here." Mr. Black walked off.

A few minutes later, Wolfenhaus came into the snug carrying a pint glass, followed by Jane with a plate of chicken, potatoes, and peas. He nodded to us, and then began to eat the dinner Jane set before him.

By the time he finished eating, we were ready to depart. I looked over at him and said, "How do you find the cooking at your new establishment?"

I felt Sir John, standing beside me, freeze.

"The food is very good, Mrs. Redmond. Good night."

"What? You've bought this building off Sir Douglas?" Sir John asked.

"No. Sir Rupert left it to me in his will." Wolfenhaus looked at me as he added, "He left me quite a bit, all unentailed, in his will."

"You've seen this will?" Sir John sounded aghast.

"I was with him when Sir Rupert went into the solicitor's office to sign it on my last visit to England."

"Why did he leave it to you? Why not one of his children?" Sir John wasn't going to let it go.

Jane slipped in and took away the empty plate.

"It was very good, Fraulein," Wolfenhaus told her. Then he turned to Sir John. "My friend was angry with Douglas..."

"Sir Douglas," Sir John corrected him.

"Sir Douglas, and Freddy couldn't manage a sack of potatoes."

"And Joan?" I asked.

"She's a woman." His tone held scorn.

I wanted to slap him.

"So, he left this property to you, did he?" Sir John asked, sounding skeptical.

"Among others. Sir Rupert was very generous."

Sir John turned on his heel and marched out, the three of us following.

I knew all we could do was leave. And then Adam and I would have to try to answer Sir John's questions in the car. Most of them we didn't have answers to.

* * *

When Adam and I came down to breakfast the next morning, Sir John was the only one at the table and he was finishing his coffee.

"Oh, Livvy, you might be interested in what Dr. Wheeler told me this morning. He's finished both postmortems in the hospital morgue in Ratherminster. It appears Hal Ames was killed before Sir Rupert. At least on average."

"Excuse me?" I was lost when he started talking about averages. Was there an average death?

"I'm putting it badly." Sir John set down his coffee cup. "The Ames lad was killed between six and nine Saturday evening, and Sir Rupert between eight and ten that same night."

"Therefore, they might not have been killed by the same person." That would make finding Hal Ames's killer harder.

"Yes. And while there are several people who might want to have killed Sir Rupert, I can't imagine why anyone would have wanted to kill that young man," Abby said, walking into the room.

"Sally's family wanted to kill him," I suggested.

"But they wouldn't have. Would they?" Sir John asked.

"The first hour, from six to seven, the family would have been around each other, or at least aware of each other, as they dressed for dinner. From seven to eight, they would have all been together having dinner. It was after eight that each one would have gone their separate ways looking for Sally. Any one of them could have killed him then," Abby said. "The Hall doesn't run any differently than any other good-sized house in southern England."

"You think someone came upon Hal Ames and killed him since he didn't have Sally with him?" Adam asked.

"Yes, and that leaves out Freddy and Anne, since they were together. Anne has enough sense not to kill anyone, and Freddy doesn't care enough about anything or anyone to kill them." Abby poured herself a cup of tea.

"Dr. Wheeler is now certain Ames's body was moved," Sir John told us. "Why?"

Why, indeed?

"Abby, would you mind paying a sympathy call on Mrs. Glenfell?" I asked.

"This morning?" she answered, looking resigned.

"Yes."

"I'll need more tea for fortification. She can be a very trying person."

I pressed my lips together in an effort not to smile.

"When was Sir Rupert's last expedition?" Adam asked Sir John. "I seem to remember they were looking for minerals in northern Greenland."

"Well, some Germans were looking for the minerals. Sir Rupert was looking for a reason to go on an expedition. It was four years ago. Something along those lines." Sir John was frowning, trying to dredge up the memory. "There was quite a stink when they returned with one of their party in a casket."

"Who?" I asked. Could it have anything to do with the two murders we'd just had?

"A young German. Don't remember his name. He was some sort of geologist. An ice slide got him. Or he fell off a cliff. Dangerous place, Greenland."

"How awful." Abby said what I was thinking.

"Who would know the whole story?" I asked. I couldn't hear a mystery such as this without wanting to know more.

"Wolfenhaus. He was on that expedition. All the later expeditions Sir Rupert went on were organized by Friedrich von Marten," Sir John told me, "and Wolfenhaus was part of the group."

I doubted Wolfenhaus wanted to talk to me after the announcement I'd made in the pub that led him to tell Sir

John and the village gossips about his inheritance. "Anyone else?"

"Anyone on the expedition, I'd think. I don't remember who else was on them."

"And you have quite enough to investigate," Adam said with a glance at Sir John.

"Quite right," Sir John said. "And you ladies have a sympathy call to make. Be sure to get the car back in time. I have to be at the inquest."

"Can we come, too?" I asked. From the looks I received, my eagerness must have shown.

A half hour later, we were dropping off our cards with Mrs. Thompson when Joan drifted into the front hall. "I suppose you want to see Louisa? She's the lady of the house now."

"My dear Joan. We came to see you," Abby said, stepping forward and kissing Mrs. Glenfell in the air by both cheeks. "How are you?"

Mrs. Glenfell glanced at Mrs. Thompson and told Abby, "Come into the drawing room."

We followed her in and took chairs by the empty fireplace. Joan Glenfell sat across from us, looking clearer of eye than she had two days before. "It's very kind of you to call on me, but please do not give me sympathy on the death of that—monster. Save that for Douglas or Freddy, although they'll laugh in your face if you do."

"It's unfortunate that you and your father never found..." I ground to a halt.

"Mutual forgiveness? An appreciation of each other's

good qualities?" She lit a cigarette and blew the smoke out toward the fireplace. "He killed my son. I can't forgive him. He knew that from the beginning. And he had no good qualities. Not after he fell in with Wolfenhaus."

Chapter Fifteen

"Killed your son?" I looked at her, shocked. It was one thing for her to have said that in a moment of distress. Quite another when she was calm, such as now.

"Last summer, my father and Wolfenhaus took my son Jack hiking in Scotland. He fell down a cliff and died. It was ruled an accident, but my father was responsible." Joan Glenfell clenched her hands into fists. "My father was responsible for Jack's death. I haven't been able to forgive him."

"And now supposedly your father has left Wolfenhaus a number of properties in the village," I said.

"That was just the way my father was, not valuing any of us," Joan said with a sigh.

"Growing up here must have been difficult." I had thought my father was horrible, but Sir Rupert beat him by a great deal.

"Not really. He ignored my existence. It was much harder on Douglas and Freddy," Joan said. "He expected brilliant achievements from them."

"Did you move away when you married?"

"Of course. Until Philip lost all our money in the crash and we had to come crawling back to my father. He never let Philip or me forget it, either." She rose gracefully and walked to the window. "Philip and I were happy until we returned here. Philip didn't believe how soul-sucking life with Sir Rupert could be. He knows now."

"Who killed Hal Ames?"

"I honestly don't know."

I took a chance. "You took your pills that evening?"

"Aaah," she groaned. "You know about my pills. Everyone knows. Sir Rupert's answer to every problem a female might pose. And this time it killed him."

Her voice lost its hysterical note once she returned to her chair. "I am sorry about the Ames boy. He closely resembled his father. Did you know that? My father hated him on sight."

Finally, a connection between the murders. "How did you feel about your daughter dating him?"

"I wasn't happy about it, but it would have blown over by autumn. I certainly didn't kill him. And neither would Philip."

"How much do you remember about that night?"

"Only bits and pieces from dinner until you turned up here. The police are livid. Apparently, I slept through everything important. Sometimes, I carry on conversations and don't remember them later." She shrugged, her tone flat, indifferent.

"Were you and Mick Ames friends?" I asked, earning me a puzzled look from Abby.

"We were when I was a girl. By the time he died, I was married and living in London with Philip."

"Just how friendly were you, Joan?" Louisa said,

coming into the room, sounding the way she used to at school when she caught someone breaking the rules. Pleased with herself and very superior. "I used to hear Sir Rupert curse every time he saw Hal Ames, but half the time he'd call him 'Mick.'"

I saw Abby shrink back in her chair as Joan rose and strode toward Louisa. "It was a harmless flirtation. We were both very young and flirting was part of the game. My father didn't approve. Mick was a laborer's son. Not our class. It wasn't as if either of us thought it would go any further."

"Your father did," Louisa told her, a sly smile on her face.

"My father was rather a stupid man." Joan Glenfell was looking less pale. I wondered if she'd ever felt safe expressing her thoughts before.

A wide smile crossed Louisa's bloodred lips. "Oh, Joan, I do believe I like this new you."

I wouldn't have trusted that smile for a moment. I knew Louisa from years before. Her smile could change from friendly to venomous with a snap of her red nail-polished fingers.

"I'm the same me I've always been. I'm just free to let you know now," Joan said. "Or maybe you're finally paying attention to me."

"Then please tell me your opinion on what should be done with Sir Rupert's trophy room. Clear it out or leave it be?" Louisa asked.

"Clear it out." Her voice was forceful. I'd never heard

Joan Glenfell sound that way before.

"Would you like a tour before we empty it forever?" Louisa asked, turning her head so her black bob swung out away from her face. "Minus the murder weapon, of course."

"Surely they won't give us that back," Joan said.

"I hope not, at least until after the trial."

"Trial?" Joan paled at Louisa's words.

"Well, someone ran that tusk through him. He didn't do it to himself."

I found I liked some things about the adult Louisa. Her words could have been something I would say. "What will you do with Sir Rupert's trophies if you don't keep them?" I asked, rising and following her to the door. "Give them to a museum?"

"Sell them," Louisa said, "and the sooner, the better. We need the money. Sir Rupert emptied our coffers."

When I walked in, I realized the carpet with the bloodstain along one edge was gone. "What happened to the carpet? Did the police take it away?"

"I had it burned," Louisa said. "It was drawing flies to the bloodstain."

"It was a nice Oriental carpet. Worn, but good quality. Worth a pretty penny," Joan said from the doorway.

"It was horrid," Louisa said. "All that blood. And the police cut chunks of the bloodied part out. Ruined it. I had it burned."

"Is there a market for relics of the Arctic?" Abby asked quickly, before anyone else could speak.

"Oh, yes," Louisa said. "There are always men who want to decorate their studies and libraries with trophies. Douglas has already made contact with some people who are interested. According to Douglas, they're willing to spend a fortune and we need the money."

"Father wouldn't have left us destitute," Joan said, hanging back in the doorway to the trophy room. "Would he?"

"He would and he did. Apparently, he spent every shilling he could get his hands on and then gave away much of our inheritance in his will. The only question is, what did he do with all the money? This?" Louisa asked, walking to the center of the trophy room and holding her arms out wide.

"He went on expeditions collecting trophies," I suggested.

"No. Before, he had always been tight-fisted, but he was burning through cash in the last few years. Since he came back from that last expedition." Louisa shook her black bob, making it swing. "Douglas can't figure out where all the money went."

"Surely the accounts must contain a clue, or the bank, or..." Abby began.

"It all went out in cash," Louisa said. "To Sir Rupert."

"Blackmail." I didn't realize I'd spoken aloud until I saw everyone staring at me. "Well, it's a possibility."

"Oh, Sir Rupert did everything out in the open. There was never any doubt about how he felt or what he thought about anything," Louisa replied. "It was never a secret."

"And I don't see where anyone around here gained from our money. Certainly not Mrs. Ames and Hal," Joan added.

"Well, then, it must be something else." What, I couldn't imagine, but it opened up a whole new line of inquiry. Sir Rupert was a nasty-enough man that someone had killed him. Perhaps that meant he was horrible enough that he'd done something someone could blackmail him for as well.

Or tried to blackmail him. If Hal Ames had attempted it, would Sir Rupert have killed him?

I remembered the meeting at the church hall where I had been summoned at the last minute to plead my case for marrying in St. Athanasius. We'd thought everything was already settled. I found Sir Rupert waiting in the room when I arrived. Despite all our preparations, Sir Rupert had created such a furor that I had to convince the church wardens that Sir John and I wanted the wedding to proceed in St. Athanasius.

Every time I tried to answer a question put to me by a member of the church council, Sir Rupert would interrupt me. He would carry on conversations with church wardens about other issues while I was speaking.

I had tried to be on my best behavior, knowing I couldn't win over the church council by being rude to a baronet and landowner. The fourth or fifth time this happened, I caught the eye of the council chairman and made a slight face.

As soon as Sir Rupert paused for breath, I began, "As

I was saying—"

"Nobody cares what you were saying," Sir Rupert said.

"The council chairman might. He asked the question," I pointed out.

"He's just making small talk. Now, about that retaining wall..." He continued on for five minutes. I sat there and kept my face blank of all expression.

They took a vote, the motion passed, and they thanked Sir Rupert for his interest in a two-hundred-year-old wall behind the churchyard. Then the chairman asked me the question he had posed before the pointless discussion about the retaining wall.

"She shouldn't be here. She's not a member," Sir Rupert objected once again.

"Sir Rupert, what did you think of the vicar's sermon last Sunday?" I asked him.

"I didn't think anything of it."

"Really? Why not?"

"I don't have to discuss it with you, you little slum brat."

"You didn't hear it, did you?" When he colored slightly, I said, "What about the Sunday before? Or the Sunday before that?"

"You little..." Sir Rupert began.

"Churchgoer?" I asked in a sugary voice. "You weren't in church last Sunday. You didn't show up any time in June. Or in May. And you say I'm not a member? I would think showing up for services on occasion would be a prerequisite."

"I'm Sir Rupert Manning, and I'm a major contributor to this church. I live within the boundaries of this parish. What are you, you little slug?"

"The daughter of a baronet and a relative of Colonel Sir John Summersby, the biggest contributor to this parish. A woman who wants to be married in her family's home church and who has had the banns read on three Sundays during service. Without a single objection from anyone present." I stared hard at him, glad we'd had the banns read before this meeting. Otherwise, I was sure he would have attended church service the following Sunday for the pleasure of objecting.

He stared back at me for a full minute before rising and storming out of the hall.

"Well," the parish council chairman said, mopping his brow, "if there are no objections, I see no reason why the wedding cannot take place in St. Athanasius on the eighth of July."

If the meeting had gone the other way, I might have murdered Sir Rupert myself.

I stopped daydreaming in time to hear Abby say, "We know he was passionate about exploration. Could he have been funding some sort of Arctic travel for a friend? Or for himself?"

"No," Joan said, "my father was only excited about explorations that he was part of, and he didn't want to go to the Arctic again, not after his last trip."

"Why?" I asked.

Abby walked over to a bookcase and pulled out one

of a series of scrapbooks. She opened it and began studying the newspaper clippings.

"He wouldn't talk about it. He just said he was through with it." Joan looked at me. "I think it was because a young man died falling on an ice floe. He went over a cliff onto the rocks by the sea."

"He wasn't getting any younger, and there hadn't been as much glory in exploration recently. Too much work and no reward. Or maybe," and at this Louisa smiled widely, "he was afraid next time it would be him."

"That was an accident. The expedition leaders said so," Joan snapped at her sister-in-law.

"If that's what you choose to believe. If it made living with that monster easier," Louisa shot back. "He was an evil, rotten..."

"Nothing made it easier to live with my father," Joan snapped at her.

"Especially after he killed your son," Louisa said.

Wordlessly, Joan left the trophy room, her footsteps growing faster as she hurried down the hall. Pulling the door open, she dashed into the drawing room, not bothering to shut it. Shocked, Abby and I held our breath.

"Oh, dear," Louisa said with a sigh. "Excuse me." She followed Joan, shutting the drawing room door after her.

"I think it's time for us to leave," Abby said, setting down the scrapbook. "John will want the car soon."

"Wait." I glanced over the yellowed newsprint. Most of the stories were in German and they were all dated 1935. One thing I noticed quickly was that Friedrich von

Marten was definitely in charge of the last expedition, not Wolfenhaus or Sir Rupert.

And one page that had displayed something large attached with corner holders, such as used on a photograph in an album, was now blank. The page held fade marks around the edges and one corner holder was still attached to the paper.

"Look. The year of the expedition is marked on the front cover of the scrapbook." I flipped through the shelf of red leather-covered binders. "There's even one here from 1899. Sir Rupert explored over a very long period of time."

Raised voices could be heard from the drawing room. "I really think we should leave," Abby said.

I gladly set the scrapbook back on the shelf with the others and followed Abby to the front hall, where we found Mrs. Thompson coming toward us. "Is there anything I can do for you?" she asked as she opened the front door in a not too subtle hint to leave.

I paused before I reached the door. "How many motor vehicles are there in this household?"

Her face showed her surprise, but she had been well trained to respond to requests, no matter how bizarre. "There are two automobiles, Sir Douglas's and Mr. Glenfell's. The farm lorry and the machinery are kept with them in the closest barn, the vehicle barn, but they belong to the estate."

"Would you have noticed if someone took a vehicle from the barn?"

"Only if I was on duty. When I go off duty, I stay in the servants' quarters and I don't come out for anything or anyone." She took a half-step back, opening the door a little wider. Her invitation to leave was unmistakable.

Chapter Sixteen

"Well," said Abby, climbing into the driver's seat of Sir John's car, "that was enlightening."

"Do you think Sir Rupert was being blackmailed?" I asked, climbing in the opposite side. I had left the window lowered when we went into the house, so I didn't need to crank it down again to get some air flowing through once the car began to move. Already the day was getting warm. My navy blue short-sleeved dress felt similar to a heavy coat in the heat and humidity.

"I suppose anyone could be blackmailed." Abby started up the engine and put the gear shift into first. We rolled away from the house and picked up speed as we moved down the drive.

"Who would have blackmailed him? The Ames family was chronically short of cash, so it couldn't have been them. At least they weren't successful if they'd tried. Has anyone in the district been spending freely in the last few years?"

"No. Perhaps Sir Rupert had been going up to London to gamble. If he'd been buying quality horseflesh or milkers or some sort of livestock for the estate, we'd all know about it. If he'd been reroofing buildings or building new fences, we'd have heard. But gambling in the private clubs in London? No one would have a clue." Abby glanced over at me before she shifted gears. "I wonder how long it'll be before the Glenfells move to town?"

"I suppose that will depend on when Mr. Glenfell can get a position in London and whether any of them killed Sir Rupert."

"Theoretically, even Sally could have," Abby said.

"Even if she hadn't been stranded in Brighton, she's just a little thing." The narwhal tusk was long and would be awkward to maneuver.

"I know. But that doesn't mean she couldn't have shoved a spear through her grandfather. If she were angry enough, and what young girl can't get furiously angry, she could have hurried toward him and her momentum would have taken care of the rest." With a nod, Abby said, "Oh, yes. And if she could have killed Sir Rupert that way, any of them could have."

I considered her words. "I think you're right."

* * *

When we returned to Summersby House, I went in search of Adam. I found him in the library in a high-backed leather chair by an open window, poring over a book.

"What do you have there?" I asked, leaning over the top of the chair on the side away from the window.

"An account of the last two of Sir Rupert's expeditions to Greenland, written in German. They were definitely hunting for mineral deposits for German industry."

I then noticed a German-English dictionary on the edge of the chair next to him. "When were they?"

"In 1933 and 1935."

"So, he stopped exploring the Arctic with Germans a few years after the Nazis came to power."

Adam shook his head. "I don't think it was his choice. My written German isn't that strong, but I'm getting the impression something happened on the last expedition that assured he'd never join another."

"The death of the geologist?" Was this going to explain Sir Rupert's death all these years later? "Was it only Sir Rupert who wasn't invited back, or was everyone on the expedition prevented from going to Greenland again?"

"I don't know. When I go back to work on Monday, I'll ask around while I learn what anyone knows about Wolfenhaus touring the south coast. That shouldn't have been allowed."

"People didn't tell Sir Rupert 'No' very often, did they?"

"It seems they did in the case of these expeditions." Adam patted my hand. "Do you mind if I keep reading, at least until after you get back from the inquests?"

"You don't want to attend?"

He made a face. "Are you joking?"

"Stay here. Maybe you'll break the case wide open." I kissed the short blond hair on the top of his head. "You might look for the name Friedrich von Marten. According to a newspaper cutting in a scrapbook in the trophy room at Manning Hall, he was in charge of the 1935 expedition."

I sauntered out of the library, heading for the garden

where I knew Abby would be.

"Oh, Mrs. Redmond," Mrs. Goodfellow called out from the kitchen as I passed by, "any luck?"

"Not so far." Then I decided to go fishing. I walked into the kitchen and asked, "Did anyone give Eleanor Ames cash? Quite anonymously, of course."

"No. It would have been a blessing if someone had. They've limped along ever since Mick was killed, and now with Hal gone, I don't know how she'll survive."

I had no idea how that problem would be solved. The investigation might prove easier. "I wish I knew when Hal Ames returned to the village on Saturday night. Then we would know what time to ask everyone if they'd seen him. Someone must have, if he returned before dark." Then I looked at the problem from the viewpoint of a country dweller. "It was a fair night out. People would have been outside."

"I'm sure they were." A smile slowly crossed Mrs. Goodfellow's face. "I could ask Tad. He'd know."

"Who's Tad?"

"Our local bobby. Constable Wiggins. They're investigating both deaths out of the police station in Ratherminster."

I was hesitant. "I don't want to get you or him into trouble."

"No trouble. He's a cousin of a niece's husband." She made it sound as if it was the simplest task in the world. "I'll see him at the inquest."

"Mrs. Goodfellow, you're a dear. Thank you." I left the

kitchen with a spring in my step, ready to hear what there was to learn at the inquest.

When I climbed into the back seat of Sir John's car, I told him and Abby what Mrs. Goodfellow planned to learn for me.

"She'll probably learn every detail of where he went on Saturday night for you. The locals here—the true locals, not those of us in the big houses—know every detail of everyone else's life going back generations. It's almost scary the way they know more about me than I do about any of them. Even Mrs. Goodfellow, who's been here since John's mother's day."

The inquests were heard, one right after the other, in the primary school hall in the village. It was sunny and warm outside and there was little ventilation in the hall. Soon, an atmosphere as if we were being surrounded by a flock of warm, furry sheep engulfed us.

I hoped they'd make this quick.

A dried-up looking man serving as the coroner called the inquest into the death of Hal Ames to order. Inspector Parsons gave his evidence first. We learned that Hal Ames returned on the last bus from Brighton on Saturday night a little after eight o'clock, but wasn't seen alive after that.

Dr. Wheeler said he was killed less than an hour later by a blow to the back of the head and asked that the body be released for burial. That was granted, and then Mr. Long was called to describe the discovery of the body the next morning.

The first jury was released into one of the classrooms

to deliberate after only a little more than half an hour.

Then the second inquest was held. Inspector Parsons reported a call from Manning Hall at ten minutes after midnight and the police response.

Dr. Wheeler reported Sir Rupert died from a narwhal tusk to the chest, and then described the damage done inside his body. Then he had to describe narwhal tusks before he could ask that this body also be buried.

Marjorie Lenard was called next. She was a thin, sallow-complexioned woman wearing a shiny, dark blue dress with a tiny pattern and a flat-crowned, dark blue straw hat. She testified in a weak voice that she had served Sir Rupert his evening tea at eight o'clock as instructed and went to her room for the night. She told the coroner she wasn't one to linger. She had to be up at four the next morning.

Then Sir John went to the front of the room and told the gathering about the three of us finding Sir Rupert at a few minutes after midnight. He spoke loudly, clearly, and calmly, showing years of practice with the judicial system.

This time the inquest took forty-five minutes. The second coroner's jury went into another classroom and the first batch of men returned to report that they found Hal Ames was murdered by person or persons unknown.

We still had to wait for the second jury to give their decision.

Most of the audience, including me, went outdoors, where it was neither so hot nor stuffy. I saw Mrs. Goodfellow in conference with Constable Wiggins and

Eleanor Ames, and decided to find out what she had learned later.

I turned and found myself face to face with Lady Louisa. "I think they'll call it justified."

I felt my eyes widen. "Why?"

She smiled. "A jury of narwhals would think so."

"I don't think this is the place to joke about Sir Rupert's death," I told her in a low voice.

"That's because you didn't live with him. Life is so much better now. He needed to be killed."

Louisa walked off, and I found Inspector Parsons had been standing behind us as he watched her walk away. And a little to one side stood Wolfenhaus.

Joan walked up to me and said, "There's the next man to be murdered, if there's any justice in the world."

"Who?"

"Wolfenhaus, of course."

Inspector Parsons's eyes narrowed. He'd heard Joan, too.

When the second jury came in a few minutes later, they also determined that the death of Sir Rupert Manning was murder by person or persons unknown.

* * *

Adam was quiet during our late lunch. Near the end of the meal, he told Sir John, "Livvy says there are scrapbooks of each of Sir Rupert's expeditions, with newspaper cuttings in English and in German, in the trophy room at Manning Hall. I'm going to ask Sir Douglas if I can borrow them, at least the last few, and bring them back here to read."

"That sounds to be an excellent suggestion. Particularly if you want to learn more about Wolfenhaus. Are you going with him, Livvy?"

"Yes, if Adam would like the company." I looked at him, fluttering my eyelashes, trying for an innocent expression, and he grinned in return.

"How could I say no to that face?"

Sir John lent Adam his automobile, and after lunch we set off. Adam's first stop was Jones's Garage to fill up the car with petrol, since we'd been using Sir John's vehicle so much.

Gary Jones came out to fill up the tank and to say hello.

"Not busy today?" I asked, getting out of the car. Adam had already climbed out to work the pump before Gary appeared.

"No. The middle of the week is usually as slow as this. And Saturday morning I leave on the first train to go to my depot, leaving my father to run this place alone." Gary seemed to survey the garage, the road, and the surrounding fields as if he was memorizing the view.

"One of the militiamen going for training?" Adam asked, offering his hand.

"Militiamen. Yeah." Gary snorted. "Thirty-four thousand men have been ordered to do six months of training while praying the war doesn't start until we can finish up and come home." He shook Adam's hand. "Not much chance of that, is there?"

"I think we're both in for the duration."

The two men held each other's gaze, and in their tones, I caught a glimpse of something I would never experience or understand. The camaraderie of soldiers. A few times, I'd seen it between Sir John or my father and someone who'd served in the Great War. This was the first time I'd viewed it in relation to the coming war.

It made me very proud. And very frightened.

"You haven't heard of anyone who saw Hal Ames on Saturday night after he returned to the village, have you?" I asked.

Gary shook his head. "I want to know what happened. We were friends, and Hal didn't deserve—what he got. It wasn't fair, and it wasn't right." He took a deep breath and said, "There. That's you topped up."

Adam gave him some brotherly advice about following orders no matter how silly they were, paid for the petrol, and we drove on to Manning Hall.

Mrs. Thompson answered the door. She informed us that Sir Douglas was out in the barns and shut the door on us. Adam and I walked around the side of the house and up a slope to the barns. Sir Douglas and a middle-aged man I didn't recognize were bringing in sacks of grain.

"Captain Redmond. Mrs. Redmond. What can I do for you?" Sir Douglas asked. It wasn't a warm greeting, but he didn't sound annoyed either. Just busy, I decided.

"I wondered if I could borrow those scrapbooks in the trophy room about Sir Rupert's expeditions," Adam said.

"You want to read those? Bored with your marriage

already?" he asked. When he saw my face, he turned pink. "Er, of course. Tell Mrs. Thompson you have my permission to take them all away. Just return them when you finish reading what a hero my father was." He poured scorn on the word "hero."

"Who put them together?" I asked.

"He did, of course." When I looked surprised, Sir Douglas said, "You don't think anyone was as interested in his career as he was, do you?"

We thanked him and walked back toward the house. The two men had forgotten us before we were a few steps away.

This time when Mrs. Thompson answered the door, Adam told her what he wanted before she could shut the door on us. She led us into the trophy room and stood guard while we picked up all the scrapbooks.

I looked through them twice and then looked around the room. The scrapbook I'd been looking at earlier, from Sir Rupert's last expedition, was missing. "Mrs. Thompson, do you know where the scrapbook from the 1935 expedition is?"

"It should be with the others." Her tone said she had too much to do to worry about old scrapbooks.

"It's not. It doesn't appear to be anywhere here."

The housekeeper made a *mmpfh* sound and began to look through all the scrapbooks. "That's odd. It's one of the ones with a reddish cover, isn't it?"

"Yes."

"The last people to look at these were you and Lady

Summersby. Perhaps she has it."

"No. You saw us when we left. We certainly didn't walk out with anything as large as a scrapbook. We set it back on the shelf as we left." I frowned at her.

She shook her head. "I can't explain it. Perhaps someone in the household picked it up to read through."

"If you find it, would you save it for me to read? I've always been impressed with Sir Rupert and I'd enjoy reading these old stories in the newspapers," Adam said.

"Of course, sir."

"Sir" made me think of Sir Douglas, which immediately led me to think of Lady Louisa. She had been out on the estate Saturday night looking for Sally, and she'd seen the estate manager, Jim Eggerton, out in the farm lorry along the fence line on the road to Sykes's Mill. Possibly near where Hal Ames's body was found.

"Thanks for your help," I told Mrs. Thompson. "Here, I'll help you take these out to the car," I added to Adam as I took part of the tall stack that he held.

When we reached the auto, I dumped my stack in the back seat and said, "Come on."

Adam set his stack down and hurried after me, his longer legs making it easy for him to catch up. When we reached the barn, both Sir Douglas and the middle-aged man were finishing their task.

"Excuse me," I said, "but are you Jim Eggerton?"

"Yes. How may I help you?" the middle-aged man asked. Sir Douglas stood looking from one of us to another.

"Lady Louisa was out on the estate Saturday night looking for her niece, who was missing at that time. She said she saw you in the farm lorry about nine o'clock on the road to Sykes's Mill checking the fence."

"I don't see how she could have," he said with a smile. "The vet and I were trying to save a cow who was giving birth to twins. Both breech. Worst delivery either of us had ever seen."

"When was this?"

"Started late afternoon and went on until two or three Sunday morning. We were lucky." He grinned at Sir Douglas. "All three survived. They're all still alive." He said it the same way football players said they scored a goal.

Sir Douglas smiled in return. "Jim's as good an estate manager as I've ever seen."

"This wasn't in the barn where you keep the vehicles, was it?"

"Good grief, no. We were in the cow barn. Why would you think we'd put the cows in with the vehicles?" Eggerton's tone clearly said "city girl."

Anyone could have taken the farm lorry and not been noticed. But who? And why?

Chapter Seventeen

We made it back to Summersby House shortly before tea. Since we had the opportunity, we carried all the scrapbooks into the library and sat down to read them. Adam took the one from 1933 to match up the clippings with the book he had been reading. I took one from the 1931 trip and began scanning the newspaper articles.

It wasn't long before I found the name Friedrich von Marten, along with a quote on how they had found mineral deposits in the very northernmost part of Norway and how they were now working on a trade deal between Norway and Germany. Von Marten was listed as the leader of the expedition and a vice chairman of the German Scientific Research Organization.

I found a photograph of him in another clipping. He was perhaps in his late forties, with fair hair and a thin face. He was good-looking in an outdoor enthusiast way, but his narrow eyes made him appear angry. I wouldn't want to cross him.

There were mentions of both Jürgen Wolfenhaus and Sir Rupert Manning as explorers attached to this expedition, along with two men who were experts in mineral deposits. One had a German name, the other's name was Polish. Another man with a French name was listed as an engineer. At least in 1931, the expedition was multinational.

I wondered if they'd held expeditions after 1935, and if they were made up of men from different nations.

I wondered how long von Marten, Wolfenhaus, and Sir Rupert had worked together on these expeditions. Glancing through the earlier scrapbooks, I found the first time Sir Rupert had worked with these Germans was in 1922, and since 1925, these men were the only ones he'd gone to the Arctic with.

Sir Rupert had traveled on his first expedition in 1899 with some British naval officers. There were other, smaller scrapbooks, each one celebrating one expedition to the Arctic, until the Great War began. After a six-year hiatus, the scrapbooks began again with one more British expedition before the 1922 trip with the Germans.

"What was the name of the man who died in Greenland during the 1935 expedition?" I asked Adam.

"I've forgotten." He started leafing through the book when Abby came in.

"You are back. The boys said they'd seen you. We're about to have tea."

Adam snapped the book shut. "Great. Translating all that German was beginning to give me a headache."

We left the scrapbooks and the old book Adam had been reading and went into the dining room. Mark, after his second sandwich, asked us what we were doing in the library when it was so nice outside.

"Reading Sir Rupert Manning's scrapbooks about his

expeditions. Most of it in German," Adam said.

"Maybe Gerhard can translate it for you." Mark started on his third sandwich with a thirteen-year-old's zeal as he looked at his younger foster brother.

Ten-year-old Gerhard and six-year-old Henry, once Heinrich, had been typical German schoolboys until a few months earlier, when their father was caught spying for the British in the very heart of the German government. He'd died in Sachsenhausen, but not before he'd extracted a promise from the British embassy to arrange for his wife and sons to leave Germany.

The spy's wife was murdered during the escape I'd orchestrated, but I'd brought the two boys to England safely. I couldn't care for them in my flat and go to work all day, so I'd asked Sir John and Abby to take the boys in.

It was love at first sight on both sides, and when Matthew and Mark came home from school at the end of term a few weeks later, it was to find they suddenly had two younger brothers. Matthew and Gerhard bonded over tinkering with old bicycles, Mark was thrilled to no longer be the baby of the family, and Henry discovered a secure homelife ruled by the unflappable Lady Abby instead of the fears of his frequently hysterical mother.

Gerhard, who didn't share his brother's appetite, set down his second sandwich and asked, "Is it technical?"

"No. Newspaper articles, mostly. They were scientific expeditions, but the engineering and geological details weren't reported in the general press." Adam stopped and glanced at me. "There must have been technical reports, but I've not seen any evidence of them in Sir Rupert's scrapbooks."

"There wouldn't be," Sir John said, setting down his tea-cup. "Sir Rupert was never big on detail. He was always about the grand gesture. Being famous and smiling for the camera. Douglas will make a much better farmer than his father. Manning Farm should be more successful with Douglas at the head."

"Is that why he had a random collection of stuffed Arctic animals and camping gear in that trophy room of his?" I asked. "There didn't seem to be anything scientific about its organization."

"There wouldn't be. Sir Rupert saw those animals as nothing but trophies to stuff and mount and show off. They were his proof that he had been to the Arctic, that he had braved the elements. It was the same with the camping gear. He was saying 'look what I survived on.'" Sir John had another sip of tea.

"Just as he didn't try to do anything scientific with his farming. As long as he received his money at harvest, he didn't care." Sir John shook his head. "I suspect that his income from the farm had been steadily dropping."

"Maybe that's why his children are so hard up now," Abby said.

Sir John considered this. "No, he was still getting enough in rents and farm produce for all of them to live comfortably. At least from what I heard from his tenants."

"Could he have been raising rents in the village to cover the drop in income from the farm?" I asked.

Looking around the table, Sir John said, "This is not to go any further. Boys? I'm serious."

We all nodded solemnly, even Henry, who wouldn't understand any of the economic details that were about to be revealed.

"I've been asking around, here and there, and I've confirmed that Sir Rupert had raised rent in the village in January, then in May, and now for August. Sir Douglas has canceled the August increase, but many of the tenants are still upset. Especially the tenant farmers, who only pay once a year at harvesttime. They can't raise their prices enough to cover Sir Rupert's huge yearly increase in land rent. They'll lose their tenancy."

"Does anyone know why he demanded all these increases?" Abby asked.

"No. And a sillier group of rumors I've seldom heard. Someone even suggested Sir Rupert was gathering a huge dowry for Sally to enable her to marry a prince. He didn't care a bit about that girl. And any prince so interested in a dowry he could forget about her family background would have lost his throne and lands after the Great War."

I wouldn't tell him about the discussion Abby and I had about blackmail or gambling as the possible reason Sir Rupert needed large amounts of cash. He'd probably declare our reasons the silliest of all.

After tea, the boys went out to kick a ball around, Adam went back to translating the book on Sir Rupert's last two expeditions, and I went upstairs to change into gardening clothes to help Abby. When I came back down,

I walked through the kitchen hall and heard Mrs. Goodfellow call out my name.

I went into the kitchen. "Tea was very good, Mrs. Goodfellow. I particularly liked your cakes."

"Thank you, Mrs. Redmond." She walked over to me and said in a low voice, "I talked to Tad."

I had seen them, heads close together, at the inquest. "What did Constable Wiggins tell you?"

"They showed Hal's picture around, and he was definitely on the last bus, which stopped in the village at about five minutes after eight. He was seen sitting in the bus shelter for a few minutes before he walked away in the direction of Manning Hall."

"That narrows down the time when he could have been murdered. Did Tad tell you anything else?"

"He was carrying a satchel when he got off the bus and walked down the road. But it wasn't found where the body was discovered and no one has returned it to Mrs. Ames or the police."

"It was definitely Hal's satchel and not Sally's?"

That silenced her for a moment. "I don't know," she admitted. "You'd better find out."

I needed to speak to Sally again. Having decided I might have worn out my welcome at Manning Hall, I turned around and headed for the telephone in the hall.

Both houses were on party lines. I'd have to be careful about what I said.

Mrs. Thompson answered the telephone, and a minute later Sally came on.

"Sally, this is Mrs. Redmond, Matthew's cousin."

"Yes?" She sounded wary. I couldn't blame her.

"When you went to the seaside with Hal, did he have a satchel with him?"

"Yes. We both did." There was no hesitancy in her tone. Then her tone turned suspicious as she asked, "Why?"

"No one has seen Hal's since he came back that evening. You wouldn't happen to know where it is, would you?"

"No. He wouldn't carry mine. Said it was too heavy and girls should learn to travel lighter. When he left, he took his satchel, an old brown school thing, and I took mine."

"Do you know what he had in it?"

"His swimming trunks. An undershirt. A pair of short pants. A change purse. A comb."

She'd taken quite an inventory. "Are you sure?"

"Yes. I looked. I held it for him while he went into the gents by the pier."

"If you happen to see—"

"Gotta go. I'm going to get a driving lesson. On the old farm lorry, not the vehicle I want to drive, but I get to drive it." She sounded thrilled.

"Sally, wait. Where do you keep the keys for the farm lorry?"

"I don't know. Coming," she called out. I heard "Good-bye," and a click before the line went dead.

I walked outside to the flower beds where Abby was

working on removing a particularly stubborn weed. "Ah, there you are," she said, straightening up with one hand pressing on her lower back. "Grab that hoe and give me a hand here."

I did as I was told, my thoughts still on what I'd learned. Or hadn't learned. Once we'd removed all the roots from a tenacious weed, Abby said, "Now. What are you thinking about? It certainly isn't gardening."

"I found out Hal Ames did come back on the last bus and walked off down the road with his old school satchel. It hasn't been seen since. And Louisa said she saw their farm lorry that night along the road where Hal's body was later found, but it wasn't driven by the farm manager. He was busy with a cow, and the vet is his alibi."

Abby deadheaded some mums. "Then someone else in the household drove it. No mystery there."

"But who? Glenfell and Sir Douglas drove their own cars that night. Freddy and Anne walked to the village. Joan stayed in the house after taking some of her pills. Louisa was out on the grounds on foot. The nursemaid was in with the two boys. The rest of the staff were hiding so they wouldn't be called on to do anything else. I suspect they work hard in that household and want to be left alone at the end of the day."

"It could be someone else's farm lorry. The Mannings aren't the only people to own one."

"Do you know who else around here has one?"

"We don't. John feels that Mullins is more economical pulling the wagon than anything that requires petrol," she said, referring to the plow horse. "And he says we'll all have to go back to horsepower once the war starts and petrol will be rationed."

"Who would know all the farm lorries in the district?"

"Ask John. He's been looking at them wistfully, even though he knows it's impractical until the war is over."

"Where is he?"

"At home farm. He should be back in time for dinner."

Wonderful. Every time I had something to check, some clue to follow, either I had to wait for someone or they hung up on me. And time was running out if I was going to help Eleanor Ames learn who killed her son.

Chapter Eighteen

I was already in our room getting dressed for dinner when Adam came upstairs. "How is your translating coming along?" I asked.

"I've learned that the personnel for the 1933 and 1935 expeditions were nearly identical. They were all German, except for Sir Rupert. The only difference I could see was the addition in 1935 of a German national, Matthias Tomperglich, as one of the geologists who replaced another German. Apparently, he was a respected mineralogist or mining expert. My translation on that is weak. He was the one who died."

"Did you learn any of the details?" He may have fallen, but I pictured any death in the Arctic to be due to the cold.

"It was summer and apparently the higher temperatures weakened a stretch of glacier. It collapsed under Tomperglich's weight, sending him to his death on the rocks below, very close to the sea. It turns out Tomperglich, Wolfenhaus, and Sir Rupert were the only ones in the area, and Sir Rupert had cross words with the dead man in the days preceding the man's death."

"Was it investigated by the police?"

"Not really. The Danish police sent investigators, who asked questions and saw the site, but they must have been stonewalled. Their report said the area was unsafe and no mining should be undertaken there. The Germans were not happy, but the Danes stood firm. No mining concessions were given."

"So, all they really had to go by was Sir Rupert's and Wolfenhaus's story, and they both said the ice gave way. It was an accident."

"It was ruled as one, but the Germans wouldn't have Sir Rupert travel with them anymore." Adam held up two ties.

I pointed to the one in his left hand, but my mind was on his words. "Was Wolfenhaus allowed to go on expedition with them again?"

"Yes." Adam raised his eyebrows.

Two men were present at an accident. One was allowed to continue with his work, the other wasn't hired again. And yet the two men remained friends.

Was it only an excuse not to use a British national on the German expeditions after 1935? Or was Sir Rupert dangerous to be around?

I wanted to speak to Wolfenhaus. "Was Friedrich von Marten in charge of both expeditions? Was he actually in the camp?" I asked Adam.

"In 1935, he was in charge but had left the day before the death." Adam looked in the mirror as he looped one end of the tie through the knot.

"Was Sir Rupert not invited back, or was he told not to show up because he wouldn't be allowed to travel with them?" There was a vast difference in emphasis. "And how many more expeditions did the Germans have that Sir Rupert wasn't invited to join?"

"They had two more, in 1936 and 1937, in northern Norway, and I believe there's one more going on currently. I saw something about it in the paper last week or the week before."

"And how did the Germans feel about having Sir Rupert participate after the death?" That was what I was really interested in.

"I can't tell from the book if they just ignored him or came right out and told him not to join them. And that would depend on how strongly they believed Sir Rupert was guilty of wrongdoing in Tomperglich's fall." Adam looked at me. "Aren't you ready yet?"

While I'd been listening to Adam, he'd finished dressing for dinner. I still wasn't ready. I hurried to finish and then walked downstairs with him.

We entered the drawing room to find everyone waiting for us. The boys looked ready to jump up and race into the dining room. Sir John and Abby both had their eyebrows raised.

"It was my fault," I said. "Adam has been finding out some things about the expeditions Sir Rupert went on and I wanted to hear all about it. In fact, Sir John—"

"Let's go into dinner first. We can talk later," Sir John said.

It wasn't until the fish course, caught by the boys in a nearby river and for which they were all praised, that I was able to pose the question I hoped Sir John had the answer for.

"Small farm lorries in the entire district? Not more than half a dozen, and probably less. Let's see…" He thought for a moment. "I can only think of five, but I could be wrong."

"Which one is closest to the Manning home farm?"

"Probably the Geoffreys's. They have a large farm over toward Engleside. Perhaps three or four miles from Manning farm. Why?"

"Louisa claims on Saturday evening about dusk, she saw a farm lorry along their fence line on the road to Sykes's Mill. None of the family had their lorry out, and the farm manager and the vet were busy with a breech birth. I wondered whose farm lorry it could have been."

"Well, the vet has one, but it sounds as if he was also out of the picture." Sir John thought a minute and added, "Could it have been Hal Ames? He knew how to drive their lorry, and he'd know where they kept the keys."

"If he was borrowing it to get Sally from the seaside, would he have stopped to ask permission?" Adam asked.

"Of course. Otherwise, if the Ames boy had taken the lorry and rescued Sally, when they returned, Sir Rupert would have had him arrested for theft."

"That's rotten," Matthew said.

"Perhaps, son, but Sir Rupert would have been within his rights. Don't you get any ideas about borrowing a vehicle without permission to learn to drive." Sir John gazed at his oldest.

I had a sudden, unpleasant thought. "But there was

no one to ask except Sir Rupert."

"Have you thought about getting a farm lorry for home farm? It would be useful for hauling things longer distances than Mullins wants to go, and—" Matthew began.

His father interrupted. "Lorries run on petrol. Mullins runs on hay. Which do you think will be rationed when the war comes?"

Matthew gave a weary sigh. "But—"

"We'll see after the war," his father said.

"Matthew," I asked, "do you know enough about farm lorries to know if there's a place to hide a satchel? I wonder if Hal left his satchel in the farm lorry and went to find someone to ask permission to get Sally or to have someone drive him over to get her?"

"Depends on whether there's a bench in the back of the Mannings' lorry for tool storage or sitting on. I've never seen their lorry close up."

"Sally's getting driving lessons on it."

"Lucky!" Matthew said. Mark and Gerhard watched Sir John and Matthew with interest.

"I'm thinking of going over to Manning Hall tomorrow to see if I could look over the farm lorry, and I wondered if you'd care to come along for technical assistance."

"May I?" Matthew looked from his father to his mother.

"What about Adam?" Abby asked.

"I'm reading that book on the 1935 expedition, and the translation's going slowly," Adam told her.

"If you want, I could give you a hand while they're gone," Sir John offered.

It began to feel as if we might make some progress after all. If luck was with us.

* * *

The next morning, Abby called Manning Hall and spoke to Louisa. Or Lady Louisa, as Abby was careful to call her. I kept my ear close by the receiver so I'd know how much sleuthing I could get away with. "And when Matthew heard Sally was taking driving lessons on the farm lorry, he wanted to come over and see the lorry. Find more reasons for his father to buy one," Abby said.

"Of course, please come over. I know how young men are about cars and lorries. Sally must be around somewhere. I'll tell her Matthew is coming over. That will cheer her up."

"She's still upset about the Ames boy, I imagine."

"We're all still upset about everything that happened on Saturday night," Louisa replied in a lofty tone. Then she added, "That odious police inspector has been around again, practically accusing me of killing Sir Rupert. Not that it wasn't a good idea, but I didn't think of it until it was too late. Someone beat me to it."

"We'll be over in a little while, and hopefully, at least Matthew can be of use cheering up Sally."

"There's nothing worse than a sixteen-year-old girl moping about the house," Louisa said before she hung up.

When we arrived at Manning Hall and rang the bell, Sally was in the hall almost as soon as Mrs. Thompson opened the door. Matthew followed us in, looking nervous with his head down and his shoulders slumped. If he'd known how to become invisible, he would have in a heartbeat.

Mrs. Thompson headed toward the back of the house.

"Matthew, Aunt Louisa said you wanted to look at the farm lorry," Sally said with enthusiasm. "It's really fun. Mr. Eggerton says I can't ruin the gears or the clutch because they're made to last forever. I've had my first lesson on it."

Matthew looked relieved. "Can we go look at it?"

"Certainly." She turned to the grown-ups. "We'll be in the car barn." Then the two of them took off.

I turned to our hostess. "Lady Louisa, when we were here last, there was a scrapbook of the 1935 expedition that wasn't there when we returned to take all the scrapbooks to Summersby House to read through them. Have you seen it? It had a reddish cover."

"No. I thought Douglas said you had them all."

"Only the last one is missing, and I have a feeling it's important."

Louisa looked at me, her bright red lips in a puzzled "O." "How could it be important? Are you searching for clues? You always were a bold girl."

"I think it has a clue to your father-in-law's death. Wolfenhaus and those Germans can come and go between Germany and England easily, and they may have had a hand in his death."

"Well, I wish someone would solve that mystery," Louisa said, lighting a cigarette. "I'm so tired of those policemen showing up here day after day that I could scream."

Despite the fact there had only been four days since the murders. "I've been asking about farm lorries. That's how Matthew learned about Sally taking driving lessons. Apparently, there's only five in the district and two of them, yours and the vet's, were here that night. The next closest is in Engleside."

"How clever of you," Louisa said. "But I don't see how it helps."

"It made me wonder if Hal Ames had come here to borrow your lorry to get Sally back from the seaside. He caught the last bus, but she didn't."

"Why didn't he just tell us? Someone would have gone to get her."

"Perhaps he did. The only people here were Sir Rupert and Joan Glenfell. And Joan might not..." I didn't know how to finish the sentence without being rude.

"If Hal was here that night, I don't remember it. I only remember bits and pieces, Sir Rupert shouting, someone running. Nothing helpful," Joan Glenfell said, frustration evident in her voice as she came into the hall.

The three of us turned to look at her. Again, I couldn't help notice how much better she looked than she had the first time I saw her, since she only had her natural fair complexion and not her drugged pallor.

She shook her head and continued. "I'm embarrassed that I let my father goad me into taking my pills that night. I've since thrown them out, determined in the future to face whatever comes my way."

"That is good news," Abby said, her voice warm with encouragement.

"What was the doctor's name who prescribed those terrible pills for you?" I asked.

"I don't remember his name, if indeed I ever heard it. He was a psychoanalyst, I remember that. He immediately gave me a shot at my father's insistence. Philip was against it, but the doctor was hired by my father and only listened to him. The next several weeks are a blank. I don't even remember my son's funeral."

Tears began to leak down her cheeks. "What kind of a mother am I, that I can't remember my child's funeral?"

"One who was fed narcotics against her will," Louisa said.

"Why would my father do that to me?" came out as a plaintive cry. "He was a hateful, selfish man. I hated him so much..."

"Maybe he acted out of guilt, that he should have taken better care of your child, and didn't?" I suggested.

"Philip never thought it was guilt. He thought that my father was directly to blame. That he'd done it on purpose." The tears stopped with a sniff, but her shoulders were rounded under some invisible weight.

"Did he have any particular reason to believe that?" I asked.

"I don't know. We've never been able to talk about it."

"Maybe you should," Louisa said, sounding more as if

she was ordering Joan to talk to her husband. "You'll both feel better if you cleared the air between you."

"It always helps," Abby added. "Always."

I paid attention to their advice. It sounded sensible, but would Adam and I be able to if something as terrible as losing a child happened to us? I hoped so.

And no doctor of my father's would be able to get within a mile of me.

Louisa moved over to hug Joan as rapid footsteps approached. "Mum, look. It's Hal's satchel," Sally exclaimed. "We found it inside the bench in the back of the farm lorry. He must have been here Saturday night after he left me at the seashore. But why didn't he tell you where I was, if he was here at the farm?"

"Or tell your grandfather?" Louisa said. "Rupert was so evil, though, that he probably wouldn't have driven to the village to rescue you, much less Brighton."

I glanced over at the door to see Matthew looking at us, a flat-headed shovel in his hand. The back of the shovel blade was discolored, with something thick spread on it. Thick and rust colored. Not mud. His eyes were rounded and his voice was weak as he said, "Mum?"

Chapter Nineteen

"Is that blood on that shovel? Where did you find it?" I asked.

"In the cabinet with the satchel. In the back of the farm lorry," Matthew answered, standing frozen in place with the short-handled flat shovel held out before him as if he wanted to drop it and wipe off his hands.

"Is that Hal's blood?" Sally asked, backing away from Matthew and into the embrace of her mother and aunt.

I walked into the hall and telephoned the police station in Ratherminster. When I returned to the drawing room, I learned Louisa had asked Mrs. Thompson to make tea.

Sally kept repeating, "Hal came here to have someone bring me home from the pier. Why didn't you?"

"I'd taken those terrible pills, darling, when I realized you were missing. After Jack..." Joan Glenfell sobbed and then wailed, "I couldn't lose you both."

"Well, you didn't lose me, and I wish you'd throw out those wretched pills." I was glad to see Sally could sound firm when she needed to, as well as concerned for her mother.

"I have. They went into the dustbin yesterday." Mother and daughter exchanged a hug.

"Why didn't your grandfather do something?" I asked. "He was here at the house, and he hadn't taken any pills."

"And he was always in favor of doing something," Louisa added. "Except this time. He hated his grandchildren. I think it made him feel old to be a grandfather."

We fell silent as Mrs. Thompson brought in the tea tray, and then waited as Lady Louisa poured. By the time she finished, the police had arrived.

They declined tea as the constable took possession of the shovel from Matthew. As soon as it left his hand, Matthew, who'd been standing the whole time, dropped into a chair. Sally handed him a cup of tea, and he gulped it down.

"We also found Hal's satchel," Sally said, handing it to the detective inspector.

"Where did you find it?" the inspector asked as he quickly ran a hand through the bag's contents. "And are you sure this is Hal Ames's?"

"Yes, I'm sure it's his, and we found it with the shovel. Matthew and I did. In the cabinet in the back of the farm lorry."

"Would you show the constable?"

Matthew and Sally set down their cups and hurried out of the room, Constable Wiggins following with the evidence in his large hand.

Inspector Parsons took a seat facing us. "Now, ladies, you realize this gives us a closer connection between the two murders in location as well as time. And all of you, except you, Lady Summersby, seem to have been on the scene at about the time of the murders or shortly thereafter. Perhaps you'd want to start, Mrs. Glenfell? You never left the house, did you?" The inspector's tone said he wanted the truth now.

"I took a sedative after dinner, and I really don't remember anything until I heard a car pull up. Thinking it was my husband, I hurried downstairs and found Sir John Summersby and Captain and Mrs. Redmond in front of the house. That's when I learned the black-out curtains in my father's room were down."

"So, you still claim you remember nothing after dinner until nearly midnight."

"Good grief, Inspector. Sir Rupert nearly forced the pills down her throat when she began to sob. And it was two pills, not just one." Louisa came close to shouting.

"Why did you tell me you only took one?" the inspector said, staring at Joan.

"Because my father said there was only one pill in his hand."

"He gave you the pills? He put them in your mouth?"

Joan Glenfell nodded, staring at the carpet.

The inspector kept an expressionless face. "And you, Mrs. Redmond. Did you see Hal Ames anywhere while you were out checking blackout curtains?"

"No. Not until the next day, after the police had been called."

"Did you see anyone out at all?"

"Constable Wiggins in the village. Mrs. Glenfell, Lady

Louisa, and Sir Rupert here at Manning House. Philip Glenfell had stopped by Summersby House a little after ten to find out if Matthew knew what Sally's plans had been for that day. And we nearly ran Sir Douglas over when we drove past the site of his accident in the dark. After we found Sir Rupert's body."

"You gave him a lift home?"

"Of course." If this was all the police were capable of, they'd never solve either murder. Which had happened at nearly the same time and in nearly the same place, if the satchel and shovel were telling us the truth.

"And you, Lady Louisa, how do you know Sir Rupert gave Mrs. Glenfell two pills?"

"I saw him do it. He didn't hide the beastly things he did to us." She had turned her head away from him.

"What beastly things did he do to you?"

"It's not important." Louisa glared at him. "You wouldn't find it important."

I wondered. The possibilities were frightening.

The inspector continued. "And you saw the farm lorry out on Sykes's Mill Road along your fence line. Near the area where Hal Ames's body was found the next morning."

"Yes."

"At what time?"

"About nine."

"Was the lorry moving?"

She stared into the distance past the walls around us. "It was at first. Then it stopped."

"And you said this was your farm lorry."

"I assumed it was ours, until I found out Jim Eggerton and the vet were busy with a cow, so it couldn't have been ours."

"How do you know it couldn't have been yours?" the inspector asked.

"Who would have been driving it?"

"Hal Ames, going to get Sally from the seaside town where he left her?" The inspector stared hard at Louisa.

She sat back, startled. "Good heavens. He'd driven it before, he knew where the keys were kept, the lorry would have easily taken him that far and back."

Inspector Parsons pressed on. "But why would he have been on Sykes's Mill Road? That runs in the wrong direction to get to the coast."

"Then I doubt it was Hal Ames driving the farm lorry to get Sally." Louisa shrugged.

"Then who was driving, Lady Louisa?" The inspector was in her face now.

"I don't know. You think someone came along, killed Hal, dumped his body, and then drove the lorry back to the barn without anyone noticing." After thinking about this for a moment, she added, "Why? Why return the farm lorry?"

"To be where they were supposed to be as quickly as possible. And that means they should have been here at Manning Hall or the farm." The inspector continued to stare at her. I had the uncomfortable feeling that he wanted Louisa to incriminate herself.

Louisa shrugged, ignoring his insinuation. "The only

people who live on the farm are Jim Eggerton and the Smiths."

"Who are the Smiths?" the inspector asked, flipping over the pages in his notebook to take more notes.

"An old couple and their sons. They've lived here as tenants forever."

"How do I find their house?" the inspector asked.

Louisa burst out laughing. "May I watch you question them? I've never heard Mr. Smith put three words together at a time. Tom Smith just grunts, the poor boy is simple, and his brother Tim is terribly shy. He'll probably see you coming and run. And Mrs. Smith. Oh, dear. Well, she has to be heard to be believed."

"Nevertheless, they were here at the time, I take it?"

"Oh, yes." Louisa was enjoying herself.

The inspector seemed to be steeling himself. "Then I'd be remiss if I didn't ask if they'd seen or heard anything."

"You can ask," Louisa said. "I'm not certain they'll answer."

"Could they have taken the lorry out on Saturday night?" the inspector asked.

"Anything's possible, but I'd think it was highly unlikely," Louisa said. The more the inspector was disconcerted, the happier Louisa appeared.

"Unless Mr. Smith thought it was his duty to ride around looking for Sally," Joan said.

"I doubt he'd do anything, even if he thought it was his duty. Sir Douglas has better luck with them than Sir Rupert ever did, and he still finds them a trial to deal with,"

Louisa replied.

"Do the Smiths know Mrs. Ames or Hal? Do they get along?" I asked. If they were part of the local residents whose families had been here forever, this might have an effect on how they'd respond to a plea to find Hal or Sally.

"Oh, they came here on the ark," Louisa said. "They must know Eleanor and Hal Ames."

"They're related to every other Smith in the district," Joan said. "The family's been here for hundreds of years."

"Then I'm sure they know the Ames family." And if the police didn't learn anything from them, I'd talk to Mrs. Goodfellow about how to approach them.

Matthew and Sally returned at that point with Constable Wiggins. "I've seen where they found the shovel and satchel, sir. There are bloodstains on the inside of the rear cabinet of the farm lorry that match streaks that a shovel, sliding around, might make. I've spoken to Mr. Eggerton and the Smiths, who live in the two cottages in the back. They all claim to have seen nothing and heard nothing."

"I told your inspector you'd get nothing out of the Smiths," Louisa said.

"Oh, we got plenty out of Mrs. Smith. It just wasn't helpful," Sally said with a grin. "I thought she was going to hit Constable Wiggins with her broom."

Constable Wiggins turned red, but he remained silent.

"Two people were killed here Saturday evening. The only person who was out wandering around without an alibi is you, Lady Manning," the inspector said. "And you are the only one who supposedly saw the lorry where we found Hal Ames's body. And you and your husband were the only ones who directly benefitted from Sir Rupert's death."

"I don't think that's true," Louisa said. The color had drained from her skin, making her lips and hair stand out brightly against the whiteness of her face.

"You're now the lady of the manor. You're in charge. The farm and the income come to your husband instead of your tightfisted father-in-law. That's what you called him, didn't you?"

"Well, he was," Louisa said defiantly.

"You can get rid of the artifacts that include at least one murder weapon. You burned the rug with the bloodstain, I understand. That was rather quick."

"After you put a hole in it. You were quick to do that," she said, glaring at the inspector.

"I think that's all for right now," the inspector said, rising from his chair.

"Inspector, you've forgotten Herr Wolfenhaus," I said.

"Who?"

"A friend of Sir Rupert's who claims to have arrived here Monday. He might have arrived earlier. And he says Sir Rupert's last will and testament gives him the unentailed properties. He had motive, means, and quite possibly opportunity." I smiled at the inspector, hoping I'd deflected his interest from Louisa.

"Do you know where he's staying?"

"The Hawk and Anvil."

The inspector made a note. "Thank you, ladies. Come along, Constable. And Lady Manning, don't go anywhere without telling us first."

"Of course." Louisa bit at a polished fingernail. I hadn't seen her do that since our early days at St. Agnes School.

The two men left before Matthew and Sally looked at each other. "Poor Wiggins," Sally said. "Mrs. Smith went after him for suggesting a 'good God-fearing woman' could be mixed up in murdering 'that nice Ames boy.' It was a sin and the Smiths have no business dealings with the devil."

Matthew looked confused. "When Constable Wiggins asked if she'd seen this devil, Mrs. Smith said maybe she had and maybe she hadn't, but it made no difference now."

"Why would she say that?" I asked.

Matthew shrugged.

"Why are you interested, Olivia?" Louisa asked.

"The farm lorry may have no involvement with the murders, but then again, it may. I believe you saw it, even if the inspector doesn't. We need to find out who was driving the lorry, and why, before we can set it aside. So far, Louisa, you may have had the best glimpse of the murderer, but I'm hopeful someone out there saw more than you did."

I took a deep breath and continued, "From Mrs. Smith's strange reply, I think we need to find out what she knows. If she was just giving Constable Wiggins trouble, we need to find out so we can move on. If she saw the farm lorry that night, here or on the road, we need to discover how much she saw."

"Don't look at me. Mrs. Smith and I can't abide each other, the judgmental little harpy," Louisa said, lighting a cigarette. I noticed her hands shook.

"Do you want me to try?" Joan asked. "She's always glad to tell me how to run my life, and I always let her. I had good practice with my father."

"May I come along?" I asked.

"Of course. I don't think your presence will make any difference."

Excusing ourselves, Joan and I walked the short distance through a field to the Smith cottage, in the center of a small barnyard busy with chickens and kittens. Joan knocked on a door that was in need of a coat of paint and then stepped back. I stood beside her, wondering what would happen.

A short, thin woman with leathery, wrinkled skin, wearing a housedress and boots, answered the door. She wore what I thought had been called a mobcap over her straight, gray hair. "What do you want, Mrs. Glenfell?" she asked with a decided lack of welcome. Her eyes kept straying past us to the edges of her farmyard.

"Sally told me what you said to the constable, Mrs. Smith, and we wondered if there was more you could tell us," Joan said.

"Wouldn't have to if you wouldn't take the devil's medicine," Mrs. Smith said as she began to shut the door.

"Do you like Mrs. Ames?" I asked.

"Why?" The door stopped moving.

"She asked me to find out what happened to Hal."

"Why would she do that? Won't bring him back." She appeared to try to stare me down.

I'd dealt with Nazi border guards who could teach her a few things about looking ominous. "That's her decision. She's the one who lost a son."

She considered that for a moment, glancing past us to the edges of the farmyard. "Why did she ask you?"

"I've had experience finding killers."

"You?" Her voice was full of scorn.

"Yes, and if you have any regard for Mrs. Ames, you'll tell us what you know about the farm lorry on Saturday night." I was tired of spending my honeymoon dealing with other people's troubles, and I seemed to be getting nowhere. It put a hard edge in my voice.

"You think you're tough, don't you? But you know nothing about Manning Farm or the people who live here."

"Why don't you straighten me out?" I made it a challenge.

She stuck her head outdoors and looked around. "All right, but not here. Meet me in the vehicle barn tonight at nine."

"Who are you afraid of?"

She slammed the door in our faces.

Chapter Twenty

We returned to the main house to find Abby and Louisa in the front hall. "Of course, we'll be there. One o'clock?" Abby said.

"Thank you, Lady Abby. And please, come to tea afterward. I suspect I'll be in need of support by then," Louisa said. "Especially with that wretched policeman."

"We'd love to."

"Could I speak to Marjorie if she's not busy at the moment?" I asked.

"Of course. Mrs. Thompson, where is Marjorie?"

The housekeeper appeared out of the gloom at the back of the front hall. "I'll get her."

A minute or two later, Marjorie arrived in the front hall at Mrs. Thompson's side. Marjorie was looking pale beneath her sallow skin, and she was shrinking away from Mrs. Thompson. Did she think she was in trouble?

"Marjorie, let's take a walk outside and talk a little," I said, hoping I could relieve her mind. "Mrs. Ames asked me to talk to you."

Marjorie's wrinkled face creased into a smile. "She's my cousin."

We went outdoors and walked along the lane toward the road. No one could overhear us there. "Remember last

Saturday morning? Did you see Sally leave to catch the bus to the pier?"

"Yes. Mrs. Thompson and I saw her off. She was going with Hal Ames."

"Yes. What happened that night when Sally didn't return?"

"Sally didn't return, and the household was in a horrible muddle. Miss Joan was fretting, so Sir Rupert slapped her. Then he tried to make her take her pills, but I saw her spit out at least one of them later."

So, Sir Rupert was a bully, he hit women, and Joan Glenfell didn't take the number of pills she led the inspector to believe. "Did Sir Rupert ever hit any of the other women?"

"Miss Louisa, yes, but not Miss Anne. The only time he hit her, she punched him back in the nose. Freddy and Douglas tried to hold him back, but Anne told them to let him go. She said she had studied boxing and wrestling, and she would beat him every time."

Marjorie smiled at the memory. "Then she said, why don't we call it a draw and never speak of this again? He stormed off, but it never happened again to my knowledge." She looked satisfied, and I had a clear impression that she didn't care too much for Sir Rupert.

"You work in an exciting household." Did she ever. "Did you see anyone take the farm lorry out Saturday night?"

"No. I took Sir Rupert his tea and then I went to my room. I was tired."

"And you didn't see Hal Ames come up to the house?"

"No. Was he here?"

I gave her a smile as I turned us back to the house. "Thank you, Marjorie. I appreciate you talking to me."

"I've worked for the Mannings for fifty years. I do what they say, and I don't ask no questions." She said her words firmly.

"Which of the Mannings tell you what to do?"

"Sir Rupert did, and Miss Joan and the new lady. Louisa, that is. And once in a while Sir Douglas and Freddy and Anne. Sally when she wants something. And Mrs. Thompson gives me my cleaning directions."

"That's quite a lot of people giving you orders."

She smiled. There was pride in her voice when she said, "I don't mind. I get it all done."

I stepped in front of her. "Did you like Sir Rupert?"

"He was all right. I liked his father better. Now, he was a good man. But liking him or not didn't change the work."

"Is there something the Mannings told you not to tell me?"

"No." But I saw fear in her eyes as she stopped and took a half-step backward. When we walked into the front hall, Marjorie immediately disappeared toward the kitchen.

Then Abby called, "Come along, Matthew."

He appeared at her side, Sally right behind him.

"Are you going to Hal Ames's funeral?" I asked. "It's this afternoon."

"I don't think we'd be welcome. Do you?" Louisa

asked. "The police seem to think I had something to do with his death."

"I think I should attend, Mummy," Sally said, staring at her mother. "Why didn't you tell me?"

"We'll talk about it later," Joan said.

I watched Joan, wondering how much she really did remember from Saturday night.

Sensing a battle brewing, Abby called me. We escaped into the car after the minimum of pleasantries and drove off.

"Well, I put my foot in that," I said. "But I heard you mention something about one o'clock. What is at one o'clock?"

"Sir Rupert's funeral tomorrow. And yes, we're going," Abby told me as Matthew groaned. "To both."

"Sally's found a new favorite?" I asked, turning around to see him.

He groaned again. Then he said, "She's okay, but she's a girl. She knows nothing about cricket and she wants to take up all my time, the way she did with Hal."

"You're both too young for that, and you may tell her I said so," Abby said.

Matthew turned frightened eyes on me from the back seat.

"You're welcome to stick close to Adam and me if you'd prefer," I told him.

He mouthed, "Thank you."

We returned home in time for lunch. Over the rabbit and vegetable stew I told Adam what Mrs. Smith had said.

"I'm going with you," he told me.

"Thank you, but please don't feel obligated..." I began.

"Livvy, there may be a killer living there. I don't feel obligated. I'm insisting."

"Mrs. Smith would make a great killer," Matthew said after a gulp of milk. "She's mean enough."

"Matthew," his parents said in unison.

"She even scares Constable Wiggins."

"But she's afraid of someone or something. I don't know what," I told Matthew. "Did you see her looking out her door to see who else was there when she was talking to Constable Wiggins? Someone along her farmyard fence line?"

He thought a moment. "Yes. How did you know? Were you watching?"

"No, but she did the same thing to us. She was all bluster, but she wasn't taking a step outside her door."

"Who do you think she's afraid of?" Gerhard asked.

"The killer."

"Terrific," Mark said with an enthusiasm his mother didn't share.

"Mark, that is quite enough."

"Could we—?" he began eagerly.

"Go over to Manning Hall and hunt for a killer?" his father asked. "No."

"But—?"

"No."

I felt sorry for Sir John and Abby, knowing how I'd behaved as a child. I almost felt sorry for my father.

No. I refused to feel sorry for my father.

"Do you want to take a walk after lunch?" Adam asked me.

"No," Abby said. "We have a funeral to attend."

I remembered that Hal Ames's funeral was that day. "Of course. I can't believe it nearly slipped my mind."

"Sir Rupert is being buried tomorrow. The Ames boy is being buried today, and we're going to show support for Mrs. Ames." Abby sounded quite determined.

Sir John looked at Adam and shrugged in some sort of masculine solidarity.

Before I went upstairs to dress, I went into the kitchen and asked Mrs. Goodfellow to tell me everything she could about Mrs. Smith and her relationship with Eleanor Ames.

"I heard Tad Wiggins tried to question Martha Smith this morning about what she saw on Saturday night." She dried her hands and sat on a stool by the tall table with a cup of tea.

I pulled out a stool across from her. "She told the constable that maybe she saw something and maybe she didn't. The way she searches the perimeter of her yard with her eyes from her doorway makes me think she's afraid of someone. When I mentioned Mrs. Ames wanted to know what happened to her son, Mrs. Smith agreed to talk to me tonight at nine in the vehicle barn."

"Mick Ames and Martha Smith were some degree of cousins. Third, I think. That makes Hal Ames a relative, and Martha has a duty to help find his killer. Doesn't matter if she wants to tell you or not. She has to help. It's as simple as that." Mrs. Goodfellow sounded determined that old customs be upheld.

"What do you think she knows?"

"Oh, Mrs. Redmond, I have no idea. It's impossible to see the drive running from the house to the road from their windows. The cottage is situated in a little dip in the land. You can't see the entrance to the barn where the vehicles are kept from their cottage, either." She studied me over her mug of tea. "If she saw something, she had to have left her cottage and garden at night for some reason, and that doesn't sound like her."

"Do you think she'll turn up tonight?"

"Yes. But be careful. She's being cagey because someone at Manning Farm is a killer, and she knows it."

"Captain Redmond is going with me to meet her."

"That's a good idea." She nodded her gray head. "The captain seems to be a handy man to have nearby when you find yourself in difficulties."

"He is." I smiled when I thought of him. "Is Marjorie Lenard a truthful person?"

"Yes. I've found her so."

"Is she an observant person?"

"Yes." Mrs. Goodfellow scowled. "What has she told you?"

"It may have no bearing on Hal's murder, or it may point to a witness. I'm not sure." I hoped it would help me sort out what happened.

"Your tea is ready in the larder, and dinner just needs to be popped in the oven. Now, I need to get ready." She rose from her stool.

"You're going to the funeral?"

"Of course. He was my nephew."

I felt my face heat when I realized I had forgotten. "Do you have a way to get there?" The village and the church weren't too far to walk for a countrywoman such as Mrs. Goodfellow, but I imagined she'd want to look her best despite traversing currently dusty paths.

"The Longs are giving me a lift."

I grinned at her. "Are you going to the funeral tomorrow?"

"Sir Rupert? Now, why would I do that?" she scoffed. "He had no feelings for this village."

I rose and left the kitchen, thanking Mrs. Goodfellow as I went.

Adam and I rode down to the church with Sir John, Abby, and Matthew. The village shops were closed when we passed, and the verge by the church was parked up as if it were Christmas. The beautiful, chilly, old stone church was packed.

We took seats near the back of the church and I looked around at the somberly dressed congregation. The Smiths were across the aisle and forward a little. When I didn't spot anyone from Manning Hall, I whispered to Matthew, "Isn't Sally coming?"

"I don't know. She told me she wanted to."

Half a minute later, I heard a rustle of fabric sliding along the pew and turned to see Sally, Mrs. Thompson, and Marjorie squeeze in the row behind us.

Then the magnificent organ began the first hymn and everyone rose.

The Reverend Garner did a good job of delivering a funeral sermon, admonishing the congregation to take care of those grieving and telling God to raise up Hal and strike down his killer. Certainly better than at our wedding, when he threatened us with eternal damnation if we committed adultery or I failed to obey.

With the final hymn, we followed the casket out to the churchyard and around to the back. Hal was being buried next to his father. We encircled the grave while Reverend Garner stood at the head and recited the familiar prayers. Sally slipped in next to Matthew, a handkerchief balled up in one hand.

Her face looked as if she hadn't had to use it.

Once the final prayers were said, the symbolic handfuls of dirt were thrown on the coffin by Mr. Long and Mr. Jones. Mrs. Ames sobbed too hard to do anything but be led away to her cottage by Mrs. Long and Mrs. Jones. Several of the older village women, Mrs. Goodfellow among them, joined the procession down the path that led from the back of the churchyard to come out on the lane across from the Ames cottage.

The rest of us stood around in front of the church, not certain what to do next. After a minute or two of chatter, shopkeepers walked back to their stores and we headed to Sir John's auto. I noticed Sally, Marjorie Lenard, and Mrs. Thompson go back to Douglas Manning's newly repaired car, and Mrs. Thompson got behind the wheel.

I needed to add her to my list of possible drivers at Manning Hall the previous Saturday. Since Mrs. Thompson knew how to drive and she ran the household, Hal could have gone to her to get permission to drive the lorry or to take him to pick up Sally at the pier. But that hadn't happened, and I couldn't begin to guess why Mrs. Thompson would have killed Hal Ames.

Mrs. Thompson got along well with Sally, and she seemed levelheaded enough not to worry where the girl's relationship with Hal Ames was headed. It wouldn't have affected her, anyway.

We returned home to a cold tea served by Mary, but at least the tea itself was hot. The boys didn't seem to notice any difference with Mrs. Goodfellow out of the house. Then I realized she would have at least a half day off every week and probably more time off than that, since Abby would be a generous employer.

"What if Mrs. Goodfellow doesn't get back in time for dinner?" I asked Abby quietly when she walked over to pour herself more tea. It was a thought I'd never worried about before.

"I'm sure she has it already prepared. All Mary will have to do is put it in the oven and take it out again to serve it. Don't worry. You'll get fed."

"That wasn't exactly what I was thinking."

"You're wondering what you're going to do about feeding Adam in the future. I suggest you learn how to cook. I did. It's a handy skill in an emergency." She gave me a smile and took her tea over to see the board game

Henry and Gerhard were playing.

Actually, I had learned to cook when I was married to Reggie Denis. His suffering through burnt meat and soggy vegetables meant that Adam would miss the worst of my mistakes.

The sky was still light when Adam and I drove over to Manning Hall at precisely nine o'clock. We drove past the house and up to the outbuilding I'd learned was where they garaged all the vehicles and the farm machinery.

The doors were shut. Thinking Mrs. Smith hadn't shown up yet, we waited outside for a few minutes. Finally, I said, "This is ridiculous," and started to walk over to the Smith cottage, Adam right behind me. I was aware he was looking around, but I preferred to think of it as curiosity rather than defensiveness.

I knocked on the door as Joan had earlier and then stepped back.

An old man opened the door. "Are you the woman who came out here to see Martha?"

"Yes."

"Well, she doesn't want to see you."

Great. A wasted trip. "Why not?"

"We've been tenants here for three generations. My father and grandfather lived in our cottage for nearly a hundred years before we took over. Don't want to lose that. Where would we go?"

"Do you really believe Sir Douglas would throw you out if Mrs. Smith speaks the truth?" Then I realized what his words meant. "Sir Douglas was driving the farm lorry?"

"No." He looked horrified. "That's not what she said."

"Then what did she say? Did she accuse Lady Louisa?" I couldn't believe either of them had any reason to kill Hal Ames. Sir Rupert, possibly, but even there I didn't see a strong motive, or any link between Sir Rupert's killing and the wandering lorry. I had an idea what the inspector was thinking, and he was wrong.

"Of course not. Lady Louisa came to our door looking for Jim Eggerton after she saw the farm lorry, wondering if it had anything to do with Miss Sally." Mr. Smith glanced past me to the edge of the farmyard.

"So, you saw Lady Louisa shortly after nine o'clock on Saturday night?" Why hadn't she told me that?

"Yes. Another five minutes and I'd have been abed and asleep."

"And Mrs. Smith also?"

"Yes."

"And being dedicated to your employers, the two of you went out to check on the farm lorry?"

He shook his head. "Martha took Tom with her."

Tom, the son who was slow and wouldn't have drawn any conclusions from anything he saw. I needed to speak to Mrs. Smith.

"And what did she see?" Adam asked, sounding belligerent. He was as unhappy about wasting what little time we had to spend together as I was.

I put out my hand and wrapped his fist with it. "I don't intend to spend my honeymoon begging you to tell me what you saw. I'll just tell Mrs. Ames that you and Mrs.

Smith have evidence concerning what happened to her son, but you won't tell anyone. I'll let her deal with you."

I turned away from the door, furious with the Smiths. "Come on, Adam."

Chapter Twenty-One

A woman's voice said, "Wait."

We turned to face the doorway.

Mrs. Smith stuck her long face out of the doorway enough to see us and waved us to come closer. When we finally drew close enough to satisfy her, she whispered, "We've been warned not to say anything or we'll lose our place here. And where are we going to go at our ages?"

"Who told you that?"

"A friend."

I crossed my arms over my chest. "One of the family who doesn't want us to get to the truth of Hal Ames's death."

"No. Not the family."

A picture of Mrs. Thompson driving Sally home from the boy's funeral came to my mind. "The housekeeper."

"Oh, I'm saying nothing."

Which told me everything. "She's wrong. Sir Douglas wouldn't put you out for telling what you know about the lorry, unless you named either him or Lady Louisa." I didn't think Douglas cared about anyone else in the house.

"Not them."

"Then who?"

Mrs. Smith looked around and then said, "The old

man."

"Sir Rupert? But he was dead then." I remembered the timeline the doctor had developed. "Oh, no. Wait. He wasn't."

"Can't tell tales about the old lord. It's not right."

"Saying you saw him with the farm lorry is not pointing any blame on him. He owned it," Adam said in a patient voice.

"Did you see him with the lorry out by the mill road?" I asked.

"When we went out there, he was driving it back into the barn."

"And this was after Lady Louisa came to your door looking for Mr. Eggerton?"

The old woman nodded.

"Was anyone else out? Did anyone else see him?"

"Not that I saw."

"Did you see Lady Louisa outside when the farm lorry returned?"

"No."

"I wonder where she went," I said aloud.

Mrs. Smith glowered at me, but she didn't say a word.

Mr. Smith grumbled, "Oh, for pity's sake. She'd have gone into the garden and sat on the bench. Hates walking the fields even during the day."

Not exactly the best alibi in the world, but I could understand her sitting on a garden bench rather than wandering the fields looking for a girl who had enough sense not to be out there at night with the bugs and the little creatures.

I suggested very strongly that the old tenant farmwife tell Constable Wiggins what she had seen, and then Adam and I went back to the car. From there we could hear raised voices.

"That's the whole point of the funeral. My father is dead. I'm in charge now, and I'll do things my way, thank you." It had to be Sir Douglas talking, but who was he talking to?

With a glance at Adam, who shook his head, I walked along the grass rather than the gravel drive to find out who was having the argument. Did it have anything to do with Sir Rupert taking the lorry out the night Sally was missing? Did it have anything to do with Sir Rupert's murder?

"How long do you think you'll be in charge when the will is read?" a man with a thick German accent spoke with malice in his tone.

"I'm his heir. The new baronet. That's what the solicitor will say."

"You don't want your father's reputation to be blackened, do you?" the other male voice said. "It will make it hard for you to maintain the respect of the villagers. Or the other baronets. It would bring shame on the entire family." I peered around the bushes at the corner of the house. In the glow of the porchlight, I could see the other man was blond the same as Joan Glenfell, perhaps in his fifties, and lean.

As I'd guessed—Herr Jürgen Wolfenhaus.

Sir Douglas said, "I don't care about my father's

reputation."

"And your own shame, as his son?"

"Not at the price you're charging. Now, get out."

I noticed a taxi waiting on the drive. The man was fortunate, because it would be a long walk in the dark to the village otherwise.

"You know my terms. I will see you tomorrow. It will be your last chance." Wolfenhaus gave him a smile made evil by the way the light fell on him.

"Stay away from me and my family." Sir Douglas stepped back into the house and slammed the door.

Wolfenhaus laughed as he walked to the taxi and climbed in.

Why had he come out here? Terms? The terms of the inheritance would be spelled out in the will. Was Wolfenhaus a blackmailer? Was Sir Rupert his target, or Sir Douglas?

* * *

After breakfast the next morning, I found Mrs. Goodfellow in the kitchen working on lunch. I realized feeding a household of eight plus the servants had to be a full-time occupation, and one I didn't want. Considering some of my culinary failures, this was a task no one else would want me to attempt, either.

"The next time you talk to Constable Wiggins, find out if Mrs. Smith has told him what she saw on Saturday night."

I had her full attention as she faced me, her chopping forgotten. "You know who killed Hal?"

"I have a suspicion. The police may think the same thing after they talk to Martha Smith. And they can do more following up on a suspicion than I can."

She sat again and began chopping. "You have no proof."

"No proof. Just answers to questions I didn't have answers to before."

"Are you going to tell Eleanor Ames?" Her knife hovered over the carrots.

"I hope you will come with me when I do."

"It'll have to be after dinner tonight."

"That's fine. I'd appreciate it if you came with me." I left the kitchen and was walking down the main hall past the telephone as it rang. I answered it more out of habit than a desire to find out who was calling.

"Mrs. Redmond," a young voice said, "can you bring Matthew over here?"

"Sally?" I hoped for Matthew's sake I guessed right. Confusing one teenaged girl with another wouldn't help his reputation.

"Yes."

"What's wrong?" She seemed to be whispering, so I whispered, too.

"Some evil German man is here arguing with Uncle Douglas, and now Mummy is crying and my father is wringing his hands and Aunt Louisa is threatening to kill him. And we have to dress for the funeral soon."

"Sally, get dressed for the funeral and try to get your mother dressed for it as well. We'll be over shortly to bring you to Summersby House before the funeral so things can settle down."

As soon as I hung up, I went into the dining room and said, "May I borrow the car, Abby? There seems to be some sort of ruckus at Manning Hall and Sally wants us to rescue her and her mother before the funeral."

Adam immediately rose. "I guess you want me to drive." He knew I had never properly learned.

"And I suppose she wants Matthew to come along," Abby said in a dry tone.

"Yes and yes."

Sir John was busy with his estate agent, so Abby gave her blessing and Adam, an unwilling Matthew, and I headed for Manning Hall. We pulled in behind a taxi and could hear the sound of raised voices from the porch before we rang the bell.

Sally must have been waiting for us, because she threw open the door and nearly leaped into Matthew's arms. Matthew looked at me with a shocked expression and a quiet "Eep."

Leaving Matthew and Sally outside the door, Adam and I marched in. Mrs. Thompson stood at the far end of the hall, blocked from answering the door by all the Mannings facing one man. Joan was wailing, her hands in fists. Philip was holding her back from striking the intruder. Douglas was shouting, "I inherited the baronetcy and the estate. Until I am told otherwise, I am in charge and you are to leave immediately."

"When is the will to be read?" the fair-haired German

asked, as if commenting on the weather. Wolfenhaus again. I wondered what he was up to.

"Here, after the funeral. Not that it has anything to do with you," Louisa said in her lady of the manor voice. "Now leave."

"Ah, but it has quite a bit to do with me. I've given you my price. You have until the will is read to decide what to do." The man looked down the front hall and added in German, "Soon you will be working for me."

The Glenfells and the Mannings looked puzzled. I had heard none of them, except for Joan, spoke any German. I doubted if Joan had worked a day in her life. Was Wolfenhaus threatening her with some sort of slavery? Maybe he just meant that they would have to manage their properties to pay him the owner's share.

"Good day, Mr. Wolfenhaus." Sir Douglas raised his voice in clear English.

Wolfenhaus nodded to us as he walked out of the house, setting his hat on his head as he stepped outdoors.

"What are we going to do?" Louisa asked, staring at her husband and ignoring us.

Douglas shook his head slowly, the beet-red color beginning to leave his face.

Joan's wails were diminishing to sobs punctuated with, "He killed my baby boy. He will be the next to die."

It was Freddy, sauntering into the hall with Anne following, who first noticed us. "Hello. Are you here with Sally's friend?"

"Yes. She called and asked us to come over. I'm sorry

if we came at a bad time." I gave him a neighborly smile.

"These Germans. They think they can take over our country one farm at a time," Philip Glenfell said.

"That's enough, Philip," Sir Douglas said. "It's nothing for the Redmonds to worry about. Nor is Sally. Louisa and I sent our boys away to her parents this morning because of the deaths and the chaos."

"And their mother being suspected of murder," Louisa said, hurt and scorn in her tone.

Her husband ignored her. "Get your daughter in line, Glenfell, and we'll go to the funeral together. As a family."

That sounded as if it was a good plan to me. Apologizing, Adam and I walked outside with Glenfell to extricate Matthew from Sally and leave.

Once back at Summersby House, all four of the boys pleaded with Abby and Sir John to allow Matthew to stay home from the funeral. They made rash promises and came up with strange reasons why Matthew needed to stay home to watch over the younger three. Henry came up with the best reason—"He wasn't a friend of Matthew's"—that left me clamping my lips shut to keep from laughing.

"Sally needs a little time away from Matthew," I suggested.

"She needs to be locked in a nunnery," Abby murmured so only I could hear her. Once again, I had to bite back my laughter.

Matthew prevailed.

After a light lunch, we readied for the funeral and we

four adults drove to the church. I wore the same black skirt and gray blouse I'd worn the day before. Adam and Sir John were lucky; men's suits were appropriate for all solemn occasions, but with the present weather, they had to be uncomfortably hot.

Parking wasn't as difficult as it had been the day before. The autos were newer models than had been present at Hal Ames's funeral, and the people going into church were dressed in higher heels and had crisper creases without a wrinkle in sight. Several gray-haired people were seen walking from the station to the church, no doubt having just arrived on the train from London.

"Herr Wolfenhaus will be here," I told Sir John. "He is anxious for them to read the will. He was at Manning Hall last night and then again this morning when Sally called us."

Sir John stopped on the pavement in front of the church and turned to stare at me. "What was he doing there?"

"Trying to get some sort of agreement from Sir Douglas before the will is read. And Philip Glenfell said something about the Germans trying to take over England one farm at a time."

"Good heavens. He doesn't think he can be willed the estate, does he? It's entailed to Douglas, and Douglas's older son."

"Is it?" Abby asked.

"Yes, much the same as ours is to Matthew. The home farm certainly is, but the rest of the holdings may not be, in the case of the Mannings."

"You mean such as the pub?" I asked, remembering how Sir Rupert had owned the building the pub was in and Wolfenhaus's comments there on Monday night.

"Exactly. Sir Rupert would be free to leave the buildings he owned in the village, his collection of trophies from the Arctic, and whatever else to whomever he wanted."

"That could be a lucrative inheritance," Adam said. "I wonder what the will says."

"Wolfenhaus said something odd. In German. He said they'd be working for him. But none of them appeared to understand German."

"None of the children speak anything but English. Well, Joan speaks traveler German. It was a sore point for Sir Rupert," Sir John said.

We went inside the beautiful cool stone church and today sat halfway down on the right. The Manning family and staff sat on the right at the front. Wolfenhaus sat on the left a few rows ahead of us.

I gave the correct responses and sang the correct hymns, but my mind was wondering if someone had killed Sir Rupert for their inheritance. What did Joan and Freddy receive from their father? What about Wolfenhaus? If we were soon to be at war with Germany, was he anxious to get his part of the estate in cash so he could take it back to Germany with him?

Was Wolfenhaus in England at the time Sir Rupert was murdered?

We weren't at war yet, so he could have been.

As the funeral ended, we walked out the front of the church and around to the side where Sir Rupert would be interred. Sally looked at us, realized Matthew wasn't with us, and then ignored us. The servants made a line behind the family. Wolfenhaus stood across the grave from the family and near us, looking solemn and cynical.

The graveside service was long, befitting a local leader. When it ended and the ceremonial clods of dirt were thrown onto the casket now lowered into the grave, I realized Louisa Manning wasn't there, nor were Joan Glenfell, the Manning servants, or Herr Wolfenhaus. As soon as they decently could, the rest of the congregation dispersed, everyone going in a different direction.

I walked with Adam, Sir John, and Abby across the lane toward the car. Glancing behind us toward the front of the church, I saw Louisa follow our path along the side of the church to join her husband in accepting condolences. She hadn't been anywhere in the churchyard that I could see a moment before.

Then Joan appeared from around the far side of the church to join the family in the front. What had she been doing, going the long way around to stand with the others?

While I was wondering where Louisa and Joan had come from, Eleanor Ames hurried out from the front of the church toward us. Excusing myself, I walked over to her.

"Mrs. Smith spoke to Constable Wiggins. They think

Sir Rupert killed my boy. Why would they think that now, when they didn't think there was any reason Sir Rupert would want to harm him before?" Her voice was rising to a wail.

I took her arm and walked her past the open grave toward the back of the churchyard and the path toward her home. I didn't want her to carry on within hearing distance of the Mannings and upset them. They didn't deserve it, not that day. And they'd had nothing to do with Sir Rupert's wickedness. "Obviously, the police can't prove Sir Rupert killed your son, not in court, but it seems likely. Can you accept that as the conclusion?"

Eleanor's face twisted as if she was fighting off tears as she marched across the back of the churchyard and started along the path toward her house. She seemed unaware of my presence behind her, her back rigid and a stricken look on her face as she stopped, staring ahead and down, when I caught up.

"I know it doesn't seem fair, but..." My voice faded as I glanced over to where she was looking when she'd halted.

The lean body of Wolfenhaus lay in the shade along the grassy verge of the path, a large carving knife sticking out of the back of his suit jacket.

Chapter Twenty-Two

Leaving Mrs. Ames to stare with a horrified expression, I ran to Adam and Sir John. "It looks as if Wolfenhaus has been murdered," I gasped out when I reached them.

"What?"

"He's behind the church, in the grass beside the path toward the Ames cottage." I pointed, as if it might make my words clearer.

Adam took off at a sprint, gaining the attention of lingering members of the congregation, with Sir John hurrying behind him. Abby and I walked quickly to follow and, as we started off, heard Eleanor Ames finally let loose with a scream.

That gained the attention of Constable Wiggins, who was directing traffic out on the road, and Reverend Garner on the front steps leading into the church. The Mannings and the Glenfells, who had gathered in front of the church to thank people for their presence, drifted around to the back.

I reached the small group in time to see Adam take his fingers off the man's neck and rise, shaking his head.

Constable Wiggins reached us then and asked everyone to step back. Since only Adam and Sir John had come within five feet of the body, they were the only ones who needed to follow his directions. "Sir John," Wiggins said, "would you please call Dr. Wheeler and the police station?"

"You can use the phone in the vestry," the Reverend Garner said as he arrived and led Sir John up the path toward the front of the church. As they walked away, I heard the vicar say, "How terrible. And at a funeral."

I kept wondering who wanted Herr Wolfenhaus dead. I knew of no one outside the Manning family who had reason to kill him. Or even knew him. But who felt so strongly that they actually took his life?

Dr. Wheeler arrived at the same time that Sir John and the Reverend Garner returned and quickly proclaimed Herr Wolfenhaus deceased. After a hurried conference with the constable, the doctor left.

I noticed the Glenfells and Freddy and Anne Manning, who'd been in the crowd of onlookers, had already left.

Sir Douglas moved beside Sir John. "I'd appreciate it if you'd join us for some refreshments and to hear the terms of the will. I suspect there will be some legal issues that you as a magistrate would have some thoughts on."

"What about your solicitor?"

"He's so old and confused that I doubt he'll be of any help. And he long ago learned to do exactly as my father insisted, whether it was legal or not."

Sir John glanced back at us. "I'll need to take Abby and the Redmonds home first."

"Bring them along," Lady Louisa told him. "I'd enjoy their company. And their common sense."

It was quickly decided that we'd follow Sir Douglas's car. Sir John had a few words with the constable and then we were all free to leave as more policemen arrived on the narrow path to deal with the crime scene.

When we arrived at Manning Hall, Mrs. Thompson opened the door for us wearing a frilly white maid's apron over her black dress. Sally came up behind her, saw Matthew wasn't there, and stomped away, up the stairs.

"Did you and Marjorie get a ride back to the house?" I asked Mrs. Thompson once we entered the hallway.

"No."

When my shock at her curt dismissal registered on my face, she straightened her shoulders and said, "We left the funeral early and took the shortcut back, stopping at a shop on the way. If you'll excuse me." She turned away from me then and walked into the dining room.

I glanced into the trophy room to find many of the displays had been dismantled and boxed up. "I'll be glad when all of this is gone," Anne Manning said as she walked up beside me. "Maybe then the house won't reek of death. Dead animals. Dead people."

"What will you use the room for?"

"The library. Then the current library can be opened up and used for the family drawing room. The views out the library windows are superb."

"I thought it odd this room doesn't have any windows," I said.

"It used to have windows until Sir Rupert's father extended the kitchen and the servants' areas. Now it's just closed in." Anne shook her head. "Sir Rupert thought it was perfect for his trophies. They wouldn't fade."

We heard noise by the front door and went into the hall. A desiccated, white-haired man carrying a briefcase in one bony hand came in and was greeted by Sir Douglas. The two of them, and Sir John, walked off to what I guessed was Sir Douglas's study.

When Philip Glenfell went to follow them in, Sir Douglas stopped him. "I just want to find out our legal position in regard to that dead German. There will be time enough for questions and hearing the will later."

Douglas shut the door, very quietly, in Philip's face. Philip turned away, his back rigid, and marched out of the house. Joan hurried after him with a squeal, but Lady Louisa caught her at the front door and guided her into the drawing room.

"We all want to hear the will read," Louisa said, "but first, they need to figure out how to handle any mention of Wolfenhaus."

"He's a German, and he killed my son. He should get nothing. He's received everything he deserved." Joan stalked out of the house after her husband.

Anne looked at Louisa and shrugged. Then she turned to me and said, "We know so little about that man, despite how often he came here while my father-in-law was alive."

"Did you like him?"

"Freddy thought he was all right. I thought he was odious."

"Why, Anne?" I was interested in hearing someone

else's impressions of Sir Rupert's good friend.

"He acted as if he was as much in charge of the house as Sir Rupert. As if he owned the estate, and everyone living here. As if he was superior, being part of the master race."

"Surely the English are considered part of Hitler's master race," I said.

"I felt as if Wolfenhaus saw us as poor relations," Anne replied.

"I don't think that was it," Louisa said. "I've known Wolfenhaus longer than you, having lived here longer. It wasn't until after the expedition of 1935 that Wolfenhaus started to act as if he owned the place. The odd thing was, Sir Rupert allowed him to order him around."

"That doesn't sound like Sir Rupert," I said.

"No, Wolfenhaus was the only one who could control him. The rest of us got the crumbs," Louisa said.

I hoped she'd confirm what I had heard. "Is it certain Wolfenhaus was supposed to get a large legacy from Sir Rupert's will?" I asked Louisa.

Color left Louisa's skin, making her bloodred lips and black hair stand out more against her face. "He told Douglas he was getting anything that wasn't entailed." She gave a small sob. "We'd be ruined."

"Then you've had a lucky break, if he can't inherit because of death or German citizenship," I said.

"I'm sure the police will be here at any moment saying the same thing." Louisa glared at me and strode into the center of the drawing room, taking in a deep breath. "Lady

Abby, would you care for another cup of tea?"

Marjorie, in a fancy white apron matching Mrs. Thompson's over her black dress, hurried over to Abby. The only time I'd seen Mary in an apron was for the most formal of gatherings that Sir John and Abby held. I realized with a start that I'd never known a death at Summersby House.

The doorbell rang, and Marjorie jumped, sloshing the tea from the cup into the saucer. As she apologized, Inspector Parsons and Constable Wiggins came in the drawing room. "Is there somewhere we can talk, Lady Louisa?"

She lifted her chin. "We just buried my father-in-law. It's all family here, except for my friends Lady Abby Summersby and Captain Redmond, and I went to school with Olivia Redmond. I've known her forever. Say what you have to say and leave."

Inspector Parsons took a deep breath and said, "We've been talking to people at the funeral. They tell us you and Herr Wolfenhaus left the graveside service to go behind the church. One of the nosier ones saw you go beyond the wall to the path into the village. Toward where Wolfenhaus's body was found."

"Did this person tell you I came back immediately when I couldn't find Mrs. Thompson and Marjorie? And I didn't go as far as where Wolfenhaus—was found."

"Why did you go after your servants?"

"Why would anyone? I had further instructions for them."

"What instructions?"

The chin went a little higher. "I—I don't remember now."

"Surely you don't suspect Lady Louisa," Abby said.

"We have to ask questions of everyone. Particularly when we believe someone can aid us in our inquiries," the inspector said.

"I told you about the farm lorry, and you didn't believe me," Louisa said, her face flushed and her eyes narrowed.

"Yes, thank you for telling us about that. It was very helpful," the inspector said. "We've now heard from someone who saw the lorry put away by your father-in-law after nine o'clock, so that narrows the time of death considerably. Where were you from nine o'clock on, Lady Louisa?"

"I've already sent my children away to my parents because of these constant invasions by the police," she snapped at him. "It's not healthy for them."

"Nine o'clock, Lady Louisa?" Inspector Parsons repeated.

"I don't know. I was tired of looking. I wanted to put my feet up and I wished the silly girl would come home. I sat on the garden bench for a while." Louisa walked over to a golden cigarette box on an end table. She took one out and lit it with a slight tremble in her hands.

"How long?"

"I don't remember."

"It would be very helpful if you could remember."

"Yes, inspector. But not today. Right now, we are waiting for the reading of the will. Then the luncheon after the funeral."

"Are you relieved, Lady Louisa?" he asked.

At that moment, a crash was heard from the direction of the kitchen.

Rather than annoyed, she looked shattered. "Relieved? Why would I be relieved? Please, you must go. Now."

"Of course. And where is your sister-in-law, Joan Glenfell?"

"What could you possibly want with Joan?" Louisa asked.

"She was also seen on the path behind the churchyard. What was she doing there, Lady Louisa?"

"How would I know? She's outside somewhere. Ask her."

"Oh, we will. Good day, Lady Louisa." The inspector, followed by Constable Wiggins nodding to various people, left the house.

Lady Louisa headed toward the kitchen. A minute later, Mrs. Thompson came out with the teapot. When Abby asked if everything was all right as her cup was refilled, Mrs. Thompson said, "Yes. I think it's Marjorie's age, poor dear."

Ten minutes later, Sir John, Sir Douglas, and the old man I was told was the solicitor came out to where we all waited in the drawing room. Sir John suggested we leave the family to grieve in peace, and Abby and I said our farewells before rescuing Adam from Freddy's description of the perfect martini.

We walked to the car and saw the Glenfells come toward us from the area of the barns. Philip headed into the house, but I hurried over and stopped Joan. "I've heard you're quite good at spitting out the pills your father gave you."

She shut her eyes for a moment. "Marjorie saw me. Yes, it's true. For the last month or two, I've learned to hold them in my mouth and spit out as much as I could after he walked off. They dissolve quickly, so I can only remove so much."

"And Saturday night? What really happened?"

"I stayed in my room, listening for the telephone or anyone coming into the house."

"Did you hear the telephone ring?"

"Yes. Once. I fell asleep and awoke to the ring. By the time I got to the stairs, it had stopped. Then I heard someone come in the front door, so I hid in the upstairs hall so no one would see me. I heard raised voices, then shouts, then running footsteps."

Joan shook her head. "Just another friendly conversation in Manning Hall. I went back to my room. A little later, I thought I heard footsteps in the attic. Then nothing until you arrived."

"Who would have been in the attic?"

"How would I know? I haven't been up there in years. Now, I need to go inside." Joan walked off, leaving me puzzled as I rejoined Adam by the car.

Once we were on our way, Abby said, "They all seemed to be a bundle of nerves. And that Inspector Parsons questioned Lady Louisa in front of us. He really upset her."

"They must know that individually and as a group they'll be suspected of murder," Sir John said. "What did the inspector ask her?"

Abby and I told him.

"What was Herr Wolfenhaus supposed to get according to the will?" It would be a breach of confidence, but I hoped Sir John would tell me. The German's legacy might give a clue as to the identity of the killer.

"This doesn't go any further." Sir John glanced back at me.

"Understood."

"One hundred pounds."

"Is that all?" I asked. "Why was everyone so worried?"

"He told them he would be getting the deeds to certain properties, money, and jewels. He offered to make a deal with them for a cash buyout of three thousand pounds, but the offer was only good until the will was read."

"Did they believe him?"

"No one had any idea of the contents of Sir Rupert's will. They believed him."

"What did they do?" I asked. "They must have been worried sick."

Sir John said, "I'm sure they were. Sir Douglas admitted to having begun negotiations with Wolfenhaus, who was proving to be a tough adversary."

"They must have believed Wolfenhaus's claims." But was that enough to turn one of them into a killer?

"What was Mrs. Glenfell talking about when she said Wolfenhaus killed her son?" Adam asked.

I quickly described the hiking trip where Jack Glenfell fell off a cliff while in the company of Sir Rupert and Wolfenhaus.

"Reason for her to kill them both," he told me.

"But would she?" Sir John said. "She doesn't appear to be the most stable of women, but she seems too frail to kill a big strong man."

"But when Sir Rupert was killed, she wasn't knocked out with all of those pills he gave her." I told them what Joan told me about trying to spit out her pills and the fight she had heard, the phone ringing and someone walking in the front door.

"Did she hear or see any hint of who came in the front door?" Adam asked me.

"No. She says she hid so whoever it was wouldn't see her."

"Blaming Wolfenhaus for her son's death would be a powerful motive. Perhaps easier than pinning it all on her father. If she surprised him coming around the back of the church, she could have followed him and struck him with the knife and walked away in a moment." Adam watched me to see how I'd take his suggestion.

"Wouldn't she have been splattered with blood?"

"How could you tell with that dull black dress she was

wearing?" Adam said.

Abby turned halfway around in her seat. "It depends on how much blood went flying. If it was just specks, it wouldn't have been too noticeable. If it was a large patch, it would have been damp and that would have shown up."

"Is there any way to tell?" I asked Adam.

"Did anyone take a close look at her dress?" he replied.

"No," I admitted. "Will the police check their clothing for blood?"

"I'm sure they will," Sir John said, "if only for the purposes of elimination."

When we returned to Summersby House, we went upstairs to change into more casual clothes. Adam sat down on the bed and said, "Livvy, should I just go back to London now?"

"Heavens, no. Why would you?"

"We're not having much of a honeymoon, are we?"

I dropped onto the bed next to him. "It hasn't been much fun for you, has it?"

"Do you want me to answer that?" His hazel eyes looked sad and solemn.

"Do you want us to go back to London now? Tomorrow morning?" I stared into his eyes. "When?"

"Do you feel you owe it to Sir John and Lady Abby to solve these murders? There seems to be evidence that Sir Rupert killed Hal Ames when he went to Manning Hall to find someone to go to Brighton and collect Sally Glenfell. You've done what you promised to do."

"That's true," I said, "but if Sir Rupert killed Hal Ames and threw his body in a ditch outside of the Manning estate, why didn't he rescue his granddaughter? And why did he kill the young man?"

"He either didn't have time to leave to get her before he was killed, or he wasn't going to get her because he was doing something he thought was more important."

Interesting. I hoped Adam had some ideas. I was out. "Such as?"

"Something to do with taking Wolfenhaus around the south coast? Something that has to do with his pro-German leanings?" He raised my brows.

I knew Adam was aware of a great deal more than I was concerning German spies within our borders. It was his job. I just seemed to find spies and killers while doing something else.

I really wished I wouldn't.

"Such as what?" I needed direction in my hunt for a killer.

"You tell me." He stared at me, his words a challenge.

I spread my hands in a helpless gesture. "I don't know. A wireless station to broadcast everything you can see from the pier? A safe house for parachutists or sailors who've come to invade us?" I gave him a small smile. "Putting a great big arrow on the roof pointing to London that German bombers could see while flying at night?"

He scowled. "Really. But how could you prove it, and what difference does it make now that Sir Rupert's dead?"

"He didn't know he was going to be dead when he was

doing whatever he was seen doing that necessitated him killing Hal Ames."

His shoulders drooped. "You're right."

We sat side by side in silence for a full minute before I said, "How do we find out what he was doing? And did his killer stop whatever it was Sir Rupert was planning, or did he or she take over the enterprise?"

Chapter Twenty-Three

"That assumes someone else in the household is also aiding the Nazi cause, if you think Sir Rupert was killed so someone could take over his activities." Adam looked glum, as if he didn't want to consider the possibility of another traitor.

"No, it just needs to be someone local who could walk over in the blackout, confident of not being seen. Particularly since we think Hal Ames walked over to Manning Hall from the village."

"That certainly widens the field," he grumbled. "I think you're going to have to agree with Mrs. Smith's testimony that after the farm lorry was seen where Hal's body was found, Sir Rupert was seen putting the lorry away, and that means that Sir Rupert probably killed Hal. That's all you promised to find out, and we can enjoy the last three days of our honeymoon."

"But why, Adam? Why did Sir Rupert kill Hal?" It made no sense. "And why kill him in the trophy room, when his knapsack and the murder weapon were found in the lorry?"

I must have looked as if I were begging, because Adam flopped back on the bed and said, "You're not going to give up on this, are you?"

"No. But I'll wait until you go back to work and then I'll come back down here and—"

"And if I want to have you in London with me for as long as I get to stay posted there, I need to help you solve the why of this murder now." He didn't sound happy about it, but he didn't sound completely against it either. "I want to have you with me as much as I can before we're separated for who knows how long."

"This investigation is part of your job. Finding Nazi sympathizers embedded in our country." I smiled down at him lying on his back, looking so handsome and strong and vibrant. It was his assignment, but that task would be taking him away from me soon, once the war started.

Was my curiosity worth the time it was stealing from us now?

Adam sat up. "You're right. I have a duty to king and country to root out traitors. That's what I'm trained for. If Sir Rupert was a traitor, was he killed by someone who planned to take over his task? If he wasn't, and he killed Hal for some random reason or other, was it a would-be traitor who came upon Hal Ames's murder and saw the perfect opportunity to kill Sir Rupert and take over his position and the money he presumably gets for selling out his country?"

That grabbed my attention. "Would Sir Rupert be paid for whatever treasonous thing he was doing?"

"I would think so. Traitors usually demand good money for the risks they are taking," Adam told me.

"But Sir Rupert was burning through money. He left

his family very badly off." It made no sense. For a moment, I was sorry I'd convinced Adam to continue this investigation with me instead of letting him drag me away.

Then I took a deep breath and said, "I think Sir Rupert, if he wasn't a traitor, was only moving around the edges of treason, and maybe that's why the Nazis weren't paying him. He had contacts in Germany, he didn't believe we'd survive an invasion, he was friendly with the Duke of Marshburn and his crowd, and he took a German for a trip along the south coast." Perhaps I'd guessed his reason. "Maybe he acted out of friendship or belief instead of for the money they offered."

"All of this makes me suspicious, and normally, I'd be looking for the cash," Adam said. "But for this to hold together as a reason for his death without a profit motive, Sir Rupert had to be doing something obvious during the evening of the blackout. When most of his family was out of the house and the servants were in their quarters."

"And we haven't seen any obvious signs of what he was doing before we arrived and found him dead." I held Adam's gaze. "How do we find out what he was doing? And how do we find out what the police have learned?"

"The first thing we do is talk to Sir John. As a magistrate, he has contacts within the local police that we can use." He rose. "Come on, let's go down to tea."

After the boys had cleaned up every morsel from the tea tray, they asked to be excused and Sir John nodded. Once I judged that they were out of earshot, I said, "Are you able to find out what the police know and suspect in the murders of Hal Ames and Sir Rupert?"

"I am, but why do you think I should?"

I told him all the ideas, crazy and not, that Adam and I had come up with.

Sir John looked at Adam. "Do you really think Sir Rupert was a danger to Britain? What could he possibly have been doing to threaten our safety?"

"I'm particularly concerned about his trips along the south coast with Wolfenhaus, sir. If he and Wolfenhaus were in league to send sensitive information back to Germany, they knew Wolfenhaus wouldn't be able to carry it back once the war starts. Sir Rupert could still collect information, but how would he transmit it to Germany?"

Sir John nodded as he reached for his pipe. "You want to know if the police are thinking along these lines?"

"Yes," I said. "And I want to know if they have any information on why Sir Rupert would have killed Hal Ames other than Hal having caught him doing something potentially illegal."

"Or at least embarrassing," Adam added. "Such as bringing over a group of Nazi-supporting Germans or setting up a wireless network. That's not illegal yet."

"And did they check the clothes of the people in Manning Hall for blood after the funeral because of Wolfenhaus's death?" I asked.

"You want me to go over to the police station in Ratherminster tomorrow and ask Inspector Parsons if they've had any luck, or even any thoughts, along those lines?" Sir John got his pipe to draw and shook out his match.

"Please. I'd like to know if we're on the right path," I told him. "I want to be as certain as I can be for Eleanor Ames."

"And Mrs. Goodfellow wants you to be certain for Mrs. Ames, which would make life here easier," Abby added without looking at Sir John.

Sir John looked wistfully at the empty tray of tea cakes and sandwiches and nodded. "I'll go over first thing in the morning."

* * *

I spent the rest of the time until dinner helping Abby in the garden while Adam continued to translate the book on Sir Rupert's last two explorations.

First thing after dinner while Mary cleaned the kitchen, Mrs. Goodfellow walked with me to Eleanor Ames's cottage. I told her I still believed Sir Rupert killed her son, but I was pursuing some other ideas in the hope I could find proof.

"Why did he kill my son?"

"I don't know. Yet."

Mrs. Ames showed me the door. "Don't come back until you know something that will explain what happened to my poor boy."

I slipped outside. Mrs. Goodfellow patted her shoulder on the way out, and then walked back to Summersby House with me.

Then over coffee, since Abby had insisted they wait

for me, we played the same game being played in homes across the country. What would Hitler do? What would the government do? Could we stop the invasion?

Our guesses were as good as anyone else's. It added a poignancy to our bedtime that night. Adam would be back at work for the army on Monday, and war was drawing closer.

We came down to breakfast the next morning to learn we'd just missed Sir John, who'd gone into Ratherminster after a long telephone conversation with the inspector. Too late for me to make a last-minute appeal for more information. I'd have to trust Sir John to get us every detail he could.

I was getting used to these huge breakfasts sitting at Abby's table. I was enjoying porridge and grilled tomatoes and eggs when Gerhard came into the room. At ten, he was more Henry's size than Mark's, but I suspected he would soon grow taller at the same speed that Mark currently was.

Having no siblings, I found the relationships and the squabbles between these boys fascinating.

Gerhard took a plate from the sideboard and soon had a hearty breakfast of sausage and toast. He sat down across from Adam and said, "Was the man who was killed behind the churchyard yesterday a Nazi?"

"We believe so, yes," Adam answered as solemnly as Gerhard had spoken.

"And he was a good friend of Sir Rupert Manning?"

"He was mentioned in Sir Rupert's will, so yes, I think

so."

Gerhard took a bite of his sausage and seemed lost in thought. Mary set a cup of tea in front of him and he gave her a smile.

"If you're worried that Sir Rupert and Wolfenhaus were working with the people who tried to kidnap you and Henry, I can tell you they weren't. The Nazis aren't going to try to grab you and Henry now," I assured him.

He gave me a grown-up look. "I know. I heard some of the older guys talking at cricket practice, and they said Sir Rupert wouldn't let any of them near the house. And it wasn't about Sally. They said he had no interest in his granddaughter because she's a girl." Gerhard sounded as if this was sensible.

"Then why wouldn't he let any young men near the house?" Adam asked.

"Something about ropes. Then they realized I was listening and stopped talking."

"Ropes?" Adam asked, scowling slightly.

Gerhard nodded seriously and ate more of his sausage.

"What could he be so secretive about that had to do with ropes?" I asked Adam.

"Possibly parachute cords. Possibly imprisoning someone," he said and shrugged. "I can't think of anything else."

"Does he have an airplane? Unless he wanted to jump off the cliffs into the Channel." It sounded crazier than most of my ideas, but I mentioned it anyway.

Adam sat still for a moment. "Wait. Ropes. Abseiling."

"What?" I gave him a puzzled look.

"Abseiling. For scaling heights and depths. Using ropes to get up and down cliffs too steep to climb without them. In the book Sir John has that I've been reading, or trying to," he made a face at his efforts in translation, "Sir Rupert and Wolfenhaus did a lot of abseiling in Greenland. It was while scaling a rocky ice cliff with them to check out mineral deposits that the geologist, who wasn't familiar with abseiling, fell to his death."

"Didn't you say the Danes came to investigate the death?"

"Yes. And it seems that after the police asked their questions, the Germans were asked to leave and forget about any mining in northern Greenland."

"Was anyone charged with negligence?"

Adam shook his head. "But that was Sir Rupert's last expedition with the Germans. In fact, his last expedition, period."

"If they were similar to the men my father worked for, the failure to set up a mine for the German government would get Sir Rupert, Herr Wolfenhaus, and everyone else fired," Gerhard said. "Thank you," he added as Mary refilled his teacup.

"When did you hear the older lads talking about this?" I asked.

"The Sunday before your wedding. At the cricket practice." The boy then shoveled a forkful of breakfast in.

"Was Hal Ames one of the young men doing the

talking?" Adam asked.

Gerhard nodded, his mouth full.

"Who else?"

We waited until he finished. "Gary Jones, Hal Ames, and a fellow I didn't know. Matthew probably knows him."

"Thank you, Gerhard. This has been very useful," I told him as I heard footsteps coming toward the dining room.

A moment later, Henry and Mark came in and began filling their plates. Gerhard gave me a pleading look. Apparently, he didn't want me to share what he'd said, but I couldn't imagine why. But then, I didn't understand siblings.

We finished breakfast and walked around the garden waiting for Sir John to return. "We need to talk to Gary Jones today. He leaves for six months of militia training tomorrow."

Adam took a half-dozen paces before he said, "If only to find out what Gerhard overheard or thinks he overheard."

"He's a smart boy," I told him. "I'm sure what Gerhard told us was accurate. I want to know what he didn't overhear. It could have a lot of bearing on Hal Ames's murder."

"Wouldn't the police have heard about it by now?"

"If they were gossiping, they might not think it important enough to tell anyone. I think it could be very important." I wished Sir John would arrive home soon so we could hear what he'd learned and then question Gary Jones at the garage.

When Sir John didn't show up, we decided to study the book he had in his library that focused on Sir Rupert's last two expeditions. Other than what Adam had already told me, there didn't seem to be anything of interest.

I wondered once again what Sir Rupert's scrapbook about his final expedition would show us, and why it had disappeared. Did it hold a clue to one or more of the murders? And were all three murders committed by the same person?

Only a member of Sir Rupert's family would have been able to hide the scrapbook and have a motive for the murders. But which one? I had discovered I liked the whole family. I didn't want it to be any of them, but thinking this way wouldn't help me uncover the identity of a killer.

Chapter Twenty-Four

We were about to sit down to lunch when Sir John returned. When I looked at him inquiringly, he said, "Later," and led us into the dining room.

It was a long meal. Matthew and Mark were arguing over the relative merits of the national cricket teams of New Zealand and the West Indies despite their parents ordering them to stop bickering at the table. When the *Daily Premier* sports pages were quoted as the source of Mark's pronouncements, I was glared at by both his parents.

That was unfair. I had nothing to do with the sports pages.

Henry chattered nonstop about some birds he'd seen in the fields. Gerhard was quiet even for him.

Sir John lingered over his soup and then his fish, dragging out our time at the table. Abby shot me puzzled glances, but all I could do was shake my head. Finally, the boys squirmed enough Sir John excused them from the table.

They hurried away to spend time outside, Matthew and Mark once again debating the strengths of various cricket teams.

"Did you learn anything about what the police have

discovered?" I asked Sir John once it was only the adults at the table.

"Inspector Parsons would only say that the investigation is ongoing. When I raised some of the points that you have discovered, he assured me the police are capable of carrying out their investigations without civilian interference."

Ouch. "But Adam is a trained investigator for the army. He hunts spies for the government." I looked from Sir John to Adam.

"The inspector says when he needs the army's help, he'll ask for it."

"Oh, dear," Abby said.

Oh, dear, indeed. "I'm sorry. I'd hoped the inspector would be open-minded enough to look into some of our questions. Or would have thought of these things himself before now."

"He believes Louisa killed Sir Rupert, and then murdered the Ames lad when he caught her in the act. He'll find a reason for her to have killed Wolfenhaus by the time he's through. I suspect it will be Wolfenhaus's threat to take over a large portion of her husband's inheritance."

I looked at Sir John sadly. "I suppose he thinks she said she saw the farm lorry on the side of the road to point to someone else's guilt?"

He nodded. "Except now he knows Mrs. Smith saw Sir Rupert putting the lorry away in the barn after Louisa saw it near where Hal Ames's body was found. He'll explain that away if he can. Otherwise, he'll say Mrs. Smith was lying to keep her place as the Mannings' tenant farmer."

"Someone must have told him how much Louisa couldn't stand Sir Rupert," Abby said.

"But none of them could stand Sir Rupert," Sir John said. "The inspector says as an alternative that Joan Glenfell was putting on an act, didn't swallow her pills, and killed her father and Wolfenhaus because they killed her son. Again, Hal Ames walked in on the murder and had to be silenced."

"Does he plan to arrest anyone?" I asked.

"Not until he decides which theory he likes better, or he can prove either one. He hopes one or the other will confess."

I looked at Sir John in horror. "No wonder he keeps showing up at Manning Hall and badgering people."

Sir John made a face. "After I spoke to the inspector, I talked to Constable Wiggins. He was much more cooperative and clever."

"What did he tell you?" I asked, sitting forward in my chair.

"There weren't any obvious signs of blood on anyone's clothes or shoes after the funeral. The inspector doesn't believe anyone as famous as Sir Rupert would do anything to harm Britain and jealousy had to be the motive. He believes Wolfenhaus was nothing more than Sir Rupert's friend from those expeditions and was murdered by mistake. Possibly a robbery gone wrong. Or again, because of jealousy. He can't seem to make up his mind."

"You're joking," Adam said.

"I'm afraid not," Sir John replied.

"It sounds as if we're to find out what really happened, we'll have to find the proof ourselves." I looked around the table expectantly.

"Are you telling us a story for youngsters about determination and right winning over wrong?" Abby asked.

"If we don't believe in this, we might as well invite the Nazis in. That's what it's going to take to repel the invasion," I snapped. Then I stopped and took a deep breath. "I'm sorry, Abby. I shouldn't have spoken so rudely to you."

"No, you're right. However, we have police to deal with local crime and they are honest, if not terribly bright sometimes."

"If the inspector messes this up, Louisa could be hanged for a crime she didn't commit. Her boys will grow up without a mother, and that's wrong. She's innocent."

"So, what do you plan to do?" Adam asked.

"Search Sir Rupert's room. Perhaps there's something there that was overlooked. But first, we need to talk to Gary Jones." I told them what Gerhard had overheard.

"My car could stand to be filled up with petrol and the oil level checked," Sir John said. "Meanwhile, I need to walk over to Stonybrook Farm. Could you take care of the auto for me, Adam?"

"Yes, sir." Adam used his military voice but there was a smile tugging at the edges of his mouth.

Within a half hour, we were pulling into Jones's Garage. I let go of a breath I didn't realize I'd been holding when I saw Gary approach the car. He could have been anywhere, saying good-bye before he left for his militia training in the morning, and he'd have been hard to track down. For once, we'd been lucky.

While he pumped the petrol, I asked him about the conversation he'd had with Hal Ames and another man that Gerhard overheard the Sunday before last.

"I can't tell you much more than what Gerhard heard. Sir Rupert's been doing something with ropes. He yells at anyone who sees him with them. He doesn't want us on his land. But that's all."

"And it has nothing to do with Sally?"

"The only reason Sally was going around with Hal was because she hoped it would make her grandfather notice her. It didn't. He still didn't pay her any mind."

"Did Hal know this?" Adam asked.

"Of course. He thought Sally was a funny kid, but he felt sorry for her, with her father groveling to her grandfather and her mother walking around imitating a ghost, all silent and gloomy, and Sally losing her older brother. Hal liked Jack. We all did. And Sally misses him more than anyone realizes. Her family thinks it's just the adults who are upset about Jack's death."

"Did she talk about Jack to Hal?"

"Yeah. Jack didn't want to go on the hiking trip with his grandfather and his grandfather's German friend. He'd been on one the summer before and hated it. He knew they'd take him abseiling, and it frightened him."

"Is that how he fell from the cliff?"

"They never said, at least that Sally heard, but she thinks they were abseiling when he fell. She said her grandfather, for all his bragging about his expeditions, wasn't very good at rock climbing or abseiling or surviving in the Arctic. The stories in his scrapbooks were what he told the newspapers, not what actually happened. He thought everyone would believe the stories he had put in the newspapers and think he was a hero." Gary finished pumping the petrol and opened the bonnet to check the oil.

"How would Sally know any different?" I asked as I climbed out of the auto.

"From her mother. There were letters sent to Sir Rupert from other expedition members telling him never to approach them again."

"And her mother read them?"

"No. They were in German. Her mother only knows tourist German. Her grandfather told her mother how ungrateful the other explorers were, blaming him for everything."

"Ungrateful?" Adam said in surprise.

"Yeah." Gary laughed. "Things were always someone else's fault."

"These people had been on an expedition with him before. Why, if they didn't like him, did they let him go on the expedition in 1935?" I asked, not expecting an answer.

Gary knew the answer, though. "Sally said her

mother said that the expedition leader had kept a short leash on Sir Rupert, who complained about it in his letters home. Unfortunately, the leader left the day before a member of the team was killed."

"Sally told Hal, and he told you?"

"Yes."

I guessed I needed to get Louisa and Joan to talk to me. I'd have to plead with them to let me in on these family secrets so we could keep Louisa from the hangman's noose. Then I needed to search the house for those letters. "Did Sally know where the letters were kept? If they were kept?"

"She never said." Gary shrugged. "I don't think she knew. You need a bit of oil," he added to Adam, who'd climbed out of the car to listen to us and stood on the other side.

When Gary returned from the garage with the oil, Adam said, "Did you ever go up to Manning Hall and see what Sir Rupert was up to?"

Gary poured oil into the engine before he said, "I did. I came around a bend in the drive and saw Sir Rupert hanging from some ropes near one of the attic windows. He didn't see me. I slipped behind a tree and watched as he climbed into the window and disappeared."

"He must have been practicing abseiling." Adam paid him and wished him luck with his army training. They talked for a few minutes about what Gary faced, none of which I wanted to experience.

"Hal was supposed to go with me to training. Last

Saturday was his last day of freedom, so he decided to take Sally to the pier for some fun. I would have gone along, except my dad needed me here. And then Hal was killed." Gary shook his head. "I'll miss him."

Next, Adam drove me to Manning Hall. Mrs. Thompson answered the door and showed us into the drawing room. Louisa came in a minute later, a crystal glass containing a brownish liquid in her hand.

"Dougie's not here. He and Freddy have gone to see that desiccated little solicitor about signing some papers and to mount my defense when they arrest me." She took another swig from her glass. "Then they're going to some farm somewhere about some animals. Philip and Sally have gone up to London for the day, trying to rebuild their lives now that our dear father has departed. Joan is hiding in her room. Marjorie is off on her day out. We're all on our sad little own." Then she emptied the contents of her glass in one swallow.

Anne came in, looked at Louisa, and said, "Adam, why don't you come back for Olivia at tea time?"

"You'll be all right?" Adam asked me.

I gave him a bright smile. "Of course."

I wouldn't say he ran out of the room, but he lost no time in escaping. I was on my own now, but I was determined to help Louisa and learn the truth about what had happened.

Louisa rose and walked over to pour herself another drink. I noticed she was taking it neat. "You want one?" she asked me.

"No, thank you. I can't drink whisky without pouring all sorts of ice and water and soda into it."

"You'd be able to if you were about to be arrested for a hanging offense. Inspector Parsons came out a short time ago and asked a bunch more questions. He told me he knew I'd done it. He said it would go better for me if I confessed. I told him if the courts convict me I knew they'd hang me regardless."

Joan came in then. "Louisa has better manners than I do. I just stared at him and refused to open my mouth to any of his impertinent questions."

"That's why I came over," I told them. "Do you know where Sir Rupert put the letters he received from other members of his expeditions?"

"No."

"Did he burn them?"

Louisa shrugged. Anne watched us with a puzzled expression.

"Could they be in the study?"

Again, Louisa shrugged.

Joan said, "No. He didn't keep anything he considered important in the study. They'd be up in his room, if they're anywhere."

"Let's go look."

I'd grabbed Louisa's full attention. "Do you think it's important?"

"It could be crucial," I told her.

"How do you know about them?" Anne asked.

I told her about Sally, Hal, and Gary.

"But who told them? The letters are in German," Louisa said.

"Who do you think?" Joan asked her.

"Do you speak German?" I asked, remembering Louisa in the classroom.

"Are you kidding? And before you ask, only Joan speaks German. And then, only enough to order dinner."

"Thanks. But," Joan added, "that's about all my German is good for."

But Sir Rupert could speak the language fluently.

"All right." Louisa headed for the door. "Let's find them. Livvy can read them to us."

Anne said, "Wait. The police locked his bedroom door."

"Who has the keys?"

"Mrs. Thompson. I'll get them." Anne headed for the kitchen.

Louisa, Joan, and I went upstairs, Louisa bringing a full tumbler of whisky with her. Somehow, she kept from spilling it.

"Do you think that's wise?" I asked her, staring at the glass.

"What would you rather I do? Sit and cry copious tears? Pretend that they aren't planning to hang me? Go abseiling with my father-in-law and fall off a cliff?" She stopped then, looked at me, and giggled. "Well, I guess that's out."

"Oh, Louisa, pull yourself together," Joan said, annoyance in her tone.

I was waiting for her hysteria to start when Anne arrived, jingling the keys. We quickly unlocked the door and went inside Sir Rupert's room.

It was a good-sized bedroom, but not palatial by any means. The furniture was old and heavy and dark, and I guessed it was Victorian. Louisa sat in a comfortable-looking chair covered in tan brocade and watched us while we made quick work of the dresser and wardrobe. Joan pulled up a side chair and began to search through the desk.

Anne pulled over a wooden chair and checked on top of the wardrobe. "Nothing."

The desk was a bigger challenge. When Joan lowered the drop-leaf shelf to reveal the writing area, we discovered the space behind it was full of pigeonholes stuffed with papers. The three large drawers beneath it were likewise full of papers to the point of bursting.

"We've got work ahead of us," I murmured.

"It's all bills and receipts," Joan said. "No wonder Douglas can't get a handle on the cost of running the farm."

Anne said, "What am I looking for?"

"Anything in German, anything connected to Sir Rupert's expeditions, anything that doesn't seem right. You knew Sir Rupert better than I did. Anything someone would want to kill him over."

"Breathing," Louisa suggested.

We ignored her while Joan and I took the pigeonholes and Anne the bottom drawer. Nothing was in order. Bank statements were mixed in with invitations to social events. A bank statement for one month might be in a pigeonhole while the one for the next month might be in the bottom drawer. Bills for chicken feed were mixed in with receipts for wine.

"Was he really this hopelessly disorganized?" I asked after finding an empty ledger in the middle of a random stack of bills.

"Yes. The solicitor despairs of straightening out the estate before the end of 1940," Louisa said. "Poor Dougie. He said his father hated him. This must be his revenge."

Joan gave her a dark look, but said nothing.

We finished with the desk no wiser than when we started. "The only thing left is the bed," I said.

"Oh, he wouldn't have," Anne said, screwing up her face in distaste.

"No, really, Olivia. He wouldn't have hidden any papers there," Joan said.

A quarter hour later, they were proved correct. At least the housekeeping was good. We weren't dusty.

We then checked behind the paintings and the draperies. Nothing. The fireplace was cold and very clean, and contained an electric bar heater, so burning anything was out of the question.

Louisa laughed and then hiccupped. "I'm going to hang. Blast that man."

I slowly pivoted, studying the walls. "Where does that door go?"

"That's Louisa's room through there," Joan said. "That

used to be Lady Amelia's room. My mother's room."

"And the door is locked from the other side. I made sure of that," Louisa told me as she pointed in my general direction.

I walked over to an empty area of wall opposite the windows and looked around. Nothing. I leaned on the wall and it shifted. Jumping upright, I found a wide crack in the wall. Tugging on it, I moved the panel more, revealing a plain wooden staircase going up. It was then that I noticed there was a trip switch. The panel opened all the way when I pushed it. "Where does this go?"

"The attic," Joan said.

"Anything interesting up there?"

Louisa shrugged and took another swig of her drink.

"I haven't been up there since before my marriage. I know the boys enjoyed playing up there, but I thought it was spooky," Joan said. "They used to appear and disappear and frighten me."

"Is this the only way up?" I asked.

"The only way I know," Joan said.

Anne thought for a minute. "I've never been up there. I've never heard anyone admit they'd been up there. I'd no idea Sir Rupert had his own private way up. Strange, though," she added. "I've seen lights in the attic windows before. When I asked, my questions were just brushed aside. I was told it was a reflection or my imagination."

Chapter Twenty-Five

I was about to go charging up to the attic to look around when a practical matter made me hesitate. "Are the electrics wired or did it resemble a torch beam when you saw light in the windows?"

Joan shrugged. Neither Anne nor Louisa knew.

I didn't see a torch nearby. There were a couple of windows and it was a clear day. I climbed the stairs, not knowing what was there.

I wasn't expecting what I found. "Come on up," I called down the stairs, turning on a light.

Anne came up immediately. "Wow," she said, looking around.

Joan said from the bottom of the staircase, "No, thank you. I remember it well enough from my childhood."

"You don't remember this, I'd bet," I called down.

There was a large wireless set on a table with two chairs in front of it. There was a large table with a map of southeastern England spread out on top. A bookcase had works on Morse code, the Arctic, and abseiling, as well as tide, moon, and railroad timetables. More detailed maps of the area were stacked up on one shelf. Coils of rope lay under one of the windows, where wires that snaked inside over the sill led back to the wireless.

And there was a kneehole desk with drawers.

Anne found a letter from a man written in German in a top drawer of the desk. She handed it to me. "I can't read German."

I dropped into one of the chairs by the wireless set as I began to read. I looked up into Anne's puzzled face and said, "You'd better get Louisa and Joan."

As I translated the letter in growing amazement, I was vaguely aware of Anne and Louisa arguing downstairs. I had finished reading before I heard any footsteps on the stair treads.

Louisa came up first, a little unsteadily. "This had better be good," she declared as she dropped onto the floor and sprawled out.

Anne followed her up the stairs and began to dig around in the desk drawer again.

Joan sat on the top step, looking as if she was ready to bolt downstairs at any moment.

I began to read aloud, translating as I went.

Sir Rupert,

The Danish investigators have cleared you of any deliberate wrongdoing in the matter of the death of Matthias Tomperglich. Charges will not be brought.

However, I personally never want to see you on another expedition, and I will do everything in my power to see that no country or scientific society ever employs you in any position in any Arctic efforts. What I believe you did does not rise to the level of murder, but I am sure I can convince the members of the international scientific community that your actions, your negligence, led to Tomperglich's death.

If you attempt to join any expedition anywhere, I will go to the Danish authorities with my knowledge and my suspicions and discover if a charge of manslaughter is possible.

There is no point in blackening the name of an explorer with your many years of experience and your reputation when it can do nothing for Tomperglich now, but if you endanger anyone else with your careless disregard for the safety of others, I will speak out.

I looked at the other three women. "It's signed by Friedrich von Marten, the head of the 1935 expedition as well as several other trips before that year that Sir Rupert took part in."

"Gracious. Is that what Wolfenhaus was using to get Sir Rupert to name him in his will?" Anne asked.

"Possibly. We don't know if Sir Rupert and Wolfenhaus were close friends or if Herr Wolfenhaus was blackmailing your father-in-law," I said.

"He went around killing people and I'm the one they're threatening to hang," Louisa moaned.

"Not just you," Joan snapped.

Anne brought me over more letters in German from the kneehole desk. "Is there anything more detailed in any of these?" she asked.

I started to read. The first two were pretty much copies of von Marten's letter, but the third one was shocking.

Holding the paper out, I said, "This letter says Sir Rupert and Tomperglich disagreed about the aims of the expedition and about politics before Sir Rupert and Wolfenhaus took him out abseiling."

"Who is it from?" Anne asked.

"An Erich Rieter. He says he saw them force Tomperglich to go abseiling with them to check out a mineral deposit the geologist wanted to study. He wanted to go by boat along the coast to get there, but Sir Rupert insisted it would be faster and easier to get down to the site by going cross-country and abseiling. Wolfenhaus tried to dissuade Sir Rupert after the geologist refused, but Sir Rupert assured him it would be fun."

"Did Rieter tell the Danish authorities?" Anne asked.

I scanned the letter. "He had left before the Danes arrived. Apparently, Sir Rupert and Wolfenhaus disagreed with Rieter's politics and his complaints about how they treated the natives. When they tried to take him abseiling against his will, he took the next boat out of there. He left that day."

"Sir Rupert sounds as if he was a monster," Anne said, her eyes rounded in shock. "But then, we suspected that."

"He was a monster," Louisa said. "Think how he ordered Jack to go hiking with him and Wolfenhaus for two summers. How he forced Joan to make Jack go with them. Them and their abseiling gear."

Joan was rocking forward and back from her perch on the top step, staring into her lap.

"Do you think the same thing that happened to this

Tomperglich happened to Jack?" Anne said.

That was exactly what I was beginning to think. "A fall off a cliff that may not have been an accident? It seemed to occur frequently around Sir Rupert."

Joan's voice came softly on the hot, stale air. "I wonder if Sir Rupert called Tom-whatever a weakling the same way he did Jack? He used to tell Philip he was trying to save the boy from turning into a failure like his father. A weakling. A soft mama's boy." She shook her head, tears running down his face. "Maybe I should have killed him. He was a horrible person."

"But you shouldn't hang if you weren't his murderer," I came close to snapping at her.

Louisa snorted. "Try to convince Inspector Parsons of anyone's innocence."

"You both had good motives to kill Sir Rupert and Wolfenhaus. If Joan suspected her father wasn't as careful abseiling as he should have been and Jack died because of his recklessness, or if you believed Sir Rupert gave away half of the estate to Wolfenhaus and squandered all his money, then you had good reason to murder."

"What do the letters say about Tomperglich?" Anne asked. "Perhaps he knew how to scale cliffs. Maybe Wolfenhaus murdered him and threw his body down to the rocks below to hide his crime and got Sir Rupert to keep silent?"

"Interesting. But how would he convince Sir Rupert to stay quiet? Sir Rupert left money for Wolfenhaus in his will, not the other way around." I stopped as soon as the words were out of my mouth. "We don't know that, do we? But if Wolfenhaus was the killer, what would have convinced Sir Rupert to keep his mouth shut?"

"There was nothing to convince him. He had everything he wanted," Louisa said, sniffing. "Somebody should have killed him ages ago."

"Who?" I asked.

"I don't know. Joan?" Louisa shrugged.

"We all should have banded together to kill him." Joan's voice was stronger now and more lethal.

"There are more letters. Keep reading. Maybe we'll learn something useful," Anne said, handing me more written in German. I had to give her credit, she was as focused on helping Louisa and Joan as I was.

"Are there any letters written in English?" I asked.

"Yes. Let's see, there's an invitation from the Duke of Marshburn for a visit, addressed to Sir Rupert and Wolfenhaus. Good grief, there are poison pen letters here." Anne held one up. In cutout letters glued to a piece of paper, it read *Stop or Die.*

Louisa laughed, a note of hysteria breaking through.

Joan gasped.

"Are there more?" I asked.

"Yes. Four more." Anne held them up. The messages were similar.

"Is there any hint as to who they're from?" I asked.

Anne shook her head. "Nor any clue as to who they're addressed to."

"We need to show this stuff to the police." And this

shortwave wireless equipment to Adam, I added to myself.

"No. Don't." Joan looked at us. "Not the poison pen letters."

"Why not?" I asked.

The room was silent.

Anne said, "Joan? Why not?"

"Because I sent him those letters." She looked around at us. "I wanted to try to frighten him. Make him think someone knew the truth about what happened to Jack and not just guesses. Someone had proof."

"Did it work?"

"Not that I saw. He never accused me of sending them. Hardly mentioned them."

"He accused me," Louisa said. "I got a large bruise on my wrist where he grabbed me when he threatened me. He said if he found out I had sent them, he would let everyone know and he'd press charges." A tear trickled down her cheek. She didn't bother to wipe it away.

"All right, we'll ignore the poison pen letters. They'd just confuse Inspector Parsons. What else have you found?" I hoped for a letter from Wolfenhaus in German demanding money to keep him silent.

"Just more letters in German. This one is addressed to a 'Lili.' Who would call Sir Rupert that?" Anne looked puzzled as she handed them to me.

I translated the first part of the letter on top, blinked, and went back to read again more slowly to be sure I had the meaning correct.

"What is it?" Anne asked.

Flipping to the end, I saw the signature was "Matti." "I think this letter was from Matthias Tomperglich to his wife or girlfriend, Lili."

Looking from Anne to Joan to Louisa, who was now dozing, I said, "The date on here is July, 1935. This had to be written shortly before he was killed."

"What does it say?" Anne demanded, eagerness in her voice.

"The first part is rather explicit. Apparently, they were intimate, and he was missing parts of their relationship."

"Translate that for me later," Anne said with a grin. "What else does it say?"

I started to read aloud a little faster, my written German coming back to me after translating so many letters that afternoon. Tomperglich's letter read:

I hope to leave here in the next few days. Most of the men are scientists in various fields. They are sensible. They make this a true scientific expedition.

Unfortunately, I have to go wider afield in the search for mineral deposits. That means I spend a lot of time in the company of Manning and Wolfenhaus. They are making my life unbearable.

I expect no better from Wolfenhaus. He's a third-rate brain from a working-class family. No breeding, no education. And he's a passionate Nazi on top of everything. What do you expect? He knows no better.

I am so glad you are out of there. I hope Lady Ellsworth has sorted out your legal difficulties and you are settling in. You will be safe there, Lady E. has promised that, and I hope to join you soon.

I have had enough of Nazis and master race nonsense from these men. Von Marten leaves today. I asked him to let me leave with him, but he said I was to stay here until a replacement can be found. The need for the minerals is so great for their war apparatus. He is going to Copenhagen and will mail this for me there. He'll be back next Tuesday and he promised he'd have my replacement with him. Knowing von Marten and his reputation, he will do it.

Wolfenhaus I can handle, but Manning frightens me. He's an English Nazi despite his title—"

"Title? What title?" Anne asked.

"I guess he means that Sir Rupert was a baronet. Perhaps in Germany that is considered part of the peerage."

"Or maybe Sir Rupert played it up to be more important than a baronet really is," Anne said. "He tried that nonsense on me."

When I looked at her, puzzled, she added, "My father is a lord. A baron, if you will. I was brought up to believe baronets were rather middle-class." Her grin told me she found the whole idea amusing.

"Oh." As the daughter of a baronet without any land, I saw her point about us being middle-class, something my father would never agree with. I hurried back to my reading.

"*...and his wealth. He's careless with his equipment,*

rude to the natives even as he expects them to cater to his every want, and has a vindictive temper.

One of the men, a meteorologist named Bertel, laughed at something Manning said. Manning glared at him. When Bertel left the main hut where we all were, Manning followed him, hit him in the back with his little avalanche shovel, and left him in the snow to either be found or freeze to death.

"Good Lord," Anne said. "The man was as evil as we all thought."

"Was that the shovel that was found in the farm lorry with blood on it?" I asked.

"I believe so. His exploration equipment, including his shovel, was in one of the cases in the trophy room, or was until we started clearing everything out," Joan said.

"I guess Hal Ames wasn't the first person Sir Rupert attacked with that shovel."

"Sir Rupert killed Hal?" Anne gasped. She thought about it for a moment and added, "I can believe it."

I continued reading aloud.

Manning wants me to go abseiling tomorrow with Wolfenhaus and him. I think we should get to the site that I want to explore by boat. After all, a sea access will be needed to bring in the mining equipment, but Manning is pulling rank and insisting on taking me there over the cliffs. Unfortunately, if I want to get there, I need Manning and Wolfenhaus to take me.

I trust Wolfenhaus not to pull any tricks, but Manning is dangerous. And after our argument the other day, I don't trust him at all.

I looked up at Anne and Joan. "It ends there. Sir Rupert must have found this letter and kept it after Tomperglich's death."

"We need to call the police and have them take away these letters. But what do we do with Louisa?"

She was snoring. A half-hearted attempt to rouse her did nothing.

Anne shrugged. Joan shook her head and led the way downstairs, the letter to Lili in my hand as I brought up the rear. Once outside of Sir Rupert's bedroom, Anne locked the door.

"Why? Louisa's in there," I said.

"I don't want anyone tampering with the letters before the police can collect them. And that's the only way into the attic. Isn't it?"

"So far as I know," Joan told her. "I never wanted anything to do with that awful attic."

Anne held on to the keys as we went to the ground floor and telephoned the police.

Chapter Twenty-Six

Anne and I sat together in the drawing room, waiting for the police to arrive after she'd phoned the Ratherminster station. Neither of us made any move to see how Louisa was. I thought that letting her sleep might be the best option.

Joan said she had stayed home so she could have some quiet, and she was going to her room and didn't want to be disturbed by us or the police or anyone.

The house was silent. Philip and Sally Glenfell weren't expected to return until that night, as was the maid, Marjorie Lenard, from her day out. Sir Douglas and Freddy would be gone until past dinnertime with livestock purchase negotiations. Mrs. Thompson and the cook apparently had decided to take some time for themselves in the servants' quarters.

I couldn't say I blamed them, but after the heat in the attic and all the reading I'd done, I was parched. I would have loved a cup of tea.

After the longest twenty minutes that I could remember, a police car pulled up in front of the house and Inspector Parsons and Constable Wiggins walked up to the door and rang the bell.

Mrs. Thompson's footsteps could be heard hurrying

out of the back of the house to answer the door. The men followed her into the drawing room, their hats handed to the housekeeper as they approached us. Wiggins, at least, carried a respectful expression.

"Why have you called us out here?" the inspector asked, sounding as annoyed as he appeared.

"Did you search the attic?" I asked. "The staircase leading up to it is reached from Sir Rupert's room."

"We searched the room and didn't find any staircase."

"It's behind a hidden panel. Come along, we'll show you. And we've found some letters up there, written in German, that give another reason for Sir Rupert's murder. And there are poison pen letters in English." I thought I'd mention them just to keep Inspector Parsons on his toes. I wouldn't tell who wrote them.

Inspector Parsons harrumphed but he grudgingly followed Anne upstairs. I followed, with Constable Wiggins bringing up the rear. Anne unlocked the door and we all entered Sir Rupert's bedroom. I went over to the hidden doorway and once again tripped the switch, releasing the panel.

The panel slid open, and I saw surprise on the faces of both policemen. Good. "Louisa's up here. Asleep," I added.

The inspector picked up her empty glass and sniffed. "Hers?" he asked.

Anne and I looked at each other before nodding.

"Wonderful." He stomped up the stairs with the rest of us behind him. "All right, where are these German letters?"

"They're right…. Where did they go?" I looked at Anne, who was staring at the empty table. Then we both stared at Louisa, still sprawled, asleep, on the floor.

"Wake her up, constable. I want to know what she did with the letters," the inspector said.

"She's still sound asleep. Someone else has been up here," I told him. I was disgusted with both Louisa's self-pity and the inspector's lack of vision, and it came out in my tone of voice.

Inspector Parsons glared at me and then the constable, who bent over and shook Louisa's shoulder. She mumbled something unintelligible and rolled onto her side.

While Wiggins continued to try to awaken Louisa, I looked out the front windows, but saw no way for anyone to enter from outside. Then I walked over to where the attic met the new addition to the house built in late Victorian times. The wall looked solid.

"Get back here. I didn't give you permission to go wandering about the place," the inspector said.

"Afraid I'll make another discovery?" I asked, pushing on a section of the wall. Unfortunately, it stayed firmly in place.

"Afraid you'll waste more police time. There's nothing here. If you insist on claiming there were letters here, then I'll have to arrest Lady Louisa for destroying evidence."

"Which she obviously didn't do. And the letters were here. So, someone else has been here. The question is how?" I tried another part of the wall. Nothing.

"Sir, I don't seem to be able to wake her. Perhaps we should come back later?" Constable Wiggins asked.

"Good idea. Good day, ladies."

"Wait! I did save one of them. It's a letter Matthias Tomperglich was writing to his wife the day he died abseiling with Sir Rupert and Wolfenhaus. It's similar to what happened to Jack Glenfell." I held it out to the inspector.

"It's in German."

"They were German. They were all German except for Sir Rupert."

"I can't read it. You might as well keep it, as a souvenir of wasting police time." He turned away from me.

"I also saved one of the poison pen letters. It's in English." I handed over the one that said *Death to Killers* in letters cut out from magazines.

"How do I investigate this? It isn't even addressed to anyone." Inspector Parsons handed the letter back to me and stomped down the stairs.

I thought he'd at least be interested in the poison pen letters. They seemed to be the sort of evidence that would appeal to the inspector.

Constable Wiggins nodded to us, wearing an embarrassed expression, and followed his supervisor out.

Anne followed him. I stayed with Louisa, looking out the windows and pushing at the wall that blocked the so-called new wing from the main part of the house.

Louisa continued sleeping. If she'd slept through

someone taking the letters, then this person either had another key to Sir Rupert's bedroom or there was another way in. If she were really awake, where had she hidden the letters, and why did she take them?

Louisa had been hopeless in German class when we were in school. She couldn't have known what was in those letters, so they'd have had no value to her before I translated them.

Besides Sir Rupert, who in this house was fluent in German? I'd heard Joan could speak some travelers' German, but no one else.

Who knew of a second way into the attic? Joan, Douglas, and Freddy had grown up here. If anyone did, they would, but Joan swore she didn't know any other way into the attic and neither Douglas nor Freddy were there that afternoon.

My thoughts kept churning. In a fury, I walked over to the wall that was the only place another staircase could be hiding, and kicked it in frustration.

Pain seared my foot and ankle. I nearly screamed as fire tore through my lower leg. I hopped around, lost my balance, and fell against the wall. It swung silently inward, and I toppled over.

The area I fell into was dark and dusty, without windows or any other source of sunshine, only a patch of weak light coming in through the doorway that shone on part of the unfinished wooden floor. Picking myself up and dusting my skirt off as I moved, I hurried over, grabbed the nearest chair, and propped it against the door to make sure it didn't close on me.

I wanted a certain exit.

Then I looked around more carefully. Old furniture, bed springs, crates, boxes, lamps, and toys were stacked around the edges of the space. Dust covered every inch, and heat baked my skin. I couldn't stop myself from coughing, while hoping no one heard me.

There was a killer in Manning Hall, and these connected attics made their work easier. I didn't want the killer to discover I'd found another way to sneak through the house.

In a dark corner, I could make out a plain wooden staircase. Despite the lingering ache in my foot, I carefully walked down the steps, trying not to make a sound.

When I opened the door at the bottom of the dark staircase, it opened into a first-floor hallway I'd not been in before. I opened the first door I came to. The toys and the scuff marks low to the ground told me I'd found the nursery, unoccupied since Louisa's children were elsewhere.

The door across the hall opened to a large, well-appointed room. The same as the other rooms in the house, the fireplace wasn't used to burn wood, but there was an electric bar heater installed. The furniture was a heavy Victorian style. On top of the dressing table was one photograph in a silver frame. I recognized the female half of the couple. I was in Mrs. Thompson's room. Noting Mrs. Thompson was with a tall, thin, dark, good-looking man in the picture, I backed out quickly and shut the door.

Now I knew how someone accessed the attic and took the letters that pointed toward anyone besides Louisa as the killer.

But who? No one was in the hallway now.

I went down to the ground floor and entered the kitchen. Mrs. Thompson and the cook were fixing tea. Mrs. Thompson looked at me and said, "Could you tell the ladies that tea will be ready in, oh, five minutes?"

"Of course." Both women went back to their chores. I hoped neither had noticed how I'd entered the kitchen, or they'd thought I'd come in by the back outside door. I left by the door that opened into the main part of the house near the trophy room.

I found Anne in the main hall. "The police just left," she told me.

"Tea in five minutes." Then I added, "Come back upstairs. I have something to show you."

I led the way through Sir Rupert's room and up to the attic. Nothing had changed from when I'd been there moments before.

"Another entrance," Anne said, glancing at Louisa, who was beginning to stir.

"There's a staircase leading to the hallway in the servants' quarters." I walked over to the doorway and looked for the latch from the main part of the house. It was hidden in a knothole in the wooden boards that made up the paneling of the well-framed wall.

Anne stuck her head in the opening. "It's dusty on the other side, but not this side. Sir Rupert must have shared his secret lair with someone to have it cleaned."

I cleaned my flat myself, so I hadn't thought about cleaning arrangements in a manor house. I should have, when I noticed how clean the attic was. "Marjorie?"

Anne nodded.

"I wonder what she makes of all this?" I looked around at the wireless transmitter, the wires I assumed went to an outside antenna, and the maps of the area.

"Nothing," Anne said. "She's worked here since she was a girl. There's nothing about the last three generations of Mannings that she doesn't know."

"How did she feel about Sir Rupert's political stance?"

"I'm sure she's fine with it. If it doesn't affect this house, she wouldn't give it any thought at all."

That was definitely an easier way to look at life. That made me wonder about Anne. "Where did you stand on Sir Rupert and his pro-German sentiments?"

"I thought he was an idiot," she said, looking around the room, "until I saw this and realized he was a dangerous idiot."

"And Freddy?"

"Freddy believes in anything popular." She saw the look on my face and added, "My husband doesn't think too deeply about things, but with Douglas's help, he should turn into a first-rate farm hand. Not energetic or terribly useful, but he'll do his bit for England and this farm."

"If he believes in anything popular, I'm surprised he doesn't want to fly. That seems to be the newest fad."

"Freddy?" Anne laughed. "It would require going to school and learning things. Not Freddy's strong point."

"Then why did you marry him?" slipped out before I thought. I could have bitten my tongue off.

Anne appeared to take no offense. She simply shrugged as if my question was unimportant. "Freddy is a lot of fun on picnics and at weekend parties and dances. And that's what I wanted in a husband. That and money."

She continued, "You appear to want a husband who thinks and reads and is gainfully employed."

"Yes."

"But no money?"

"Neither of us have a hope of inheriting a dime." I grinned at her. "So, having a clever, hard-working husband is a necessity."

Louisa groaned and sat up. "I must have fallen asleep."

She looked horrible, with red marks from the floorboards on her face and wrinkled clothes.

Anne and I walked over to her. "Yes, you did. You're in the attic," Anne said.

"Come on, let's get you downstairs," I added.

Between us, we got the limp Louisa down to her room and into bed. "We need to call the police and show them the other exit from the attic," I told Anne while we closed the curtains and left the room. Mercifully, my foot wasn't hurting after I kicked the wall in a flare of temper. I was too pleased with what I'd found.

"It will keep," she responded. "Your husband should

be here any moment, and Douglas and Freddy should be home soon."

I shook my head sadly. "And the inspector will probably refuse to come out here again today."

"Exactly."

We heard the front bell ring, and footsteps in the front hall.

"What about the letters?" I asked her.

"You keep them. We can't afford to have them disappear, too, and I don't think they're safe at Manning Hall. There's something very wrong here," Anne whispered.

I couldn't have agreed more. The letters went back in my pocket.

We went downstairs to find Adam alone in the front hall. "Ready to go?" he asked.

"We want to show you something first. Something you would understand," I told him.

We exchanged a look. "Lead the way."

Adam's eyebrows rose when we led him through Sir Rupert's bedroom, opened the sliding panel, and led him to the attic. He whistled when he saw the wireless set and immediately went over to study it. Then he followed the wires to the antenna, opened the window, and stuck his head out. "How did he...?"

Then he looked at the ropes at his feet. "Oh. I don't suppose anyone saw any abseiling going on outside the house?" He looked at Anne.

"No. Not that anyone mentioned."

Adam nodded, muttered "Gary" to himself, and then looked at the maps. "Impressive." He glanced at Anne. "It looks as if he used abseiling techniques to put the antenna above roof level in the tree branches. I'm going to have to report this setup when I get to work on Monday."

"It was Sir Rupert's. Tell anyone you want." Anne looked at the radio and shook her head. "Stupid fool," she murmured. "He had dangerous friends."

"No wonder he wanted to keep this wireless transmitter and antenna quiet," Adam said. "Once the war starts, all shortwave transmitting by private citizens becomes illegal. He needed a way to send our secrets to his friend Wolfenhaus and the Nazis."

"Would messages sent out from here reach Germany?" I asked.

"Definitely. Mind if I turn this on? I want to see who or what I'll reach."

"Go ahead," Anne said.

Adam sat down in front of the wireless set, turned it on, and let it warm up. We could hear vague sorts of noises come from the machine, including some that might be a human voice, but nothing on the frequency Sir Rupert had left the machine dialed into.

"I was hoping someone would be broadcasting, but no such luck." Adam turned off the machine. "Shall we go? Abby and Sir John are waiting tea for us."

Chapter Twenty-Seven

We arrived at Summersby House in time to take tea with Sir John, Abby, and the boys.

"You both look glum," Abby said. "Is everything all right?"

"No. It's not," Adam said. "I'll tell you after tea."

Parched and hungry after my afternoon in the hot attic, I gobbled down two sandwiches and two cups of tea. Adam didn't finish his first cup of tea before he began to pace.

Sir John and Abby exchanged a look and then Sir John led Adam outside to discuss what was on his mind.

Abby and I watched them walk away across a field.

"It's that bad?" Abby asked me.

"It's worse. He doesn't know what else we found," I told her.

"What?" Henry asked, walking over so he could lean on my chair.

"Never you mind," Abby said, ruffling his hair affectionately.

"Are there any more sandwiches?" Mark asked.

"No, but this is tea, not dinner. You won't starve between now and then," Abby told him.

"He will if Mrs. Goodfellow doesn't come back,"

Henry said.

We all turned and looked at him. Mary, who'd come in with a tray to carry out dirty cups and plates, tried to back out the door with a half-filled tray before she was noticed.

"Mary, what is he talking about?" Abby asked in her deceptively mild tone.

"Well," she began, "Marjorie Lenard came over after lunch to speak to Hester Goodfellow. They whispered for a moment and then Hester told me to take care of tea and she'd be back to deal with dinner."

"Where did they go?" Abby asked.

"Eleanor Ames's, ma'am."

"Why?" I was definitely curious.

"I don't know. Whatever Marjorie said, Mrs. Goodfellow was upset about it."

"And they were going straight to Mrs. Ames?" I asked.

Mary nodded. "That's what Mrs. Goodfellow said."

"If you'll excuse me, Abby," I said, rising.

"I'll drive you. Matthew, you're in charge until your father returns."

Four pair of eyes stared at us as we hurried out. We were down the lane before Abby said, "You think Mrs. Goodfellow is in danger." There was no question in her voice.

"I think Marjorie is in a great deal more danger. You've seen how nervous she's been when we've been over there."

"I thought it was just her age." Abby drove toward the

lower side of the village.

"Because Mrs. Thompson said so."

Abby thought about it for a moment. "You're right."

"I think it's because she's afraid."

We pulled up in front of Eleanor Ames's cottage, and Mrs. Goodfellow hurried to the car. "I'm so sorry, but Marjorie came and told me something that I thought Eleanor needed to hear. I'll get right up to Summersby House and start dinner."

"Where's Marjorie?" I asked.

"She's headed back to Manning Hall."

"How long ago?"

Now Mrs. Goodfellow looked startled. "A couple of minutes ago. No more than that."

"Quick, Abby, we must reach her before she gets there," I said.

"She didn't go by the roads," Mrs. Goodfellow said, causing Abby, who'd put the car into gear, to brake suddenly. "She's taking the path."

Which went through clumps of trees and under a bridge. Plenty of places for an attacker to hide. I jumped out of the car. "Meet me where the path comes out on the road going up to Manning Hall."

I took off on the run, noting only that Mrs. Goodfellow jumped into my seat beside Abby.

The farther along I dashed, out of sight of anyone, the more a little voice said I was being foolish. I hadn't heard what Marjorie wanted to tell Mrs. Goodfellow and Mrs. Ames. I was only guessing. I had no proof.

I slowed to a quick walk along the side of a field and then by a tangle of bushes and vines before I reached another field. Marjorie Lenard was nowhere to be seen.

Speeding into a run, I crossed the field and went into a woodland that went up a hill. I knew I couldn't be far from the road now. "Marjorie," I called.

I thought I heard something ahead of me. Footsteps or a twig breaking. Some sound that wasn't a small woodland creature.

"Marjorie?"

Rounding a corner on the slope, I saw what looked like a pile of laundry off to the side of the dirt path. I rushed forward, my heart racing, until I could see the bundle had arms and legs.

"Marjorie!"

She was lying face-down in the grass and decayed leaves, a piece of rope around her neck. I turned her on her side, pulling the cord away and feeling for a pulse. It was there, weak beneath my fingers.

I rose and looked around for her attacker. No one.

Then I heard Abby call my name. I shouted back, and a moment later she and Mrs. Goodfellow came down the path from the road.

I rose to meet them. "She's alive, but barely. Get Dr. Wheeler."

Abby hurried back to her car. Mrs. Goodfellow looked around and said, "Who would do this? Hal's killer?"

I shook my head. "What did Marjorie tell you?"

"On Saturday night, she heard someone upstairs in

the attic above her room. When she finally got the nerve to find out who it was, she met Mrs. Thompson coming down the stairs. She said she'd gone up to check on the same thing, but there was something in her manner that made Marjorie not believe her. A while later, you came and found Sir Rupert dead."

Marjorie made a little whimpering sound, but when we gently shook her, we couldn't awaken her.

Kneeling next to her, I looked at Mrs. Goodfellow. "Did she know it's possible to go from the servants' quarters to Sir Rupert's bedroom by way of the attic?"

"Of course. She'd been cleaning the attic for Sir Rupert for years. He made her promise not to tell a soul what she saw up there. But she knew about the door between the two sections of the attic, since the addition was built by Sir Rupert's father." Marjorie's thin hair had come loose from her bun. Mrs. Goodfellow brushed it off her cheek. "Poor lamb."

Marjorie began to make a choking sound, so Mrs. Goodfellow and I raised the maid into a half-kneeling position. She choked some more, made a couple of whooping sounds, and began to breathe more evenly, although her eyes remained closed.

We stayed with her, watching her closely, while I kept an ear out for any danger that might be lurking ready to finish us off. Fortunately, the next sound we heard was Abby talking to Dr. Wheeler as they came down the path.

The doctor quickly examined her and then had us lay her down again so he could take a better look at her neck.

He pulled out his stethoscope and listened to her heart and her neck. After a minute or so, he stood and picked up the rope I'd tossed aside. "This was what she was strangled with?"

"Yes. I found it around her neck when I came upon her." A piece of the rope that looked familiar from the floor of the Manning Hall attic beneath the window.

"It's a good thing you arrived when you did. That is heavy rope." He put away his stethoscope and closed his bag. "Any longer and she would have been dead. As it is, she seems to be coming around. In a few minutes you can help her up the path to Lady Abby's car and give her a ride back to Manning Hall."

"Not a good idea. It was someone from Manning Hall who did this." I stared at the doctor for a moment. "Any chance we can take her to the cottage hospital in Ratherminster?"

"You want me to admit her?"

"Yes, please."

"Lady Abby," Dr. Wheeler said with eyebrows raised, "if you'd give us a ride to Ratherminster?"

"Of course, Doctor."

I helped them get Marjorie on her feet and the four of us maneuvered her up the slope to the road. Mrs. Goodfellow brought Marjorie's hat along, the shape of the blue straw by now trampled beyond recognition.

We put her in the back of the auto with the doctor while Mrs. Goodfellow rode in front with Abby. "I'll walk back and talk to Eleanor Ames before I go to Summersby

House and find something to feed the boys," I told them.

As I hurried down the hill, Mrs. Goodfellow called from the car, "There's a cold roast in the larder." Abby turned the car around on the narrow lane while I took off down the path.

I was back at the Ames cottage in a few minutes. When I banged on the door, Eleanor answered.

"Someone just tried to kill Marjorie Lenard. Dr. Wheeler is admitting her to the cottage hospital in Ratherminster. She's in bad shape," came out in gasps from running the last section of path.

She shrank back. "Oh, no."

"What did she tell you, Mrs. Ames?"

"N-nothing."

"She must have told you something worth killing for, since someone just tried to kill her." At least I hoped she had told her story more than once.

She planted her feet in the doorway and glowered at me. "Nothing that has to do with Hal's murder."

"Sir Rupert probably killed your son, but someone killed Sir Rupert, denying you the satisfaction of seeing him hang for what he did. Now we need to find his killer."

Eleanor Ames moved forward until she was glaring at me across her doorstep. "I say well done to anyone who killed that murdering devil."

I was shocked. "I'm certain the same person who killed Sir Rupert just tried to kill Marjorie. Do you say 'well done' to killing Marjorie, too?"

"Of course not. But she's not dead."

"Not yet."

When her mouth stayed clamped shut, I turned to go with a ferocious glare.

"Wait." She paused until I faced her. "It wasn't much, but then, it made no sense to me. She said she saw Mrs. Thompson coming down from the attic, and in the attic, Marjorie had seen a lot of letters and things in German. And a group photograph."

We hadn't found any photos when Anne and I had looked through the attic, but we hadn't been through everything. "What was special about what she'd found?"

"It was the photograph. In some way it bothered her."

"Did she say why? Who was in the photo?"

"She didn't say. It was just as she was leaving. She said, 'I don't understand. He shouldn't have joined them.' Then she repeated it. 'He shouldn't have joined them. He shouldn't be with anyone wearing that uniform.'"

"Was there anything else?"

Eleanor Ames shook her head. "Nothing. She was late getting back and didn't stay long. And she seemed confused. No, uncertain. She seemed uncertain."

What I heard about this addition to Marjorie's story made no sense to me, but I knew I needed to go back to the attic. I thanked her and headed to Summersby House.

When I arrived, I discovered Abby had called from the cottage hospital, and the males in the household were already braced for whatever I could dream up for a cold supper.

I steamed rolls and had Adam carve the remains of the

roast in the larder. Mary helped me throw together a salad from vegetables from the garden. I contented myself with knowing they wouldn't starve.

Sir John and Adam praised my originality. Henry, ever the optimist, said, "It's wonderful to have two teas in one day." The older boys, after receiving a warning look from Sir John, refrained from laughing. Barely.

After we finished dinner, since it was still light out, I gave Anne a call at Manning Hall. After a minute while Mrs. Thompson went to fetch her, Anne came on the line.

"Douglas received a call from Dr. Wheeler just before dinner telling us about the attack on Marjorie. It was a good thing you came upon her, or the results could have been tragic. Thank you," Anne said.

"She said something that makes me think the answer to all these attacks is in the attic. Are you willing to go up there with me this evening?"

"Douglas and Freddy are talking about walking down to the pub. Do you want me to stop them?" she said in a half-whisper.

"No. It's nothing as dramatic as that. How is Louisa doing?"

"She hasn't left her room. Neither has Joan."

Probably just as well. Hopefully, they would wake to better news tomorrow. "Well, you and I can go up and take a look around. Is that all right with you?"

"Of course. I'll see you in a little while."

After I hung up, I went to find Adam. When I told him of my plan, he groaned. "Letters you found have disappeared. The maid has been attacked. Don't you think you should wait for the police?"

"Inspector Parsons doesn't believe in the theory about blackmail, or espionage, or anything. Didn't Sir John say Abby told him the inspector was treating the attack on Marjorie as some random robbery gone wrong?"

Adam looked as if he'd bitten into a sour apple. "If you're going over there, I'm coming with you."

I wasn't sure if I was happy he wanted to protect me or annoyed he thought I needed protecting.

Chapter Twenty-Eight

After Adam went in search of Sir John to tell him where we were headed, we walked in the summer evening air toward Manning Hall. The lanes smelled of wildflowers, while birds chirped as they flew by to their nests for the night. Voices reached us before we saw Sir Douglas and Freddy walking toward us around a bend in the road.

"Coming to see us?" Douglas asked as they reached us.

"Livvy and Anne want to finish the search of the attic they started today," Adam said.

"While they do that, come join us in the pub for a pint," Freddy said.

Adam was about to decline when I said, "Go ahead. I'll see you up at the Hall in a little while."

He raised his eyebrows.

I nodded.

"Okay, just a quick one," Adam said.

The three men continued the way we had come and I continued alone to Manning Hall.

I was hot and dusty from the walk when Mrs. Thompson let me in. Anne appeared in the front hall a moment later, and the housekeeper walked back toward the kitchen. Once she was on the other side of the door, we hurried on tiptoe to Sir Rupert's room, then slid the panel back and went up the stairs to the attic.

"Is Joan going to join us?" I asked.

"She told me she didn't want tea and she didn't want to go back into the attic. She wants us to leave her alone." Anne shrugged and glanced around the attic. "What are we looking for?"

"A group photograph. There was something about it that bothered Marjorie. And it probably led to the attack."

"Have you heard how she is?"

"All I know is she was alive when she reached the hospital." I decided to take a chance. "Do you happen to know if Mrs. Thompson reads German?"

"She should. She is German. She came over and was working as a maid when she married Mr. Thompson."

"What happened to him?"

"Died, I suppose. She's never said anything to me." Anne watched me dig through the desk drawers with a scowl. "Why?"

"The letter I translated to you. It sounded as if that Lady something-or-other might have changed Tomperglich's wife's details so she could get into the country." I started to remove the desk drawers.

"I thought maids could get admittance easily," Anne said as she looked over my shoulder at the photographs I pulled out from behind the top drawer. "What were those doing back there?"

"Either they just fell, or they were deliberately

hidden." I set all the photographs on top of the desk and began to sort through them. "I suspect hidden."

I pulled out the second drawer. Nothing was hidden behind it. Then I tried the bottom one and found the letters I'd translated earlier in the day. The letters I wanted to show Inspector Parsons. "Let's hang on to these," I said and slipped some of them under the shortwave radio. Others I put under a stack of maps on the bookshelves.

Anne was looking through the photos while I'd hidden the letters. When I stepped next to her to look at the photographs, she said, "Is that who I think it is?"

It was a photo of a young couple in a park or garden. They stood, staring at the camera, in casual clothes. Since they were hatless, the camera caught all the details of their faces. "Yes, I think it is Mrs. Thompson."

I didn't mention I'd seen the same photograph in Mrs. Thompson's room earlier that day.

Anne glanced up at me. "Why did Sir Rupert have a photo of Mrs. Thompson and some man up here among his expedition paperwork?"

"I don't know. Maybe that's Thompson with her. But this stuff isn't just about expeditions. Not the shortwave radio set or the maps of southern England."

"What was that devil up to?" she asked, looking around her.

I wanted the answer to that myself. Aloud, I said, "Let's find the group photo Marjorie was concerned about."

She shook her head, still looking at the photograph of

the couple. "This makes no sense."

"Maybe Mrs. Thompson was acquainted with Sir Rupert and Wolfenhaus before she started working here?" What I didn't want to say aloud was this might become evidence of a very good motive for Mrs. Thompson to murder both men. I had no idea what that motive might be.

"There's no group photo here," Anne said, looking at the last of the glossy black and white images.

"It must be here somewhere. That seemed to be the reason Marjorie was upset when she went to see Mrs. Goodfellow and Mrs. Ames."

She handed me the photos. "I don't see anything to make her upset."

I flipped through them. Anne was right. "Let's spread out and look around. I'm going to guess, the same as the letters, that it's here somewhere."

There wasn't that much furniture to check. We searched the desk, the table holding the shortwave set, and the shelves, but there was no sign of the photograph. I looked under the maps spread out across the map table. Anne checked around the windows.

Her only comment was, "It's growing dark out. I hope it cools off tonight."

I dropped onto one of the chairs by the shortwave set, hoping that a point of reference lower to the floor would give me a new insight. At least it would let me rest in the frying heat collected beneath the eaves during the day.

Anne collapsed into the other chair and fanned

herself with her hand. "Maybe whoever hid the letters took the photograph away," she said.

"Why didn't someone take away the letters, or burn them, instead of just hiding them up here? And does the same reasoning hold true for the group photograph? They must have some value for someone. But who? And why?" I asked.

"Whoever hid them didn't want to be found with them in their possession, but they wanted to save them for some reason," Anne said.

"Maybe they wanted evidence to show Sir Rupert as the Nazi follower that he was? Or maybe..."

Anne watched me while she tapped a pencil on the table.

"Maybe," I continued, "they wanted to have all the evidence at hand to prove Sir Rupert was a murderer. You suspect Sir Rupert of killing Jack Glenfell. I suspect him of murdering Hal Ames. Neither of us have the necessary proof. But those letters provide plenty of reason to suspect Sir Rupert was a killer, at least in Greenland."

"And the group photo?"

"More of that evidence? It certainly upset Marjorie Lenard." I wasn't certain, but I was willing to wander about in confusion until we were able to figure out exactly what happened.

Anne dropped the pencil and it rolled under the desk. When she bent over to pick it up, she said, "Will you look at this."

I bent over and looked up at the bottom side of the

table. A group photograph and some stationery were pinned to the underside. We carefully detached them and put them on top of the table where we could study them.

The group photograph had mounting corners still attached to two corners, evidence that it had been in the 1935 scrapbook in the trophy room before being removed.

"Look," Anne said, "there's writing on the back of the photo. Names, I think, but the handwriting is really horrid."

"These are more letters written by Matthias Tomperglich to Lili. In German. He spends a lot of time complaining about Sir Rupert." I flipped through the pages, translating a phrase here and there.

"Why? And is there anything to lead you to believe Sir Rupert felt the same way about Tomperglich?" Anne asked.

"Apparently, Sir Rupert and Wolfenhaus said Matthias Tomperglich would have to divorce Lili because of racial purity. This says they threatened to make sure of it when they returned to Germany." Sir Rupert, so annoying before, now made me sick. How could he be so—so horrid? Awful? Disgusting? He must have enjoyed interfering with other people's marriages.

"Why?" Anne asked, but I ignored her as I tried to translate the three letters that had been pinned beneath the table.

"Here he tells Lili she must get out of the country before they return from Greenland. Here he asks if she's written to him in the past three weeks since he's had no word from her."

"Something was wrong, wasn't it?" Anne said in an angry tone of voice, "and my father-in-law was the reason things were in disarray. He could be the most infuriating man. He treated his children as if they were dirt. I'm surprised he didn't leave his unentailed property to Wolfenhaus. It would have been just like him." She folded her arms over her chest and glared at the photographs.

"And I think it was Sir Rupert's nature to even lie to Wolfenhaus."

Anne nodded.

"Something was very wrong." After I'd seen what Esther's relatives went through and the fear in the eyes of the children sent away to a safer life in England on the Kindertransport, Matthias's words in this letter made me sick. "Lili was Jewish, although I think this part," I pointed at the letter, "means half-Jewish, and Matthias was Christian. German."

"So?"

"About this time in Germany, the Nazis began their campaign to stamp out racial defilement. That was their fancy name for sexual contact between Jews and non-Jews. It didn't matter if they were married or not."

"No wonder he wanted Lili to leave Germany. Was he planning to join her?" Anne asked, looking at the letter in my hand.

I flipped through the pages. "Yes. In this letter, he writes, 'As soon as I get back to Germany, I'll come for the weekend to see you at Lady E's.'"

"Do you think it's some kind of code?"

"I doubt the German post was safe from censorship. A German writing that he was going to abandon his country in favor of joining his Jewish wife would not be popular. But we already know Matthias died in Greenland while abseiling with Sir Rupert and Wolfenhaus."

"The same way Jack died," Anne said, "but I have no idea why in Jack's case."

"An accident, perhaps? If someone is forced to perform beyond their knowledge or experience, you can get terrible accidents with scaling rock walls with ropes or rock climbing."

"And Sir Rupert had no patience for 'amateurs,' as he called them. Or weakness of any kind." Anne shook her head. "And all he said about Jack was that he fell. He was careless and he fell. Sir Rupert showed no remorse or concern over Jack's death."

"With Matthias Tomperglich, it sounds as if his fall and death were planned. While the Danish government didn't charge anyone, the letters we found from the other expedition members made it very clear his death was Sir Rupert's fault. They wanted nothing more to do with him."

"I wish the Danes had charged him with murder. Manslaughter, at least. Then maybe Jack would still be alive." Anne sounded bitter.

"And Hal Ames. All I can think is that his crime was being in the wrong place at the wrong time." And he paid with his life. Sir Rupert was a disgusting man. As I thought of him, I grew more nauseated. I wanted Sir Rupert there so I could slap him. Kick him. Murder him.

"Why? What did he see or do?" Anne asked.

I shook my head. When I glanced out the window, I saw it was full dark. Where was Adam? I didn't want to waste what little time I had left before the men returned and stopped our search for the night, but I was anxious that Adam had been away so long. Did he think my investigation was foolish? Taking a deep breath, I said, "Let's see if we can figure out who is who in this group photo."

Anne was right. The handwriting, actually two different hands in two different colors of ink, was horrible. Names were crowded together. Some were on a slant. Even if we figured out all the names, how could we be certain which name went with each face?

"I can make out the names Wolfenhaus and von Marten," I said.

Flipping the photograph over, Anne said, "Well, this is Sir Rupert and this is Wolfenhaus."

I looked back at the names and then at the photo. "This is von Marten, right in the center. Makes sense, since he was in charge."

"Was he? Look at the uniforms," Anne said.

I stopped concentrating on the faces and looked at the picture as a whole. The men were standing on a dock in front of a ship. Many were in suits, including von Marten, but several were wearing military uniforms. The black Nazi German SS uniforms of the mid-thirties.

Studying their faces, I recognized Wolfenhaus in an SS uniform. And then gasped.

Sir Rupert was part of the group.

"What was Sir Rupert doing with these SS officers? He was British. Wasn't the SS a German military group?" Puzzled, I looked at the back of the photograph. "This says these are the members of the 1935 expedition to Greenland. Several of these members were Nazis. They were SS officers."

"And now you know why the inspector thinks someone in the family killed Sir Rupert. He truly was an odious man." Anne looked as if she'd tasted something bitter.

"But none of you did, did you?" This picture was at least four years old. Sir Rupert only died last weekend. What had happened to cause someone to suddenly kill Sir Rupert after waiting so long?

"None of us did." Anne shrugged. "I don't know why. Maybe none of us felt endangered enough to strike out."

"Anger's not enough to make someone kill?"

"Anger maybe, but what I felt most was disgust. If you're asking, Olivia, I didn't kill him. Freddy loves living here. I love Freddy. Maybe someday it won't be enough, but for now it is. I had no motive for killing him."

"I believe you." Probably because if she loved Freddy, this farm was the safest place for him until the war was over. I was married to a soldier. I knew about wanting to keep my husband safe. Unfortunately, while she could do it, I couldn't.

"Thank you." Anne's tone was serious, not sarcastic. "Now, Joan might have been angry enough to kill after Jack died, but Sir Rupert made certain she was drugged most of the time."

"What about Philip?"

"What about Philip? Sir Rupert convinced him he was a weakling, or maybe he is a weakling." Anne shrugged.

"But it was Philip's son that Sir Rupert killed. Don't you think Philip would have been angry enough for revenge?"

"Maybe Philip is just a nice guy. I can't see Philip killing anybody." Anne made a face. "Sir Rupert hated nice guys."

"I wonder about Tomperglich. Was he a nice guy? Which one was he?" I searched the photograph, trying to match up faces on one side and names on the other. It appeared Tomperglich was next to Wolfenhaus.

I studied the faces, and then blinked. Digging out the photo of the couple, I looked from the man in that photo to the man I thought was Tomperglich.

I held the two photos out to Anne. "There's your answer."

She stared at them. "Oh. Oh, dear."

"Oh, dear is right. I want those photographs back," said a voice behind us.

Chapter Twenty-Nine

I felt my heart stutter and my face heat as I turned toward Mrs. Thompson. "Come in, Mrs. Lillian Thompson. Or should I say Lili Tomperglich?"

She ignored my question. "Back away from the table. I want what is mine."

I jumped up and moved hurriedly away in the direction Anne was going, both of us inspired by the large pistol the housekeeper was carrying.

"Where did you get that?" I asked.

"It was Sir Rupert's." It was the first time I'd seen her smile. Her smile frightened me more than the pistol.

"He had this gun and was waiting for me, but I showed him. I came across the attics and sneaked up on him. I ran him through before he could fire. When the tusk went in, he grabbed the curtain behind him. As he fell, he pulled the curtain and the curtain rod down."

"And then you took his pistol?" I asked.

"Yes." She gathered up the photographs and looked around for the letters. "Where are they?"

"Where are what?"

She cocked the pistol in reply.

"Are you planning to use the letters and photos for

your defense?" I hoped I could keep her talking until Adam and the Manning brothers showed up.

"No. I'm going to show the world that Sir Rupert and Wolfenhaus murdered my husband."

"Sir Rupert murdered Hal Ames, too, didn't he? Did you see him kill that young man?" This might be my one chance to find out what happened to Ames. His mother deserved the truth.

"Sir Rupert and I were arguing in the trophy room. I'd finally found the letters up here in the attic, where I searched all those nights while you thought I was in my room," she said to Anne. "These letters say that the German scientists on the expedition believed he had killed my husband. I finally had the proof I needed. Finally. And while the rest of the family was out, I wanted him to confess."

"Did he?"

"No. I had found the group photo of Sir Rupert with the SS officers in the 1935 scrapbook. When you came back for the scrapbooks, I hid that one to keep the photo, but then I found the photograph was already missing. More proof of what an evil man Sir Rupert was. I'm glad you found it."

"What did he say about that photo?"

"He was proud of it."

"Creep." That hardly covered his evil. Sir Rupert was much worse than just the snake who tried to ruin my wedding. "Did you know he had your husband's letters to you?"

"Not until I found his pile of letters in German hidden under a floorboard. After he died, I put them in the drawers to get to them more easily. I wondered why I received so few letters from Matti. He would write me, referring to something he'd mentioned in the preceding letter, which I hadn't received. I had blamed the censors. Now I know Sir Rupert was the culprit. He was a thief as well as a murderer."

"How did Sir Rupert steal mail from the sacks that would go on the supply ship?"

"I have no idea. Theft? Bribery? Blackmail?" Mrs. Thompson continued, "He was in the trophy room when I found him, reorganizing his gear, opening all the display cases, cleaning all his exploration apparatus. When I showed him the proof, he said his trophies were the only proof he needed. He was famous and honored by his country. They would believe him. That was all that mattered.

"I had entered this country without permission. He would have me deported. And then he said my husband was a weakling. Not worth having on the planet, let alone on something as important as an expedition."

"Why didn't you kill him before now?"

"I needed the proof of what he'd done. It took me months and months before I found all the evidence I needed to confront him."

"And Hal Ames walked in on the two of you?"

"Yes. He wanted one of us to drive over to Brighton and rescue Sally. Sir Rupert said it showed how weak and ineffective he was, the way his father had been. They started to argue. Hal was frantic. He couldn't abandon a young girl all alone in a seaside town.

"Then he turned to me to ask me to give him the lorry keys and he'd drive over there himself if we wouldn't protect Sally. Sir Rupert began to yell about Hal stealing his farm lorry the way his father had, picked up the shovel he used in the Arctic, and hit him over the head. Killed him instantly."

I was drawn into the story, heartbroken that an act of kindness led to the young man's death. Then I heard her words again in my head. "Wait. Did he say Hal's father stole his farm lorry? Is that why he killed him?"

She shrugged. "It sounded that way."

"What did you do?"

"What could I do? I checked on Hal and found he was dead. Then Sir Rupert told me to help him put Hal's body into the farm lorry. I said no. I ran upstairs and went in search of Sir Rupert's gun. I knew he was going to kill me. I was a witness to his actions.

"Then I heard the lorry start up and drive away. I couldn't find the pistol anywhere. I went back downstairs to the kitchen and hid, waiting for Sir Rupert's return."

"What did you—?"

"Stop right there."

I turned to where Mrs. Thompson was looking behind me. Anne had managed to get down three steps in silence.

"Get back up here." She sighted the pistol on Anne's chest.

Anne shot me a look before she came up to the top of the stairs.

"So far you haven't done anything you need to regret," I told the housekeeper. "Sir Rupert and Wolfenhaus were killers and spies against England. You'll probably get a medal for stopping them. Marjorie Lenard will hopefully recover. Don't do anything to make things worse."

"How can things be worse?" She walked toward us. At this distance, she couldn't miss no matter how bad a shot she was. "Matthias is dead."

"And nothing you or I or anyone can do will bring him back," I told her. "But we can do what we're able to stop the Nazis who killed him from destroying England the way they have Germany."

"I stopped them. I did. You saw the photograph, the one with Sir Rupert standing with Wolfenhaus and others wearing SS uniforms?"

"We did."

"They believed in that evil. That power makes right. The purity of the German people. They killed Matthias because my mother was Jewish. Can you imagine anything more terrible? He died because of my mother, who'd been dead for many years." Her face twisted with anguish. The horror of what she'd been living with in this house was finally coming out, and she was losing control. Anne and I were in danger from that pistol.

"When he returned, he went upstairs and I knew he had brought out his pistol. I followed him upstairs through the attic with a narwhal tusk in my hand. And when I came into his room through the secret door, I put everything I had into running him through, saying 'For Matthias.'" She didn't appear to be aware of us anymore, and I was glad.

Then she looked directly at us and raised the pistol.

I had to keep going, to have Mrs. Thompson tell the whole story to Anne and me. To buy us more time until the men came back from the pub. "Is that why you came to work here? To kill Sir Rupert?"

"Of course. Mrs. Manning there is the best of the bunch, along with Sir Douglas, but I wouldn't want to work for any of the others."

"Thank you, Mrs. Thompson," Anne said.

"Mrs. Tomperglich, if you don't mind, ma'am." She appeared to be regaining her composure.

Anne nodded. "Mrs. Tomperglich."

"Were you blackmailing Sir Rupert?" I asked.

"Me? No. He would not have paid me to keep his secrets. He would just have had me deported."

I felt deflated, over and above having a gun pointed at my chest. "I felt certain someone was blackmailing him. That money had to be going somewhere."

"He was paying Wolfenhaus a great deal of money."

"Why?" I wondered if she had proof of that, or what good proof would do us now.

"To keep his secrets. First, that he killed my husband, and then that he killed his grandson. Wolfenhaus saw him kill both. There are letters around here somewhere from Wolfenhaus, saying donate to this Nazi cause or that, but the money always went to Wolfenhaus when he came here."

"Why didn't Sir Rupert just kill Wolfenhaus and save himself the money?"

"Wolfenhaus was careful. His guard was always up. And he told Sir Rupert he had left a letter with a solicitor here in Britain that would tell everything if he died under suspicious circumstances."

I had to know. "But you managed to kill Wolfenhaus. How?"

"Marjorie and I left the graveside service almost immediately to walk back to the house to be ready for the reception. I sent her to the bakery to pick up more bread and I slipped away on the path with the knife in my bag. I hid behind some bushes. Wolfenhaus didn't realize I was there until the moment I stepped out on the trail behind him. I didn't hesitate. A second later, the knife sliced into his back. He never expected anyone to be so daring."

Another smile, and then, "The silly inspector looked over the family's mourning clothes for blood, but not mine or Marjorie's. We are not important. We are merely servants."

"Is that why you attacked Marjorie? Did she figure out that was when you killed Wolfenhaus?"

"No. She finally realized I was the one who had killed Sir Rupert. She didn't believe you should kill the lord of the manor no matter how much he deserved killing."

I decided Marjorie was lucky to have survived. "What do you plan to do now? I suppose you'll turn in your resignation," I said. I hoped to keep her on less volatile subjects until Adam arrived. Where was he?

"Do you think I'm stupid? You think this is such a joke. Turn in my resignation? They'll hang me for killing a peer." The pistol came back to aim directly at my chest.

"Not a peer. He was only a baronet," Anne said, scorn in her tone.

"It doesn't matter. The big hero is still dead, and I'll still hang." Mrs. Thompson could top Anne's scorn with ease.

"But you eliminated a dangerous spy and a murderer," I said. "You did England a great service. The courts should take that into consideration."

"They'll say thank you very much, and then they'll hang me. I do not wish to be hanged." She had her control back as well as her sense of her own dignity.

"Then leave." I challenged her. Probably not a bright thing to do, I decided after the words passed my lips.

"And be hunted down as if I were an animal? No, thank you."

"What do you want?" I had no idea how to shape this conversation so that Anne and I could stay alive. Especially since our husbands were taking a very long time getting back from the pub.

"I want to go free. After all I've lost, after all I've done for this country, I want to go free. I want the king to pardon me."

"Does the king pardon people?" I asked Anne.

She looked at me as if I was crazy. "How would I

know?"

"It's possible. It might be Chamberlain, as prime minister, rather than the king who pardons people. And don't you have to be charged and convicted of a crime before you can be pardoned?" With the gun still pointed at my chest, I was finding it easy to be creative, but difficult to remember what I'd learned at school.

"Oh, wait. The royal prerogative of mercy. I remember reading about it at university. The king has had the right to pardon anyone convicted of a crime since the Middle Ages." Anne looked at her. "You have to be convicted first. If you're tried and acquitted, you go free and you can never be tried again for the same crime and so no pardon is necessary."

"You're wasting my time. What chance do I have, a German, of being pardoned for killing an Englishman by the English king?" She was waving the gun around. I feared she'd pull the trigger without meaning to, but one of us would still be dead.

"That's where the power of the press comes in," I told her. "I write for the *Daily Premier.* We can get a campaign going in the London papers to show what a benefit you've provided England by eliminating dangerous spies and murderers."

"I don't believe you. Why would the English help me, a German?"

"Because you helped us," I told her.

"This is a trick to convince me to let you go. Then you'll go back on your word and I'll hang." Once again Mrs.

Tomperglich was aiming the pistol directly at my chest.

My heart pounded as if I was racing. I wanted to scream out for Adam. I was starting to feel weak, unable to take a deep breath.

If I fainted, I'd make an easy target. I tried to pull air into my lungs as I became determined to stay on my feet. I refused to make killing me any easier than it already was. "There's one thing you may know the answer to. Who sent Sir Rupert the poison pen letters?" It was a silly question that I already knew the answer to, but I wanted to keep her talking.

"The what?"

Anne looked at me as if I'd lost my mind.

All I could think was that we were running out of time, and I wanted to live. "The poison pen letters. The notes that were made out of cut-out magazine letters."

"I didn't do that."

"But you saw everything going on in this house. You must know," I told her.

"It was Joan."

Anne and I looked at each other. She knew. "Joan."

"They frightened Sir Rupert, because he did not know where the letters came from. And all the time, Joan was watching him and smiling."

"I guess it was her only way of fighting back," Anne said.

"Downstairs," the housekeeper ordered, gesturing with the pistol, "and don't try any tricks. We're going to take the car and drive far away from here. If you behave, I will let you go. Unharmed."

"Do you promise?" I asked.

"What choice do you have but to believe me?" she said in a reasonable tone.

"Come on," I said to Anne after a deep breath.

"Not so fast. First, the letters." The pistol was still pointed at me.

I took them from the two places where I had hidden them and left them on top of the table. Mrs. Tomperglich gathered them up without taking her eyes off us for a moment.

She had us go downstairs with my hands resting on Anne's shoulders so we would stay close together. I was certain Anne could feel my arms tremble. Then we crossed Sir Rupert's bedroom and went out into the hall.

I hoped Louisa would come out of her bedroom and see our strange procession, but there was not a sound coming from her bedroom. I had no idea how Anne was feeling, but my legs were shaking so badly I knew I couldn't run.

And where was Joan? There was no sign of her, either.

At the housekeeper's direction, we went down the main staircase to the ground floor and then around by the former trophy room toward the kitchen. "Why did you use a narwhal tusk on Sir Rupert? I've wondered about that," I told her. Keep her talking. Adam should arrive at any time. At least he could see which way we went.

"It was handy. It was from the Arctic, which seemed fitting. And it made a good spear. Keep moving."

"Toward the vehicle barn?" Anne asked.

"Yes."

I wondered if the cook could be seen, and signaled, in the kitchen as we went past, but she was nowhere in sight. I'd hoped someone would be around and could tell the police, or Adam, or Sir John, somebody, what had happened to us.

We'd had no luck at all. And Adam, Douglas, and Freddy still hadn't returned from the pub. I wasn't wearing a watch, but it had to have been past closing time by the time we walked out the kitchen hall door into the night air.

Where were they?

It was more difficult walking over uneven terrain outside with my hands still on top of Anne's shoulders than it had been inside. Unfortunately, athletic Anne was increasing her gait.

"Wait. Slow down," I told her, "or I'm going to trip and fall and knock you down, too."

"And then I will have to shoot you both," Mrs. Tomperglich said.

"No. Please don't," Anne said, sounding panicked for the first time as she slowed.

"We're heading for the auto. There's no reason for you to shoot us. Everything is working out according to your plan," I told her. I really didn't want Mrs. Tomperglich to get upset or unnerved. That wouldn't turn out well for Anne or me.

We were almost to the barn when I said, "Do you have the car keys?"

"Of course." She sounded calm again. "Mrs. Manning, you drive. Mrs. Redmond, get in the passenger seat. I'll ride behind you. You can be certain I will keep my pistol aimed at you all the time."

When we reached the car barn, we stopped in front of the doors. "Mrs. Manning, you open the doors. Mrs. Redmond, stand right here in front of my pistol."

Anne opened the massive doors wide and then turned back to face us while my legs shook. The housekeeper threw her the keys and Anne caught them with a grace I didn't have.

"Now, get in and start the car. Then pull it out here and we will get in."

Anne looked at me as she nodded and went into the dark cavern where only the bonnet of the car could be glimpsed in the moonlight. A moment later, I heard the car door open and shut, and then nothing.

In the distance, I heard a moo. Closer, all was silence.

"Come on," Mrs. Tomperglich snapped.

"It won't start," Anne said.

"Lift the hood and tell me what's wrong."

"I can lift the hood, but I haven't the foggiest idea about what's underneath."

"Get out and lift the hood."

When she did, the housekeeper shoved me forward so all three of us were in the wide entrance to the barn, our silhouettes obvious to anyone inside.

"Drop the gun, Mrs. Tomperglich," Adam's voice rang out from inside in the darkness.

She swung around, peered into the barn, and fired. Two shots rang out .

Chapter Thirty

Someone screamed. It might have been me, but I couldn't tell because my ears were ringing from the twin explosions. Figures raced out of the darkness inside the garage as hand torches switched on, leaving little circles of light dazzling me as they were aimed at Anne and me.

Where was Adam? Had he been shot?

Then torchlight shone on the housekeeper lying face-up on the gravel, blood covering her blouse and the pistol laying at her side.

And then Adam's strong arms encircled me as I shook with the fear and strain that I couldn't show before. Of not knowing during those long seconds what had happened to my husband. I buried my face in his shoulder as he kissed my ear and whispered, "It's okay. I'm here, Livvy. Everything's all right."

I was vaguely aware of people rushing around, of Mrs. Tomperglich being carried away in a police van, of Anne being led sobbing into the house by Freddy, of Inspector Parsons speaking to me. I couldn't make sense of what he said. Then Sir John and Abby drove up and Adam helped me into the car.

When we were back at Summersby House, they fixed me tea laced with brandy while my teeth continued to chatter and the four boys watched, wide-eyed, from the doorway. Then Adam led me to bed and piled covers over me. Despite the warmth of the July night, I shivered uncontrollably. Then Adam lay down and held me close until I stopped shaking and fell asleep.

* * *

The next morning, I awoke in the bed and found the other side empty. I dressed quickly and went downstairs to learn the story of how we came to be rescued and where my hero husband was. The full breakfast I polished off was even larger than thirteen-year-old Mark's.

Adam sat next to me, watching me eat. "We came back to Manning Hall to find Louisa, Joan, and the cook waiting for us at the end of the drive. They told us what the cook had overheard from the attic stairs leading into the servants' quarters. We decided to immobilize all the vehicles so Mrs. Thompson couldn't drive away before we planned anything else."

He grinned at me then. "We couldn't agree on any other course of action."

I stared at him, speechless. Finally, I stammered, "You mean if we hadn't come out, we were on our own?"

"We would have come up with some sort of rescue plan eventually. One that didn't include Freddy," he added, grumbling.

"How did Mrs. Thompson—Mrs. Tomperglich—fire two shots and only hit herself?" That made no sense.

Adam and Sir John exchanged glances.

"What?" How much were they hiding from me?

Adam studied his half-eaten breakfast. "I fired one of the shots. I borrowed a pistol from Sir John."

"You were carrying a gun with you when we left here yesterday evening?" My voice rose in astonishment.

Adam gave me a grim stare. "It was obvious someone had gained revenge against Sir Rupert and Wolfenhaus. The house was full of weapons, and full of people willing to use them. And you were determined to search for the final piece of proof."

"When Marjorie was attacked, and Mrs. Ames said she kept going on about a photo, I felt certain that was the proof we needed to take to Inspector Parsons. How did you get him to come to Manning Hall with you?"

"After the shooting, Sir Douglas called the police station and asked for police and an ambulance. The inspector was at the station. Fortunately, that meant they were able to arrive quickly."

"And Mrs. Tomperglich? Is she...?" I couldn't say the word. Despite her threats to kill me, I didn't want to hear she was dead. There'd been too much death already.

"They operated last night. Inspector Parsons plans to interview her this morning." Adam clutched my hand. "I had a clear shot, Livvy. I deliberately shot her in the shoulder. It was all I needed to do to stop her."

I let out a long breath and smiled at him. "I'm glad. The photo Marjorie saw? It showed Sir Rupert with Wolfenhaus, who was wearing an SS uniform. They killed Matthias Tomperglich because he was married to Mrs. Thompson, whose mother was Jewish. Mrs. Thompson had already escaped here. She was waiting for Matthias to arrive here after he left Greenland." I had to tell them what I knew.

"She'll hang for it." Abby shook her head.

"It's not fair."

"Livvy..." Adam dropped my hand so he could stroke my cheek.

"It's not fair," I all but shouted.

"It's the law," Sir John said, very quietly but with a note of finality in his voice.

"Those men were spies and murderers."

"Then it should have been proven in court so the law could take care of them," Sir John told me.

"The law has done such a good job so far." I crossed my arms over my chest and turned my face away from Adam as I seethed inside.

"As soon as the war starts, we'll be rounding up all the Nazi sympathizers," Adam assured me. "She didn't wait long enough."

"Why did she kill Sir Rupert with the narwhal tusk when she did?" Abby asked.

I told her the story Mrs. Tomperglich shared. "If she hadn't killed him first, I think Sir Rupert would have killed her to keep her silent about him killing Hal Ames."

"She can argue self-defense," Adam said, "but it doesn't explain Wolfenhaus's death."

I nodded, hating to admit it. "Sir Rupert's funeral would be her last chance to kill Wolfenhaus in revenge. He'd never return to England with Sir Rupert dead, and

Mrs. Tomperglich couldn't go back to Germany."

The telephone rang in the hallway. I could hear Mary talking, and a moment later she came in. "Inspector Parsons on the telephone for Captain and Mrs. Redmond."

"Finish your breakfast. I'll get it," Adam said, rising.

"I've lost my appetite." I'd already cleaned my plate. I stood and followed him to the telephone table in the hall.

Adam spoke into the receiver and then listened for a minute. "We'll find a way down there. We should be there within the hour."

After he hung up, he said, "Inspector Parsons wants to talk to you, and Mrs. Thompson wants to speak to me. We're both supposed to go down to the cottage hospital."

I walked into the dining room. "Anyone going into Ratherminster?"

No one was, so we borrowed the automobile. After dressing to go out, we drove into Ratherminster. Since neither of us had been to the market town before, we had to stop for directions.

When we entered the hospital, Inspector Parsons and a constable were waiting for us. "Before you see Mrs. Thompson, I want to take both your statements."

That took quite a while. I was impressed with Adam's concise report. He left nothing out, he was factual and detached, and he was honest and straightforward. I rambled, sounded hysterical, and didn't make much sense. Twice I had to stop and take a deep breath before I could continue my statement.

We were told our statements would be written up

and we could sign them later at the Ratherminster police station. Adam wisely asked for directions from the constable.

"Have you heard Mrs. Thompson's statement yet?" I asked.

"She refuses to tell us anything, but don't worry, we'll get it out of her sooner rather than later," Inspector Parsons said with a little too much enthusiasm for my liking.

"And how is Marjorie Lenard?" I asked him.

"She's gone back to Manning Hall with a sore throat and a need to get the dusting done. That woman is indestructible," the inspector added under his breath.

A young nurse led us down a ward to the far end that was screened off for privacy. I was surprised Inspector Parsons didn't have a constable posted by Mrs. Thompson's side to make sure she didn't escape, but one look at the woman told me the doctors were able to assure the police she couldn't possibly rise from her bed.

"Mrs. Tomperglich?" I said. "You asked to see my husband and me?"

"You are the one who shot me?" she asked, looking at Adam by moving only her eyes.

"Yes."

"Why didn't you finish the job?" Her voice was so soft I wasn't certain I heard her correctly.

"I beg your pardon?" Adam looked surprised.

"You leave me with a useless arm and a life that will soon be ended by a hangman. Why didn't you kill me and get it over with quickly?"

He looked down at the bed, his face a stern mask. "I'm sorry about your arm, but I only had the right to keep you from hurting my wife and the other woman, not to kill you."

"We both know what they'll do to me. A German in Britain, accused of killing an aristocrat. An explorer. A hero." I thought I heard a weak laugh come from the pale woman.

"That's for a jury to decide. Not me." Adam sounded less stern. I was proud of him for unbending a little.

"Your Inspector Parsons has already told me to confess. He says they will hang me, no matter what."

"That's not for him to decide," I said, glaring down the ward toward where the inspector must be waiting. "Do you still have your letters and photographs?"

"Yes."

"You are entitled to a defense barrister. Show him those things. Hopefully, he will show the court what kind of a man Sir Rupert was." I watched her, looking so frail and fragile. I wondered if she'd live to go to trial. She appeared to have given up. "That's what you really want, isn't it? That everyone knows what Sir Rupert was really like."

"Yes. Now, go away. I'm tired."

We said good-bye and walked down the ward in silence.

* * *

We had dinner that night listening to the four boys

chattering on, but Adam and I were both silent. When Sir John asked if we wanted to go to the pub, we both shook our heads. Neither of us had been good company since we returned from Ratherminster, and at least in my case, that wasn't going to change for a long time after we returned to London.

The telephone rang while we were finishing our coffee. Mary came in and said, "It's Lady Louisa on the telephone for Mrs. Redmond."

I went out, hoping she wasn't inviting me to anything.

"Livvy," she began, "we just heard from Inspector Parsons."

"Lucky you."

"He wanted us to know Mrs. Thompson, or whoever she was, bled to death tonight."

I slid down the wall so I was sitting on the floor, the receiver still in my hand.

"Did you hear me?" Louisa's voice sounded far away.

"Yes," came out as a whisper.

"The inspector said she was guilty of killing Sir Rupert and Wolfenhaus. I'm no longer under suspicion, and my boys will be coming home tomorrow. I'm so thrilled. Thank you, Livvy."

"For what?" I heard the surprise in my voice. Things had not ended happily.

"For helping me bring my children home. For being kind when I…" There was a pause. "I was right to tell the headmistress when you snuck in late at night at school." Her tone had changed back to snooty.

"Remember that when your children are tattled on by their classmates."

"They won't behave the way you did."

I couldn't resist getting a dig in. "Will they fall apart at the first sign of trouble the way perfect little Louisa did?"

Silence lingered until I thought she'd hung up on me. "You're right. I deserved that."

"No, you didn't," I admitted. "I'm upset about Mrs. Tomperglich. Sir Rupert killed her husband, killed Hal Ames, probably killed your nephew Jack, at least accidentally, had been giving the Nazis information, and was never charged with any crime. Mrs. Thompson killed Sir Rupert in revenge, and she would have hanged."

"She knew how it was going to end. She wanted to die," Louisa said.

"How do you know?"

"I was inside the vehicle barn when she fired that pistol. She had no idea where any of us were. She just fired into the ceiling."

"What?" I had thought she'd aimed at Adam, or at least at his voice.

"She wanted Adam, the police, someone, to kill her. When he didn't, I was told that in the hospital, she pulled off her bandages and irritated the wound site while the nurses were busy elsewhere. She died in a comfortable hospital bed in a pool of her own blood. This way, she was able to fade away rather than hang, which she didn't want to do. She was even more afraid of ending her days in a German prison."

"Inspector Parsons told you all this?"

"Yes."

"Mrs. Thompson's mother was Jewish and she killed a Nazi. I can't imagine what the Nazis would have done had they got hold of her." Louisa was right. Her housekeeper had taken the easy way out.

And I didn't blame her. Rumors of German torture were filtering in to the *Daily Premier* newsroom.

"We've hired Eleanor Ames as our new housekeeper. Dr. Wheeler encouraged her to take the post, as did Mr. Jones and Mr. Long. They negotiated a good deal for her with Douglas. She told me she's going to be in charge of this house, and I think she'll do a good job of it."

"I'm glad to hear something good has come out of all this."

After a long pause, Louisa said, "Are you going back to London soon?"

"Tomorrow."

"Have someone come down and take away the shortwave radio in the attic before anyone else does any more damage with it," she told me. "And don't be a stranger next time."

"It was good seeing you again, Louisa."

"I haven't given you good wishes on your wedding. Good luck, Livvy."

"Thanks. We'll need it." Especially when Hitler made his move. Adam would soon be doing his bit for king and country, and I—Who knew what I'd be doing?

When I rose from the floor, I hung up the phone and

went off to give Adam a big kiss. It was summertime and we had a day left to our honeymoon. I was certain we wouldn't waste it.

Despite the uncertainty of our future, I knew I was the luckiest girl on the planet.

Enjoyed **Deadly Darkness**? Be sure to read the entire Deadly Series for more of Olivia's adventures. And please, if you enjoyed this story, take a moment to leave a review on your favorite retailer and tell your friends. Word of mouth and individual reviews are still the best ways to learn about new books.

Acknowledgments

Writers can't work in a vacuum when it comes time to publish their work. My thanks to Jen Parker for her help in making this story the best it can be, Eilis Flynn for her help in editing my work, Les Floyd for removing the worst of my Americanisms, and Jennifer Brown for her eagle-eyed proofreading.

With the pandemic lockdown while I was writing this book, I am indebted to the British Library collection of newspapers that they have put online. Details reported in July, 1939 in the London newspapers appear as plot points in this story and give it a richness it would lack otherwise.

And my thanks to you, the reader, who make the final connection between my pen and the world. I hope you've enjoyed the journey.

About the Author

Kate Parker grew up reading her mother's collection of mystery books by Christie, Sayers, and others. Now she can't write a story without someone being murdered, and everyday items are studied for their lethal potential. It had taken her years to convince her husband she hadn't poisoned dinner; that funny taste is because she can't cook. Her children have grown up to be surprisingly normal, but two of them are developing their own love of literary mayhem, so the term "normal" may have to be revised.

For the time being, Kate has brought her imagination to the perilous times before and during World War II in the Deadly series. London society resembled today's lifestyle, but Victorian influences still abounded. Kate's sleuth is a young widow earning her living as a society reporter for a large daily newspaper while secretly working as a counterespionage agent for Britain's spymaster and finding danger as she tries to unmask Nazi spies while helping refugees from oppression.

As much as she loves stately architecture and vintage clothing, Kate has also developed an appreciation of central heating and air conditioning. She's discovered life in Carolina requires her to wear shorts and T-shirts while drinking hot tea and it takes a great deal of imagination to picture cool, misty weather when it's 90 degrees out and sunny.

Follow Kate and her deadly examination of history at www.KateParkerbooks.com

and www.Facebook.com/Author.Kate.Parker/

and www.bookbub.com/authors/kate-parker